Best Wi[shes]

My Dear Soul an' Days

Les Terry

Illustrated by Peter Rothwell

EDWARD GASKELL PUBLISHERS
DEVON

First Published in 1998 by
EDWARD GASKELL
The Lazarus Press
6 Grenville Street
Bideford Devon
EX39 2EA

©Les Terry 1998
Drawings by Peter Rothwell
isbn 1 -898546 -20 -7

My Dear Soul an' Days

Les Terry

Illustrated by Peter Rothwell

This book is sold subject to the condition that it shall not, by way of trade or otherwise, be lent, re-sold, hired out or otherwise circulated without the publisher's prior consent being given in writing, in any form of binding or cover other than that in which it is published and without a similar condition being imposed on the subsequent purchaser.

Typeset, printed, & bound by
The Lazarus Press
Unit 7 Caddsdown Business Park
Bideford
Devon EX39 3DX

Acknowledgements

To Angela and Steve,
for their great interest and support.

And to my good friends at Mill Farm, Whiddon Down,
who helped so much without knowing.
I only had to listen.

Dedicated to

owr maid Leeno

PROLOGUE

High above the West Country in the scattered cloud of an autumn sky, a lone raider of the German Luftwaffe flew on its mission. It was one of many, but had somehow got itself separated from the rest of its raiding party and the pilot and navigator were doing their utmost to find and rejoin them. Their efforts were doomed to failure, for now they were joined by a British Hurricane fighter that had been despatched from its squadron, chasing the main enemy group, to do something about this singleton bomber.

Far below on the ground some people who were about their work paused to watch as the two aircraft played their deadly game of hide-and-seek in and out of the clouds. The German pilot, with considerable skill, kept his Heinkel out of the Hurricane's view, as far as he was able, knowing that he would be quickly out-manoeuvred if he allowed the fighter to come too close, but in doing so he was becoming more and more separated from his group.

Pilot Officer Terry Christopher in his Hurricane decided that sooner or later his adversary would have to come down below cloud to try to pick up a landmark of some sort in order to rethink a new direction. Spotting a sizeable hole in the cloud, he cut the throttle and dropped easily through to level off just under the ceiling. He was both right and lucky, for there, less than a mile away to his left and just above him, was the enemy bomber. Slamming the throttle wide open he pulled hard on the stick and with full left rudder came right up under the belly of the raider, firing all eight wing-mounted Brownings. The German had been caught almost unawares, immediately losing his ventral machine guns and sustaining considerable damage to the tail and elevator control rods.

In a desperate effort to escape further onslaught he shouted the order to jettison his bomb load and attempted to climb back into the clouds, but there was no response to the Heinkel's controls and it was now a sitting duck for the returning fighter.

For the bomber and its crew, the war, it seemed, was going to be over quite soon.

1

Tom Dryfield and his son Joe entered the kitchen through the back door. After kicking off their boots, they took turns to wash the day's grime from their hands before sitting down at the table to partake of a hard-earned meal. Together they made a father and son partnership which ran Stoney Downe Farm, some two hundred and ten acres, give or take a few, situated about four and a half miles east of Pottles Cross, a small village ten miles north of the market town of Newton Waybrook. To the south of them and bordering on the lower sections of the farm were the rugged tors and commons of Dartmoor, which afforded them certain 'rights of grazing', and had done so for generations past. Tom was the third generation of Dryfields now farming at Stoney Downe, with the fourth one in the shape of Joe, coming on. The last but by no means least member of the Dryfield family was Bess — wife, mother, cook and housekeeper, not to mention good all-round farm-hand when the need arose. And it was to Bess now that the two men were looking with hungry eyes as she carefully tended the pot of stew bubbling on the stove.

'Won't be long,' she said, 'but this ol' rabbit wuz bigger than I thought, so the teddies and dumplins be takin a bit longer, but there now, that's right's twill ever be, I reck'n.'

Tom and Joe already had knives and forks in their hands as Bess ladled out huge helpings of food to them, and then put out a generous plateful for herself. For the next five minutes or so nothing was heard but the clatter of cutlery upon plates and the chomping of teeth around rabbit and dumpling, and in due course as empty plates were pushed back and chairs eased away from the table, no one would dispute Bess's ability at the cooking stove.

The country was now two years into the Second World War and many parts were suffering from air-raids, invasion scares, food rationing and shortages of pretty well everything, but here at Stoney Downe it almost seemed like a different world. They knew from their old wireless set what the general situation was most of the time, as long as the batteries hadn't run down, and they often heard, and sometimes saw, enemy aircraft high above them en route to wreak terrible havoc upon the industrial areas of the Midlands and the North. And there were the nights when they could look towards the south-east and just make out the search-lights and the flashes of anti-aircraft shells exploding, which told them that Plymouth was once again receiving a pounding.

But food rationing? You wouldn't have thought so here at Stoney Downe. There was always a rabbit or two, or maybe a chicken. And on occasions a young pig might do a disappearing act and turn up again sometime later hanging on several hooks down in the cellar, where it couldn't be seen by 'they that wad'n s'posed t'be lookin.'

As Bess began to clear the dishes towards the sink and Tom reached for his tobacco tin, the conversation between the family started afresh.

'Reck'n you could do with a bit of 'elp there maid,' said Tom.

'Aw no,' replied Bess. 'Twon't take me long, and there's plenty of 'ot watter on the stove. You two sit back fer minute 'r two. I dare say you've 'ad enough t'do and the weather ant bin much 'elp to ee. What've ee bin on upon anyway? Neither one of ee be lookin' zackly plaised bout somethin.'

'Well....' said Tom, looking across the table at Joe. 'Us've bin wonderin what tdo with th' 'ol sow becuz e've started t'give us a bit of trouble.'

'What sort o' trouble would 'e give ee?' asked Bess

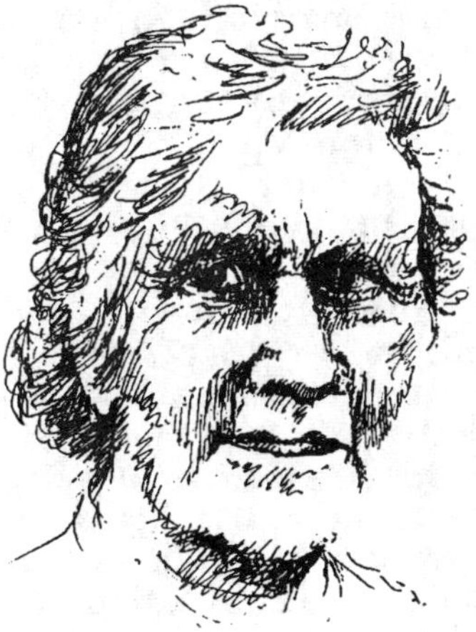

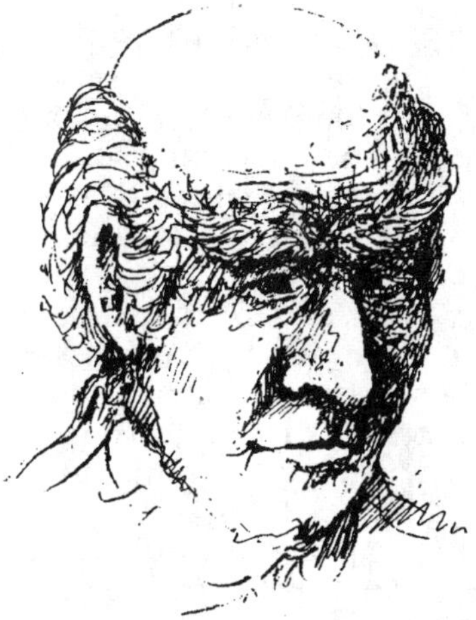

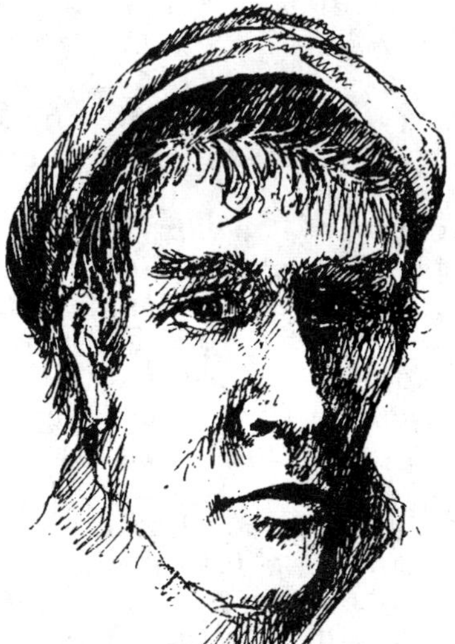

as she carried a kettle of hot water over to the sink.

'Well....' said Tom again, scratching his head, 'e've got 'eaps too fat, so 'e idn likely t'make ort much in Newton Market, and tidn very likely e'll breed any more neither. Us won't want t'keep the ol' thing yer just t'look at. What d'you say Joe? You'm keepin perty quiet, I fancy.'

'Aise, well tis up t'you really father,' said Joe at last. 'All I c'n say is that the ol' pig've bin good to us and don't owe us nort fer certain, but you knaw best what t'do.'

Joe was a bit of a quiet lad, not much past his nineteenth birthday and not yet ready, perhaps, for making big decisions. On his eighteenth birthday he had been required to register at the nearest Labour Exchange for call-up into the armed forces, but Tom had stepped in, quite rightly, and claimed him as being exempt because he needed him to help run the farm. Joe, not being particularly anxious to leave home, was happy to go along with it, saying as he did now that 'father knawed best'. In any case it was true to say that farming was a reserved occupation — someone had to plough and sow and reap and mow, as well as breed cattle and sheep to help feed the nation in these rather desperate times; and of course pigs — one of which species the family at Stoney Downe Farm had to make a decision on in the very near future.

'Didn' you say George wuz comin down t'night t'play cards?' Bess reminded her husband.

'Cawd beggar me, tha's right, 'e is,' said Tom. 'I clean fergot tiz Thursday.'

'P'raps George'll 'ave some idea bout what us c'n do with the ol' sow,' suggested Joe. 'Nobody else round yer knaws s'much about pigs as 'e do'.

Tom looked at Joe thoughtfully for a moment. 'Aise, I reckn you'm right, boy,' he said. 'George'll ave some sort of answer to it fer certain.'

George Mattford was the Dryfields' nearest neighbour and ran a smallholding of some thirty to forty acres about two miles up the road from Stoney Downe. Pigs were his speciality and there wasn't much, if anything, that anyone could tell him about them. He did, in fact, own the only decent boar pig for miles around — a huge saddleback that he had reared himself which had proved to be a good wage earner for him because farmers from a wide area brought their amorous sows along for the 'services'. This included Tom Dryfield's old sow of course, and since they were such close neighbours, George had got into the habit of dropping in on the Dryfields once a week, usually on a Thursday evening, for a game of cards and to talk farming. It always ended up with a bit of supper – a generous portion of meat pie or the like – and a mug of tea, which was no doubt the highlight of the evening for him.

Well, George had become a widower a year or two previously and, since he'd had no family, he spent most of his time alone, except for his pigs of course and several chickens that wandered around the place.

'Hark!' said Bess suddenly. 'I c'n 'ear footsteps. That'll be George now, I reck'n.'

She had correctly identified the owner of the boots, for George it surely was who, a moment later, clomped his way down the passage and into the kitchen. He was warmly greeted by all those present, for not only was this a night out for him, it was also an event for his hosts who now had somebody else to talk to for an hour or so, with a different line of conversation and usually a bit of good-natured banter. And George could almost always be relied upon for a funny story or two.

Tonight however, George wasn't quite his usual self. There was something on his mind, and Tom could sense it straight away.

'What's up with ee, my beauty?' he asked. 'You ant runned out of pigswill or ort like that, ave ee?'

'No, nuthin like that, Tom,' replied George, settling himself down at the table. 'But I get me problems sometimes, same as most other folks do. But still —' he added quickly, 'I musn' come down yer and worry you folks with em.'

'Why not, George?' asked Joe. 'Us wuz thinkin about askin your opinion on a certain matter — wad'n us, father?'

'Matter o'fact us wuz,' said Tom. 'But our troubles c'n wait. Tell us wha's on your mind first, ol' friend, then praps us c'n do summin to elp ee out.'

'I dunnaw if you can or no' said George, giving his hosts a woeful look. 'Tiz that there saddleback o' mine. I'm nearly fraid t'say it, but that there ol' boar've served his last pig!'

Tom looked at his friend aghast. 'Don't tell me e's daid!' he said with some alarm.

'Aw no,' said George. 'E idn daid, Tom, but I'm fraid I gotta get th'ol vet out. D'you knaw, this mornin 'e couldn' ardly get up on is legs.'

'Well you bin workin'n too ard,' said Tom. 'Tha's all I c'n say, onless e've et somethin that didn' agree with'n. They c'n be a bit pernickety sometimes, which I'm sure you knaw — specially they well bred ones like yours is.'

'Aise, I spose you'm right, Tom,' said George with a sigh. 'I'll let'n rest up for a day 'r two and praps e'll come round again. Anyway, wha's this yer problem you wanted t' ask me about?'

'Looks like us be both in the same boat, George,' said Tom, 'becuz I'm beggered if I knaw what I'm gwain do with that ol' sow o' mine. Where do ee think 'e wuz, fust thing this mornin'?'

'Dunnaw, where wuz'n to?' asked George.

'Well e'd broke out've the pig's 'ouse and got isself up in the trailer,' said Tom. 'I reck'n 'e must've fancied another trip up t'see your ol' saddleback – an' you knaw 'e wuz only up there day fore yesterday.'

'Well I'm beggered,' replied George, who had suddenly seen a funny side to it. 'Well, you knaw wha's wrong with 'e, don' ee?'

'No, but I should like fer you t' tell me,' said Tom, looking at George and waiting for his expert opinion. But George, who was feeling better now that he knew that Tom had a problem as well as himself, could hardly keep from laughing out loud as he said, 'Well, e's gone maaze, tha's what's the matter with 'e!'

Fortunately, because of the shadowy light thrown out by the oil lamp, George's expression was largely missed by Tom, but Bess noticed it and decided to interfere before the subject went any further. She had an idea that sparks might fly if she didn't.

'Why don't you two get on out to the Risin' Sun and ave a drink or two fer a change,' she said. 'I've gotta feelin that neither one of ee be of a mind t'play cards this evenin, so you'm only yer clutterin up the kitchen.'

'That don't sound like a bad idea, maid,' said Tom, getting to his feet. 'What d'you say George? Joe c'n drive us over in the ol' car. Tid'n very far is it?'

'Aise, twill be bit of a change,' said George, 'long as us ben't too late 'ome.' George didn't want to miss his meat pie and mug of tea for supper – but off they went in Tom's old Austin Six with Joe at the wheel. Ten minutes later they arrived outside the door of their nearest hostelry, the Rising Sun Inn, and as they entered the dimly lit bar they were greeted by Jim Collins, the landlord.

'Evenin gents,' said he. 'Unusual to see you here on a Thursday. What happened, did Lady Luck smile on ee or something?'

'T'other way round more like,' replied Tom as he ordered the drinks. 'As a matter o' fact us've bin avin' trouble with the pigs one way or nuther and twould'n take us long to get rids of one 'r two of em if us could get em off our 'ands quick.'

'Well, you never know yer luck Tom.' Jim filled their glasses and passed them over the bar. 'These are funny ol' times,' he continued. 'The war seems t' mean different things to different people. There's some who be quite happy to join up and help to protect the country, and there's they who'll look around t' see what they can make out of it.'

Then, as the three men drank their ale, he leaned over and whispered 'There's a couple o' strangers behind the settle who might be able to do ee some good. They've been asking around looking for some meat on the hoof. No doubt they'm on the wrong side o' things but play yer cards right and both of ee might make something out of it.'

Tom and George looked at each other, then turned and looked towards the two strangers. Electricity had not yet arrived in this part of the West Country and in the dim light of the pub's oil lamps they had not noticed anyone else in the bar – which was understandable perhaps because the two men were sitting more or less out of sight on the big wooden settle where they could observe, almost without being observed themselves and they were wearing dark suits and black hats, which put a touch of mystery and a slightly sinister aura about them.

'Mind what you'm bout if they get talkin' to ee,' warned Jim. 'I shouldn't think they'm zackly on the level, so watch 'em!'

The two farmers nodded their appreciation to Jim and, for a moment, studied their glasses. Joe, meanwhile, had wearied of what was going on and moved closer to the log fire where he sat on a stool and idly thumbed through the pages of an old magazine which someone had left behind. His father and George Mattford stood quietly at the bar, ordered more drinks and waited, but they had no fear of what the two strangers might try to do. Ever since they were old enough to add up, a large part of their livelihood had been in dealing with men and animals, and they had a few tricks of their own up their sleeves.

Over in the corner the two dark suits were muttering in low tones. 'Those two look like a right pair of bumpkins.' said the first man. He was slightly bigger than the other one, and the accent was of the Midlands, or thereabouts.

'Yeah,' replied the other, 'And it sounds like they might have some pigs to sell. Let's buy em a couple of drinks. These yokels are a pushover for a pint of scrumpy or whatever it is they call that stuff they drink around here.'

If they ever knew it, they had both forgotten one of the first rules of salesmanship — 'never underestimate the opposition'. Neither George or Tom, however they might appear, could be put into the bumpkin category, and neither did they drink scrumpy, so as the strangers got up and approached the bar, they had already made two mistakes, and there were more to come.

'Good evening, gentlemen' said the first man. 'It's a nice evening.'

Tom and George looked at each of the two strangers and George said 'Well, I reck'n twill be a bit better when the wust o' it's over.'

The smile stayed on the first man's face but a frown appeared also as he tried to interpret the wit, and lost a bit of ground in the process. Nevertheless

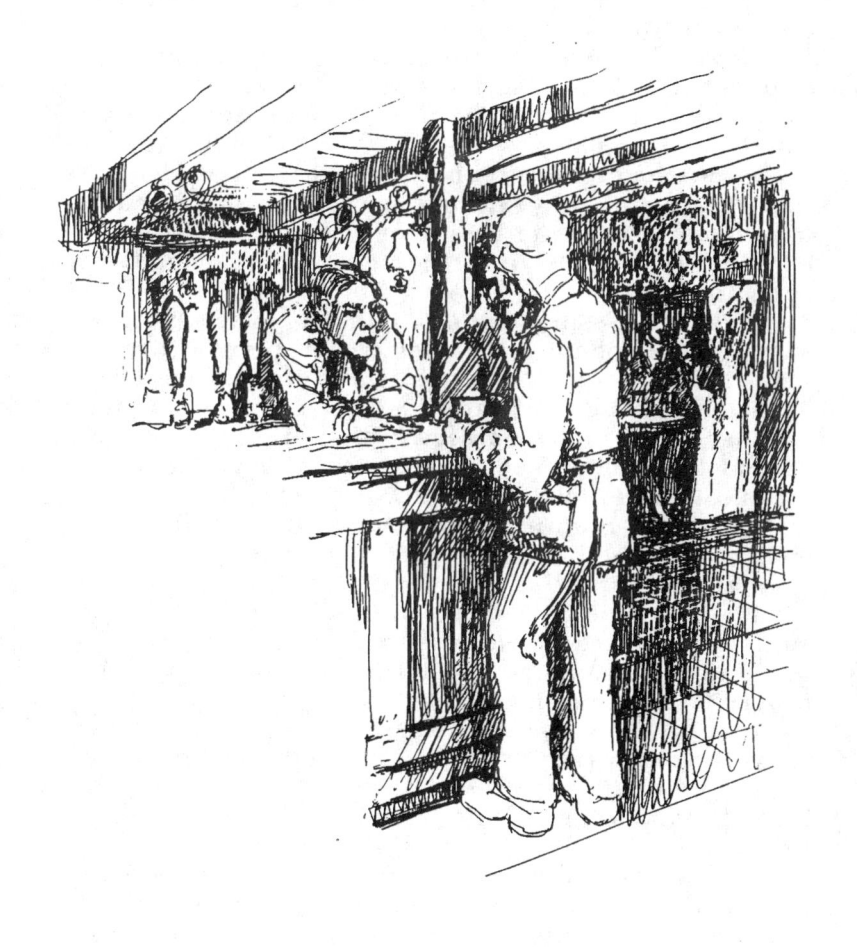

he went on, 'We are a bit weary of our own company, and we wondered if you would care to join us in a little of the local brew.'

'Thankee,' said Tom and George together, pushing their glasses forward in a gesture of acceptance, and George added, 'Us be always ready to ave a drink with a couple of gents. Idn us, Tom?'

'Never 'eard ee say a truer thing than that, George,' said Tom. 'I'll 'ave a drop o' whisky.'

'Aise, and I'll 'ave the same,' said George, 'and thankee very much.'

So much for the scrumpy drinkers, the first one thought, but he dug into his pocket and pulled out a handful of notes, the colour of which wasn't missed by the two farmers, and they glanced knowingly at each other.

'Us've 'eard that you'm lookin fer some animals,' said George, coming straight to the point. 'Pity us didn' see ee couple days ago. Only jus' moved a few fat pigs on, didn' us, Tom?'

'Aise, tha's quite correct,' answered Tom. 'I ant got nort left now 'cept that prize sow which I bin meanin to enter in this year's Christmas shaw.'

'Yer, aff a minute, Tom,' broke in George. 'That one nearly got you fust prize last year. You ben't thinkin of gettin rid of 'e, be ee?'

'Well, tid'n that I don't want t' keep'n, George,' said Tom, 'but tis costin s'much to keep e's weight up, and you knaw yourself what tis like t' get the proper feed fer em these days.'

'Aise, I knaw tha's true Tom,' said George. 'I'm 'avin the same trouble with that there saddleback o' mine, but when I see the way 'e rins round the yard like 'e do, I don't want t' think about sellin' 'e neither.'

The two strangers were listening intently to what the farmers were saying but did their best not to show too much interest. Tom and George, however, knew from long experience that a carrot was dangling in front of them and that they were itching to take a bite. After a little more to-ing and fro-ing between them in which Tom and George practically convinced themselves that no two finer pigs would be found in the whole of Devon, the second of the two strangers ventured to ask if they could possibly put some kind of value upon them.

'Well now, lemmee see, uh, aff a minute now.' George drew the wind through his teeth in the time honoured manner of the countryman when thinking of something important. 'I should say that ol' saddleback o' mine ought t'make twenty five score, and I reckn your prize sow,ll be bout the same, don' ee think so, Tom?'.

'Aise, you ben't far wrong, George,' answered Tom, and they both watched the faces of the two in the dark suits. They, in turn, were looking at each other in disbelief, not knowing what to make of it – but of course they were a little bit out of their depth here, and were about to show it.

'That seems a lot of money for one pig', said the first.

'Money?' said Tom. 'Us wad'n talkin'....' He suddenly felt George's boot against his ankle.

'No, us wouldn' think t' ask that much fer a quick sale.... that is if us decided to sell 'em,' George cut in. He was a bit quicker off the mark than Tom and realised that a 'score' to these two meant twenty pounds in money, whereas to any farmer discussing pigs, a 'score' was a reference to the animal's weight.

'Tell ee what,' he went on, 'Why don't ee come out to our place and see the animals fer yersels? Tis only a little ways out and us be fairminded folks who'll give ee a fair deal. You got some sort of transport, I take it?'

'Yes, we have,' said the first man. 'We've got a vehicle parked around the back.'

'Tha's a proper job,' said George. 'Now, le's 'ave one fer the road t'keep our strength up. Let Joe take the car back 'ome Tom, and us'll ride with these gentlemen.'

As it happened, George's 'one fer the road' led to two or three – which was a little bit more of his strategy because by the time they left the Rising Sun there was a very considerable 'good old pals' atmosphere between all of them. They located their new acquaintances' vehicle in the darkness behind the pub. It seemed to be some sort of van, and Tom and George climbed in the back and sat on what appeared to be a couple of large packing cases, then shouted directions to the two men in the front.

Meanwhile, Joe had arrived back at Stoney Downe in the old car, which he parked behind the barn and then headed for the kitchen. As he reached the stable door he heard the sound of his old sheep dog softly barking a welcome to its young master. He opened the top half and peered inside, and the old dog quietly wagged its tail on the straw bed upon which it lay, just next to the stalls.

'S'alright Ben,' he said. 'Go on back t' slape. Tidn time t' git up yet.'

The welcome from Ben would have been different had a stranger walked by but dogs, of course, always know their own. The three work horses stirred slightly at the sound of Joe's voice, then eased from one rear leg to the other and chewed another mouthful of hay before dozing off again. In the far stall the pony did likewise. The stable was very much Tom's domain really and its occupants would have a visit from him too before everyone settled down for the night.

Joe shut the stable door and went into the house. His mother sat at the table, busy, and with much dexterity, darning her menfolk's socks, while the two farm cats reclined luxuriously upon the fireside chairs. As Joe entered the kitchen the cats raised their heads and glared balefully, and waited to see which one would have to vacate its resting place for him. Joe, however, elected to sit at the table, and the cats relaxed once more.

'You'm back early, Joe,' said his mum with a smile. 'Is everything alright?'

'Aw, aise I reck'n,' said Joe with a yawn. 'Father and George met up with a couple o' strangers in the Sun. I bant sure what they'm on upon exzackly, but I shouldn' think they'll be long. George said these two fellas would give em a lift 'ome.'

'Wonder what tha's all about then,' remarked Bess with a puzzled look.

'Dunnaw,' said Joe. 'I'll go on up baid and 'ave a early night fer a change.'

'Well there's a bit o' pasty left over,' said Bess. 'Take it up baid with ee.'

'Aw thanks,' said Joe, picking up this half of a

miniature banquet. 'Just what I fancied. Night mam.'

'Night night. Joe, see ee in the mornin dear.'

Joe wondered if she ever went to bed as he stuffed down the last mouthful of the pasty. Always in the kitchen doing something. She'd be there in the morning, bright as a button, with a cup of tea for him before he went out to do the early milking, and his dad would be fed and watered too, that he knew, before this night's escapade was over. He got into bed and began to doze off, but the piece of pasty apparently had other ideas. It had seemingly decided to start a war of its own inside of Joe's stomach as it came up against the ale from the Rising Sun. Sleep was out of the question for the time being, so he got out of bed and walked up and down the room.

He belched noisily a few times and then suddenly the pasty and the ale seemed to call a truce and gave up the battle. Feeling better, he crossed to the window and peered out into the darkness. There was a moon, but the night was also cloudy. A southerly breeze sent the clouds scudding across the sky and, in between, the moon shone its beams down into the farmyard and over the mewy, next to which was the pigsty, and joining that was the orchard which bordered the lane.

Through the intermittent light of the moon Joe thought he could pick out the shape of a vehicle by the orchard gate, and though he couldn't be certain, he was almost sure that he could hear voices, and the pigs seemed a bit restless. The wind in the trees made it impossible to decipher anything properly, but he did hear the vehicle suddenly start up and slowly make its way out through the lane. He guessed it must be pretty close to midnight, and a moment or two later his father and George came in the back door and then there was some earnest conversation with Bess as she made supper for them both. With Tom in the house once more, Joe decided that all was well and got back into bed. In practically no time at all he was fast asleep.

§

Next morning Joe was up early as usual. His mother poured his cup of tea as he came down the stairs, and he quickly drank it, then went out to the cow shippens and began the milking. Tom came out to help before long and nodded the time of day to his son.

'Did ee get a lift 'ome last night, Dad?', asked Joe.

'Aise,' answered Tom. 'Twas a bit late, but me and George got back venchally.'

'Looked like a bleddy 'earse from where I wuz standin,' remarked Joe with a grin.

'Well you ben't far wrong boy,' said Tom, but didn't elaborate any further.

When the milking was done, Joe turned the cows out into the yard. They quietly made their way across the mewy and through the open gate into the meadow. Joe closed the gate and glanced thoughtfully towards the pigsty, and he was about to walk over to it when he heard his father's voice behind him.

'Got rid of the ol' sow las' night,' he said.

'You didn!' said Joe, rather taken aback.

'Aise, beggered if I didn,' said Tom, looking very pleased with himself. 'Got nearly double market price fer'n too. They two chaps in the Sun las' night didn' knaw a pig's ass frum 'is belly button, and they took George's ol' saddleback as well. Cawd, when they seed the size of em they couldn' give us the money quick enough, all in cash as well, and no questions asked.'

'You wuz perty quiet about it,' said Joe. 'I never 'eard a thing ardly. Didn' ee have t'put the knive in 'em?'

'Aw aise,' replied Tom, 'but George 'ad a stunner in 'is pocket. That soon quietened em down. Anyway, they chaps had to meet others fu'ther up the line so they didn' want t' waste too much time round yer.'

'Just as well I reckn,' said Joe thoughtfully.

'Aise, but don't say a word to nobody mind,' replied Tom. 'Us gotta keep this to oursels.'

'Aw yeah, course,' vouched Joe, and thought what a smart fellow his dad must be.

A couple of evenings later, on Saturday, Joe was again in the Rising Sun. So were Tom and George who were both in a jovial mood and looking as if they had discovered a gold mine. There were a few more locals in the bar this evening and there was a lot of talk about something called The Women's Land Army or some such thing which was due to arrive in the area in the very near future.

Tom and George were drinking up well and buying drinks for one or two people, which surprised Joe a bit, because they didn't usually do that. The evening was going along nicely, when old Maurice Bennett, who was sitting in the corner by the fire, suddenly shouted up amidst a fit of asthmatic chuckling, 'Cyaw, I'm beggered if I knaw! What the hell be us gwain read next ?!'

'What's that all about?' queried Jim Collins, the landlord.

'Tiz all in yer,' said Maurice, holding up the day's issue of the *Morning News*. 'Two chaps wuz caught speedin in a 'earse up Bristol way, an' when the police looked inside, they seed a pig's foot stickin out frum under a coffin lid !'

His wheezy chest prevented him from reading further so he passed the paper over to Jim, who read on, 'Further investigation revealed at least two pigs drawn and quartered inside the coffin together with other animal remains....'

Joe looked across to where his father and George were standing. It was easy to pick them out in the crowded bar, because they were the only ones that weren't laughing. He sidled over towards them and saw that they both were not looking at all good.

'You alright, dad?' he asked anxiously.

'I don't zackly knaw, boy,' said Tom. 'Think I'll nip outside fer a minute or two and git a bit o' fresh air. I fancy it've got a bit stuffy in yer.'

'You'm quite right,' put in George hastily. 'C'mon, Tom, I'll come out long with ee.'

Joe followed the two men outside, where Tom recovered himself somewhat, and he and George began a lengthy reconstruction of the goings on two nights previously, and tried to figure out if 'they there pigs could, in any way, be traced back to them, and if so, 'what the bleddy ell be us gwain do about it?'

'Aw, I shouldn worry too much bout that,' said Joe, doing his best to cheer them up. 'Look ow dark t'wuz las' Thursd'y night. I don't s'pose they two chaps knawed where they wuz to, when they wuz yer'.

'P'raps you'm right boy, p'raps you'm right,' replied Tom. 'But anyway, I think I'll get away 'omeward. You better stay a bit longer. Twill look a bit funny if us all disappear. What be you gwain do, George?'

'Aw, I reckn I'll come back wi' you, Tom,' said George. 'Us'll see through it all some'ow.'

George also reckoned that he would be alright for a bit of supper at Tom's house as well, and he didn't want to lose the chance of that.

'Anyway,' said Joe. 'I shan't say nuthin' to they in there,' indicating towards the bar, 'If they want to knaw where you'm to, I'll tell 'em you went 'ome early cos you got some bullocks t'see to. I'll see ee a bit later on, Father, and you too George.' And with that he turned on his heel and walked back into the pub.

'Smairt boy you got there, Tom,' said George as they made their way towards Tom's old Austin. 'Takes after 'is mother, I reckn.'

George had no intention of insinuating that there was any great difference between Bess and Tom in the brains department. This was his way of easing the tension, which he knew was building up in Tom's mind. The two men had been friends for much longer than either one of them could remember and whilst Tom would worry about things most of the time, George maintained a frivolous attitude to everything all of the time, and now as he gave Tom a sidelong glance, Tom looked at him also and chuckled quietly.

'George,' he said. 'You'm a perty ol' beauty. You be sure nough!'

§

Back inside the Sun, Joe was relieved to see that the interest had switched from the matter of funeralised pigs in a speeding hearse, to an arm wrestling contest between two of the heftiest farm hands in the vicinity. Several pints of beer and cider were bet on the outcome and by the time Jim Collins had shouted for 'last orders', most of the customers needed help to get themselves homeward bound, and few would want to remember on the coming morn what had transpired the night before.

By the time Joe got home, George had eaten his supper and gone. Tom was sitting at the table, still looking worried, while Bess fussed around putting food on a plate for Joe, which he tucked into hungrily. He looked at his father and grinned broadly.

'Charlie Gifford beat Bill Bunn at arm wrastlin, he said. 'Ol' Bill never bin beat before and 'e didn like it much, but Jim Collins must've nearly sold right out of beer and cider, th' way they wuz all drinkin on the finish of it. There'll be a few thick 'aids in th' mornin I reckn and nobody'll mind ort about that stuff in th' newspaper.'

Tom's face took on some relief. 'Aise,' he said thoughtfully, with a glimmer of a smile. 'Praps you'm right boy. Le's hope so anyway.'

It was two or three days though before he began to shake off the worry of being called to question over his and George Mattford's pigs, and their combined midnight sale caper. He quietly vowed to himself a hundred times that 'twas nivver worth it' and 'nivver agin', and gradually his old confidence began to return.

2

It was about a week later, just after the morning milking. The cows had been put into the meadow, Tom and Joe had eaten their breakfast and were now engaged in cleaning out the cow shippens. The sound of a car coming up the lane brought them both out into the yard to see who this might be, and they were just in time to watch a rather official looking black car pull up by the yard gate. The door opened and out stepped an equally official looking man. He was tall and thin. Quite the tallest thin man that Tom could ever remember seeing anywhere before. He wore a long raincoat, and on his head sat a bowler hat which was perhaps a size too big because it fitted right down on his ears, giving him a somewhat comical appearance. In fact it very briefly occurred to Tom that, if it wasn't for his ears, he would not be able to see where he was going.

'Good Morning,' said the bowler hat, as the man came through the gate. 'I'm from the Ministry of Agriculture and....'

Tom didn't hear the rest of the stranger's opening sentence, but what he had heard made his jaw sag three inches and his stomach felt as if it was touching his boots.

'You are Mr. Dryfield, I presume?'

Tom recovered slightly as he heard his name mentioned. 'Aise,' he said. 'What's yer bizness?'

'Well, I would like to speak to you if I could, on a

matter of some delicacy. Can we go indoors?'

'Come on in,' croaked Tom, who was now feeling decidedly uneasy. 'But if tis bout they there pigs....'

'Pigs ?' the man from the Ministry interrupted. 'I know nothing of pigs. Dreadful things. Not my department at all. No, this is something about which I must speak to both you and your good lady. She is at home, I trust?'

'Aise, I reckn,' said Tom, wondering whatever was coming next. He motioned to Joe to carry on with what he was doing, then led the way into the kitchen.

'This yer's the Missus,' he said, pointing to his wife, who was busy as usual, looking at something sizzling on the stove. 'I'm fraid I didn' get your name.'

'Short,' said the man from the Ministry. 'Harry Short,' and offered his hand to Bess.

'Very pleased t' meet ee, Mr. Short,' she said, giving him her best smile. 'Will ee hev a cup o' tay, and a bit o' cake praps ?'

'Ah, thank you kindly, Mrs. Dryfield. Most acceptable, most acceptable,' and he sat down at the table, placing his brief case at the side.

Tom sat down opposite and looked at their visitor. He began to feel a little less worried now, because if it wasn't anything to do with the pigs, what else could be the reason for a visit from the Ministry of Agriculture? And why would anybody, who was at least six foot three and had put a dent in his bowler hat on entering the back door, be called Mr Short ? With this thought in his mind he almost laughed out loud and had to put his hand over his mouth to hide the fact – but Mr. Short didn't notice anything. He was much too busy praising Bess's cake baking ability and had his eyes on the lump that remained in the cake tin. She didn't need any prompting and had the good sense to realise that anyone from the M. of A. should be handled with care.

'Do ee hev a piece more cake,' she said, picking up the knife.

'Well, I don't know. I shouldn't really, but alright, thank you, just a small piece if you don't mind.' Mr. Short hadn't tasted cake like this for a long time. 'Got to watch the old diet a bit you know" he added, 'but your cake is really delicious.'

Bess smiled sweetly and Tom looked at her approvingly. She knew how to get on the right side of the people that mattered, and Tom had about made up his mind that Mr. Short wasn't there to do them much harm —which, as it turned out, was near enough right.

'Now, said Mr. Short, after washing down the cake with his mug of tea, 'You are no doubt wondering what I have come to see you about.' He paused for a moment to study the two faces before him, then went on, 'You will have heard by now I am sure, that there is in existence a group of people called the Women's Land Army, which consists of selected young ladies who are ideally suited to take an active part in the farming community."

'Most of them,' he continued after giving Bess time to refill his mug with tea, 'are from the smallholdings around about and therefore quite experienced in agricultural ways, although surplus to requirements, as it were. Others have been brought up in a rural environment and are used to the countryside, but there are some from the towns and cities who have shown an earnest desire to help out on the land and they have all been put through an exhaustive course of animal husbandry and general farming practice, conducive to this area I may say, and have been adjudged suitable by us, the Ministry of Agriculture, to be of considerable assistance upon the bigger farms such as yours here at Stoney Downe."

Tom was watching his visitor very closely and taking in every word. He had not missed the meaningful look and the slightly harder tone of voice when mention of these 'young ladies being adjudged suitable by the Ministry of Agriculture' was made. His first reaction was to reject the idea that women could do a man's job on a farm. They might be alright for feeding calves and poultry and could even help with the milking, but in his mind 'maids should be in the kitchen, 'elpin mother t' cook and clane,' and he was about to put this point to Mr. Short when Bess, who had guessed what was on her husband's mind, stuck the tea pot under his nose, and with a look that Tom knew only too well, said, 'Drop more tay, my 'andsome?' and then turning to Mr. Short, 'Do ee carry on, my dear. Us be finding this very interestin.'

'Well,' continued Mr. Short, 'the situation at the moment is that we have a number of these young ladies billeted in a hostel in Newton Waybrook, and every day they are transported to various farmsteads to do their bit for the war effort, but we would like to get them farther afield and you don't need to be reminded I'm quite sure, of the distance between yourselves and Newton Waybrook. You have done the journey often enough to the market there. It must be all of sixteen miles or more, so the travelling difficulties to and fro twice a day will be obvious to you.

Now, we see the solution to the problem to be very simple. We will select one of these young ladies and bring her along to see you. If you think she is suitable, we would want her to stay with you and lodge here. You will of course receive the full allowance for her while she is with you, but I want to make it quite clear to you both that her reason for being here is to increase, or at least, help to increase the production of food. These are very difficult days for all of us, and we must all do what we can to defeat the common enemy.'

Mr. Short looked closely at Tom and Bess. 'I realise that this will be a very important decision for you to make,' he said. 'It will be as though you have acquired a new member of the family who will join in almost everything you do, at work as well as in your leisure time. She will, I feel certain, become a welcome addition to the farm and to the household, and the particular young lady that I have in mind would be well suited to you both.'

He rose to his feet. 'Now I must be on my way, but please let me bring her out to see you, for the matter is of as much importance to her as it is to your good selves and, indeed, the responsibility of putting the right person in the right place weighs heavily on my shoulders. Now I really must be going. I have more farms to visit and time, I'm afraid, waits for no one. Before I depart, however, can I ask you to give me some indication as to how you feel about it all?'

Tom looked at Bess and scratched his head thoughtfully. He wasn't quite sure what to make of it, and the expression on his wife's face puzzled him even more.

'Whaddee think about it, maid?' he said at last. Tis up t'you really.'

Bess's eyes were alight with the scheme of it all. Now someone of her own kind could be here. Someone she could talk to, woman to woman. Someone with whom she could discuss things. Feminine things. Being as isolated as they were, she rarely saw anyone except Tom and Joe, and there wasn't a lot of time for gossip on her weekly visits to the village shop to collect their rations. The only other time she came into contact with anyone was when she was able to attend Chapel, and then most of the other folks seemed to find reason or excuse to 'Get away homeward t' see t' things as soon as the service was over.

But now she looked at Tom and said 'No, my 'andsome. Tid'n up to me. You got the farm t' run, you and Joe, and tha's what we live on. Lord knaws you could do with some 'elp, both of ee, and ther's no men round yer now tha's worth much....' then tilting her head sideways....' but I would dearly like t' meet the young maid.'

Tom turned from his wife to Mr. Short. 'Well that settles it,' he said. 'You bring on the young lady and I reckn us'll find her plenty t' do, and I think you c'n be sure....' he paused and looked at Bess again, 'you c'n be sure as eggs,' he said with a smile, 'er'll 'ave a good 'ome yer.'

'Exactly as I thought,' said Mr. Short, 'and I'm very pleased to hear your decision. Now I really must be going, but we shall meet again in two or three days time.'

As he made for the door, he turned to Bess. 'Thank you again for your hospitality, and a very good day to you, Mrs. Dryfield.'

'Most welcome I'm sure,' said a very excited lady of the house.

'I better way see ee out t' the gate, Mr. Short,' said Tom as he followed his visitor through the door and into the yard. 'Us've got an ol' rooster yer th't don't take too kindly t' strangers and....'

Tom's warning was about five seconds too late.'

'Yee! Ow! Ow! ' shouted the unfortunate man from

the Ministry as he suddenly had to fend off an attack to his rear by a vicious beak and a pair of claws attached to a huge mass of feathers.

'You varmint, you'll do that once too offen!' shouted Tom as he aimed his stick at the ill-tempered old rooster and sent it scurrying across the yard. 'Sorry about that, Mr. Short. I didn' see 'e wuz so close to ee. 'E's a fair devil when 'e wants t' be, but one o' these days us'll make a bleddy good dinner out o' that one.'

Mr. Short made no reply, but thought to himself that it would be a great pleasure to lend a hand at ringing the bird's neck. He rather painfully got into his car and started the engine and with a slight wave of his hand in farewell he drove off down the lane.

'I don' reckn èll be in a 'urry to come through that gate again! Joe had walked over to join his father as he closed the gate, 'What wuz it all bout, what did 'e want t' see you and mother fer?'

'Well,' said Tom, with some relief in his voice. 'Twad'n nort to do with they there pigs like us thought, but I'm beggered if there id'n gwain be some changes round yer, I'll tell ee straight!' And he went on to explain to Joe the reason for Mr. Short's visit.

'A Land Army Girl?' queried Joe incredulously. 'What, livin' yer in our 'ouse? What-hevver d'mother think bout it, and what-hevver's a maid gwain do round yer all day?'

'I s'pose us'll 'ave to wait and see boy,' said Tom. 'Praps 'er might do somethin with the bullocks and pigs, but us'll 'ave t' see. As regards Mother, well, 'er's happy as a cat wi' two tails and c'n ardly wait fer the maid t' come in over th' door-step.'

'Aise, I c'n see Mother bein like that,' Joe said thoughtfully, 'but I can't see what a maid's gwain do out yer all day long.'

'Us'll just 'ave to wait and see,' said Tom again, 'but you better way try an' get that ol' tractor started up and workin proper, 'cuz you'm gwain 'ave to do a lot more ploughin and workin ground when 'er gets yer. That's the reason fer 'er bein' yer, so as you and me c'n grow extra crops to 'elp the war effort.'

'Pity they didn' send us out a better tractor 'stead of a Land Army Maid,' remarked Joe. 'I've tried all ways t' get that clickin thing to work proper. C'yaw, 'e must've bin 'acked to bits long 'fore us set eyes on 'n.'

'Aise, I knaw,' answered Tom. 'Tha's th' trouble with buyin things second 'and, but there tis, there's a war on so they tell us, so us just got t' do the best us can with what us've got, and tha's it and all bout it. Anyway, my innards is tellin me tis perty near to dinner time so us may as well go in and see what Mother got t'say.'

On entering the kitchen the two men were greeted by the aroma of rabbit stew and dumplings cooking away on the stove. They took their seats and waited, but there seemed to be a lot of activity upstairs, with furniture being moved around and the sound of brushing and mats being shaken out of the bedroom window.

'What the heck is 'er on upon up there?' wondered Tom.

'I dunnaw,' replied Joe, 'but I reck'n us'll soon find out.' And sure enough, after a minute or two Bess came down to the kitchen, flushed and smiling happily.

'Oh', she exclaimed upon seeing them there. 'Is it that time already? I've just been up to see where us could put our new guest. I think 'er'll be quite comfy in the back bedroom. Tis nice and cosy in there and a goodish view out over the orchard. I must get the baid aired off proper though. Don' want 'er to caitch a cold soon as 'er gets yer.'

'Well don' get too excited and worked up bout it,' said Tom. 'I don' want fer ee to be any way disappointed with what us get — not that I think us got ort to worry bout really. Mr. Short seemed a nice enough chap. Leastways 'e was 'fore th' ol' rooster got a hold to 'n'.

Both men laughed at the mention of the bad tempered rooster, but Bess clasped her hands and said, 'Oh what a pity, poor ol' fella. 'E was such a nice man too. I 'ope e'll soon get over it.'

She moved around laying up the table for the midday meal. 'I'll just put spoons out,' she said. 'You won't want knives and forks fer rabbit stew, will ee?'

'Now donnee fuss so,' said Tom. 'You'm gettin yerself all of a 'eap fer nort. Now that maid is comin yer

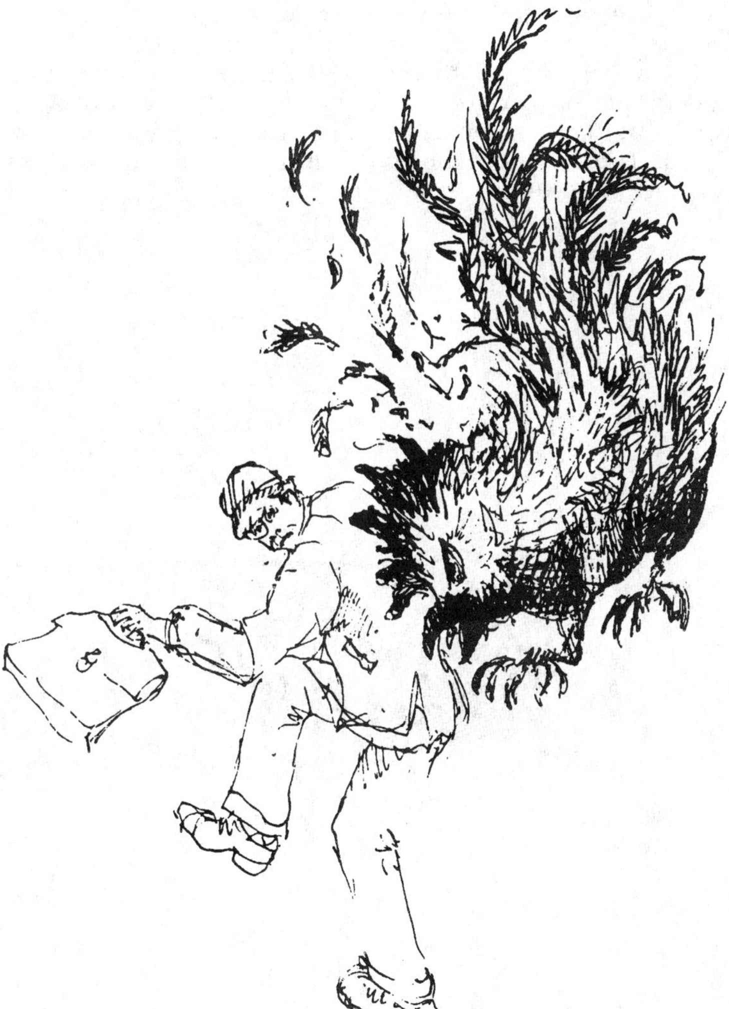

to do a job and nort else. Anybody'd think 'er wuz comin' to spend the Christmas 'olidays the way you'm gwain on.'

'Yes, I knaw, and I'm sorry, my 'andsome,' said Bess. 'But I do want 'er to feel at home yer. Poor cheel might be miles away from 'er own kin.'

'Aise I s'pose,' Tom had to admit. 'Aise, us'll 'ave to do what us can to make the maid welcome, and that includes you, Joe. Strikes me you'm keepin' a bit quiet about it , so what've ee got to say, ort 'r nort?'

'I'll tell ee more bout it when I've 'ad me rabbit stew,' replied Joe, with a grin.

3

Three days went by and Mr. Short had not returned. The fourth day came and went and still there was no sign of any visitors, and Bess was becoming a little concerned. Surely, she thought to herself, nothing could have happened to change their minds. She even began to wonder if it all hadn't been some kind of silly dream, and that Mr. Short hadn't been to see them at all. But of course he had. Wasn't it him that had enjoyed her cake so much?

For the umpteenth time she climbed the stairs and looked into the back bedroom. Not since Joe was born could she remember getting so all worked up and excited about anything. It was going to be just like Mr. Short had said.....'as though you have acquired a new member of the family.'

If she could name but one regret in her married life it would, it seemed to her, be the fact that she had not produced more children, and she often thought that Tom had felt this as well. Not that there was any apparent reason for the absence of children around the place. It was just something that had not happened. But now something which could be called 'the next best thing' maybe was going to happen, and as each hour passed, she was getting more and more het up with it all.

She crossed to the bedroom window from where she could see quite some distance down the lane. This was the only direction from which anyone would approach the farm, and she spent several minutes watching for any kind of movement. Much closer to the farm she could see Joe, who was endeavouring to repair the orchard gate — a job she knew had been crying out to be done for many a month. She smiled as she suddenly realised that from the orchard gate Joe too would have an uninterrupted view right down the lane.

When the fifth day came since Mr. Short's visit, Bess was beginning to run out of patience.

'S'pose I better go down and get some dinner on the table,' she said to herself. 'They two'll be in soon lookin fer somethin t'eat I reck'n. Oh, I do wish folks 'd do what they say they'm gwain do instead of angin' us about like this.'

She turned from the bedroom and descended the stairs towards the kitchen. As she reached the bottom she heard Tom's voice calling from the yard.

'Bess, Bess, be you in there?'

'What is it Tom?' Bess called back.

'Car comin up the lane,' shouted Tom. 'Looks like Mr. Short, and e've got somebody with 'n!'

As she dashed through the passage to the back door she wondered briefly how Tom could see who was coming up the lane from the yard, but then she saw that he was standing in the high doorway of the hay loft from where he could see just as much as Joe, up at the orchard gate. Her heart skipped a beat as she rushed back to the kitchen and took off her apron. Then, smoothing her hair with her hands, she hurried out to the yard gate, getting there just as Mr. Short pulled up in his car. Tom came down and stood behind her, but Joe elected to stay up by the orchard gate and watch from a distance.

'Thought you'd fergot all bout us,' said Bess as Mr. Short waved a cheery greeting.

'Absolutely no chance of that,' Mr. Short assured her. 'Just a little delay in procedure, that's all. But come and meet the new addition to your household.'

Bess and Tom watched as the passenger door of the car opened and a slight, shy-looking young lady stepped out. She was dressed in the uniform of the Women's Land Army — green jumper, thick corduroy breeches, brown woollen socks up to her knees and brown shoes. On her head was the regulation hat

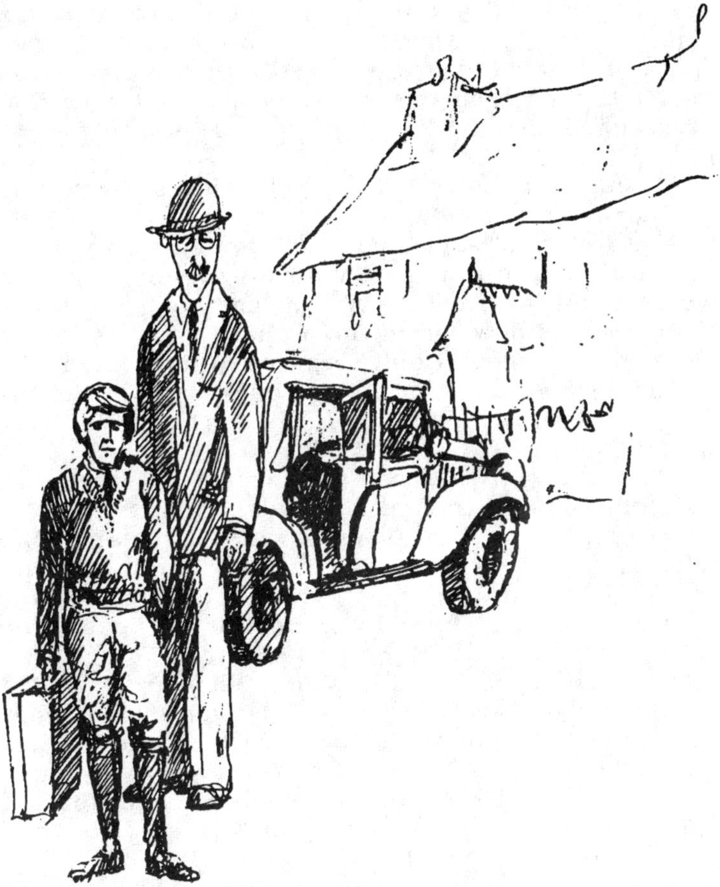

which almost covered her auburn hair, but set back just enough to reveal a pleasant, quite pretty face.

Being uncertain as to what to do next, the young lady looked first at Mr. Short and then to her new hosts.

Bess, whose heart was as big as two and was about ready to bust, decided then and there that her new charge was everything she'd hoped she would be, and reaching towards her she said, 'Welcome to our home my dear. Come on in now. I'm sure you can drink a cup o' tay. Kiddle's all on an' boilin'..... Tom, bring the maid's luggage in. Joe'll give ee a hand. You too, Mr. Short. Come on in, all of ee.' And with that she grabbed the girl by the arm and headed for the kitchen.

'All introductions when we get indoors then,' said Mr. Short.

'Aise I s'pose,' said Tom, and looking up to where Joe had been standing, 'C'mon down yer, boy, and give us a 'and with the maid's luggage.'

Joe ambled down from the orchard gate. 'Only one suitcase?' he asked. 'Don't seem much fer a maid.'

'There's another bag on the back seat,' said Mr. Short, 'but you go ahead with the case and I'll bring that one.'

Joe picked up the case and headed for the back door, followed by Tom and Mr. Short.

'P'raps,' said Tom as they walked towards the house, 'p'raps I tend to think of farm hands as bein' sort of — big and strong as you might say. 'Course I could be wrong, but the maid don't appear t'be partic'lly big, and maybe not too strong.'

Mr. Short turned towards Tom. 'Size, Mr. Dryfield,' he said, 'is not everything, and let me assure you, this young lady would not be here if my colleagues and I were not completely sure of her ability to carry out her duties. He patted Tom on the shoulder. 'I think she may well surprise you,' he said as they went through the back door.

Once inside, the two men sat down at the kitchen table and Joe, who had taken the suitcase up to the bedroom, came back down and joined them.

'Mother's up shawin the maid what's what,' he said. 'They'll be down in a minute.' And, sure enough a moment or two later a smiling Bess appeared with the new girl, also smiling and a little more relaxed — due, no doubt, to the look of her comfortable bedroom, and also to the happy chatter of this well proportioned lady of the house who was making her feel so much at home.

'Well now,' said Bess. 'What about a nice cup o' tay?'

'Ah, a wonderful idea.' Mr. Short was up on his feet. 'But first of all, I think we should all get to know each other. Now, since I know all of you, I will do the introductions.' He paused for a brief moment, then smiled as Bess said 'Well don' ee be too long bout it.'

'Mr. and Mrs. Dryfield,' he said, undeterred, 'and of course young Mr. Dryfield, please meet your new helper from the Women's Land Army, Miss Violet May Johnson.'

Tom half rose to his feet and leant across the table, stretching a calloused hand towards the girl. 'Delighted to see ee, my dear,' he said with a smile. 'I hope you'm gwain be very happy yer with us.'

Violet May looked up from a slightly bowed head, caught hold of Tom's huge fist and said, 'How d'you do, Mr. Dryfield, I'm very pleased to be here thank you.'

'C'mon now, Joe,' said Tom, 'Tis your turn. Say hullo to your new workmate.'

Joe got to his feet, awkwardly held out his hand and said, 'Ow d'ee do.'

'Pleased to meet you, Joe,' smiled Violet May, in a way that made poor Joe's ears and cheeks turn bright crimson.

Bess then said 'Now us will 'ave that cup o' tay. Violet and me've already met so I bain't gwain waste no more time talkin'. Get the cake tin out, Joe. Mr. Short, you'll be stayin fer a while, won't ee?'

'Yes indeed.' Mr. Short wasn't going to miss a slice or two of that cake. 'There are a number of details to be sorted out and some paperwork to go through. ....I was about to suggest,' he went on, 'that perhaps Joe could take Violet May around the farm and acquaint her with the surroundings. He could also perhaps point out to her what some of her duties might be.'

He paused to drink from the mug of tea that Bess had put before him. 'There are several things,' he continued, looking at Tom and Bess, 'that we must discuss before I can officially hand the young lady over to you.'

'I see,' said Tom, and turning to Joe he said, 'Soon's you've had yer tay, take the maid out round. T'won't be worth startin much now, 'fore milkin time.'

Joe nodded his head, but then Tom was forced to glance approvingly at Bess when Violet May said, 'I'll just go upstairs and put some work clothes on just in case we find something to do.' And without waiting for an answer she went up to her room and shortly reappeared wearing bib and brace overalls and an army battle dress jacket. On her feet, a pair of boots. An unbecoming outfit for a young lady? Not a bit of it! Violet May still looked as sweet as a nut and winning the admiration, and maybe a heart or two, among all those present.

'Ready, Joe?' she smiled, and Joe, who wasn't really up to being smiled at in such a manner, almost kicked the chair over as he rose from the table.

'What-hevver be ee bout, boy,' laughed Bess, much amused at Joe's embarrassment. 'Us'll want that chair again dinner time y' knaw.'

That didn't help Joe at all, so he grabbed his hat and headed for the back door before anyone else said something to add to his discomfort. 'Us'll start out in the yard,' he said to the girl, and off they went leaving Tom and Bess and Mr. Short to discuss and sort out all the relevant matters. As they disappeared out of the back door, Bess refilled the mugs with tea and replenished the plates with cake. Pulling up a chair, she took her place at the table and looked expectantly at Mr. Short.

'Well now,' he began. 'First of all, do not be too dismayed at the rather slight build of this young lady. For reasons which I shall explain to you in due course, we have kept a close watch on her during her training spell with us and I can tell you this, she has an uncanny way of being able to strike up an immediate relationship with animals, be they cows, calves, horses, pigs, sheep or whatever. I confess I've never seen anything quite like it. She has absolutely no fear of anything on four legs and I'm convinced that this must be what she was born to do. That is to say, be employed amongst animals on a farm, and I am quite sure, Mrs. Dryfield....' he paused, lifted his piece of cake and looked at Bess, 'I am quite sure that your cooking will very soon make a noticeable difference in her physique.'

'Tis nice of ee to say that, Mr. Short,' said Bess. 'Course us'll look after the maid, won' us, Tom,? I just 'ope that er'll be 'appy with us, tha's all, and Joe's a good boy and gets on well with most. Tom'll tell ee, same as I 'ave.'

'Aise, tha's true enough,' said Tom. 'Joe's a good 'ard workin boy, and never gived us a bit o' trouble.' He chuckled quietly. 'But I got t' say I'm glad t' see the maid,' he went on, 'cuz 'er ant bin yer five minutes and looks like er've made 'erself at 'ome already, and tha's a good sign to me.'

Mr. Short looked at them both and was well satisfied. But there was more to tell of Violet May's background, and he wasted no time in relating it to the people there before him. Or at least, what he knew of it.

'It would appear,' he said, 'that life has not exactly been a bed of roses for the girl. Sadly, she lost her mother whilst still at school, just when someone of that age would most need a mother's guidance, and so it was left to her father to bring her up the best way he could. He, poor fellow, was struggling along working as a mechanic, and trying to spend as much time as possible with her, even to the extent of taking her to work with him during school holidays. That way, he could at least be sure that she had something to eat at midday.'

'They were living at Eastbourne then and it seems that whenever he had time to spare, he would take her out onto the Downs and into the countryside where, I would guess, she first realised this passion for animals. They were evidently devoted to each other, but then the worst possible thing for them happened. The war broke out and Mr. Johnson was called up into the army — the Tank Corps I believe, and Violet May was sent to live with an ageing relative in Pevensey.'

'Oh the poor cheel!' exclaimed Bess, almost in tears. 'Oh, id'n it awful, Tom. What that poor maid must've gone through!'

'Well, there's no doubt it was a terrible wrench to them both,' said Mr. Short, 'and it could not have been easy for the girl, but there was worse to come, for having had only a short period of training, her father was sent overseas to the Middle East where he has apparently been involved in the heaviest fighting. His letters home to her were fairly regular at first, but they suddenly stopped coming and it has been almost four months now since she last heard from him.'

'Oh my dear soul an' days!' cried Bess with handkerchief in hand. Tom was looking down at the floor and reaching in his pocket for his baccy tin.

'Yes,' continued Mr. Short. 'it certainly hasn't been easy and there must have been times when she has feared the worst for her father. Even so she keeps remarkably cheerful and is convinced that he will return to her one day. But more than anything, I think, it is this love of animals that keeps her going and it was fortunate indeed, that upon her eighteenth birthday, no more than two months ago, she volunteered and was accepted into the Land Army. I can tell you that she has measured up extremely well in our eyes and.... well, you know the rest.'

For a moment there was silence in the kitchen. Then Tom said, 'Tis well that you've told us this, Mr. Short.' His words came slowly as he continued, 'And we must thank ee for the tellin of it. The maid will be most welcome yer, us'll all see t' that, rest assured. There'll be plenty for 'er t' do, but I don't think I need t' tell ee that er'll be well looked after. Mother'll see to that, won't ee, my 'andsome?'

'Aw aise, my dear, you c'n rest yer heart contented.' Bess meant every word. 'That maid'll be just like one of our own. But, I do 'ope 'er 'ears from 'er daddy soon.' Then, looking at Tom she said, 'Wonder 'ow 'er's gettin on with Joe?'

4

Violet May followed Joe out of the back door and almost immediately saw the dog. 'Hello, who's this?' she asked Joe.

'This is Ben,' he answered. 'I spect 'e wuz down one o' the lower fields chasin rabbits when you arrived. Mind, e comes complete with fleas and e's coat's all matted up, so I shouldn let 'n get too close to ee. 'E lives in the stable yer with th' 'orses.'

'Oh, he's a beautiful dog, aren't you, Ben?' she said, and patted him on the head and shoulders. 'I may give you a bath and a hair cut, then you'll be more beautiful than ever.' To which remarks and treatment old Ben wagged his tail, and panted with pleasure, and followed the two young people around.

Joe gave her a sidelong glance. There wasn't a great deal of difference in their ages, he was probably a year or so older, but he had begun to experience an unusual feeling of pleasure in her company and was glad to be the one given the task of showing her around the place.

'This yer's the stable,' he informed her as they arrived at the first building.

'How many horses have you got?' she asked.

'There's three of 'm, and a pony,' he answered. 'They'll be down in the bottom field now, but us fetch 'em in for the night. Father works they mostly, and uses the pony when 'e wants t' look at the sheep. There's several o' they out on the moor, but they come in a bit closer to the farm when the weather gets rough, and they start lambin. Us've got a tractor as well, which you'll see in a minute.'

'Yer's the cow shippens,' he continued as they moved on, and explained the layout of ten stalls each side of a space in the middle, where the young calves stayed that still suckled. 'Keeps the mothers 'appy y'knaw, and us leave a quarter on they that got calves so as they c'n 'ave a drink after us finish the milkin.'

She looked over the partition which separated the stalls from the middle section, and her eyes softened. There in the straw lay three calves, the oldest not more than three weeks born.

'Can I go in?' she asked.

Joe replied by opening the little entrance door for her. She entered and knelt down beside them, and he watched as she touched each one of them in turn. They showed no fear of her as they slowly got to their feet and responded by attempting to suckle her fingers.

'Well look at you,' she said softly. 'Aren't you the lucky ones to live in such luxury. Your mums will be here soon, then you'll all be happy for sure.'

Joe leant on the partition and chewed on a piece of straw, and as she rose to her feet she looked at him and said, 'Do you think I'm a bit silly?' And then, as if to answer her own question, 'But they're so innocent and helpless.'

Holding the door open for her to come out, he said 'It don't pay to get too close to 'em y'knaw. You got to mind they don't always stay that size. Two o' they is bull calves and they'll go on to the butcher's market when they'm big enough. The little heifer's the only one us'll keep.'

'Yes, I do understand,' said Violet May. 'but you see, I know what it's like to be left on my own.'

He was suddenly puzzled as to how to reply to the girl, for he had yet to learn about the difficult times she'd had to live through, and so he decided to change the subject.

'C'mon up to the loft,' he said. 'I'll shaw ee how us thraw down the hay, ready fer the cows when they come in.'

He led the way up the rickety staircase to the floor above where he seized a prong and began to throw quantities of fodder down by the stalls, and then explained that they had to bring more hay in from the ricks when the loft was empty.

'When the cows come in make sure you let 'em find their own stall,' Joe said 'and don't tie any of 'em 'till they'm in and settled, else you'm askin fer trouble. Cows c'n be funny things sometimes. They'll nearly always come in the door in the same order an' they knaw zackly where their own stall is to, but sometimes one ov'm might nip in 'fore e's 'sposed to, an' if 'e gits in th' way, th' next one'll use 'is horns to shove 'n out of it. You c'n see what'd happen if the fust one was tied up and couldn' git out o' the way. You'd 'ave a cow with some very sore ribs.'

Violet May smiled as she listened to Joe and his strong dialect and wondered how on this earth an animal with such obvious femininity could ever be referred to as 'he' and knowing 'his' place. She had yet to learn of course that in Devon, "everything is a *he* except a Tom-cat, and that one's a *she*!" Anyway, Joe was still talking, and she was still pleased to listen.

'Us be milkin sixteen cows now,' he said, 'but nineteen'll come in altogether. Three's due to calve in the next few weeks, but the Ministry wants us to increase now that you've come yer with us so Father'll be buyin two or three more soon, though I don' knaw where us be gwain put 'em.'

Leaving the shippens, they walked out across the mewy and over to the pigsty, followed by the old dog Ben. The broken apse on the door, caused by the errant sow (now deceased) still hadn't been repaired, but Joe decided not to elaborate on that for the time being. Instead, they continued down towards the barn where the car and trailer were kept and at the side of which rested the problem of Joe's life at the moment, the reluctant tractor.

'What's happened to this one?' asked the girl. 'You've got all the plugs out, is it giving you some trouble?'

'Well, tis a bit,' replied Joe. 'Trouble is, us bought 'n second 'and, an' us don' knaw much about 'em, except that 'e runs on this yer vaporisin oil after you've got 'n started up on petrol. But this ol' thing don' want t' go on anything for very long. Tis the first tractor us've ever had and I'm 'fraid t' say it, but us got a bit t' learn about 'em. Us always worked 'orses and got on alright, but now the guvverment wants us to plough up a lot more ground so us've got this one. Tis s'posed to be quicker, but us am'n found out yet whether tis or no.'

'My dad worked on tractors,' said Violet May. 'In fact, that was his job before he was called up. Quite often he would have to go out to some of the farms near where we lived, to do repairs on all sorts of farm machinery.'

'I wish he wuz 'ere now,' said Joe unknowingly.

The girl's face fell at the sound of Joe's words and for a moment she turned away.

'It's been my greatest wish for a long time,' she said. 'He's been in the army for over two years, and been sent overseas. It's nearly four months since I've heard from him.'

Poor Joe didn't know where to look or what to say. 'C'yaw, I.... I didn' mean t'....' He was absolutely lost, but she quickly came to the rescue.

'Oh no, that's alright Joe, you weren't to know anything about it. You see, according to the newspapers his regiment has been in some pretty heavy fighting out in the desert, and no mail has come through for ages. Of course, I've been moved around a bit just lately, and it could be that the post hasn't caught up with me yet, but I'm sure I'll hear from my dad again soon.'

Joe remained silent, trying to think of the best thing to say to her, but she understood, and again came to the rescue.

'During school holidays he would always take me with him if he was called out to a farm to perhaps get a tractor started and running properly. I remember that he would always tell farmers, that as they were often out in all sorts of weather, water and muck in the tanks were a tractors biggest enemy. Then he would look at me and wink his eye and say "you can always rely on farmers to have plenty of that".'

She smiled again at Joe. 'He was pretty good with tractors, and taught me quite a lot about them. I think perhaps he wished I was a boy sometimes, although he never ever said so, but I know that he missed mum terribly after she died, and he wasn't any different from most other men I suppose, and would have liked a son to sort of follow him on.'

Casting her eyes down to the assortment of tools lying around by the side of the tractor, she carefully selected one of them. Without a word, she began to disconnect one of the supply pipes from the fuel tank, and as Joe looked on a little dubiously, she spoke again.

'You know what, Joe? I wouldn't be a bit surprised if this engine is suffering from the same old trouble. See that?' She held the pipe now detached from the tank for Joe to see. 'Look at the tank. Hardly a drop has come out and it ought to be running freely with the pipe off. Is there very much fuel in it?'

'About half full I reck'n.' he replied.

She picked up another spanner and started to remove the union which connected the pipe to the tank.

'Be ready to put your thumb over the hole when this one comes out,' she warned him. 'But don't worry if you lose some fuel. It'll be mostly muck and water, but there's a gauze filter behind this union which must be absolutely choked, so watch out now, and be quick with your thumb, Joe.'

Joe complied, and could hardly believe his eyes as the union came out with the attached filter almost solid with the saturated dust of the fields.

'It's some time since that one was last seen to,' Violet May said. 'I daresay there's a lot more muck and water in there, but it always settles in the bottom so let it run out until it's good and clean. You'll lose a bit of fuel, but that can't be helped. The poor old thing has been starved, no wonder it wouldn't run!'

With the help of some of the fuel which Joe had managed to save in an old tin, she gave the union and filter a thorough clean and then deftly replaced it at the bottom of the tank. A little more fuel was wasted in the process, but a moment later the supply pipe was reconnected and then all was under control.

'You can put the plugs back now, Joe,' she said. 'I'll just clean the float chamber out and then we'll see if it will start up. I expect the petrol side is clear.

Don't ask me why, but that side never gives much trouble.'

Then, by using the two way tap with the float chamber removed, she was able to prove both tanks were running freely, while Joe could only watch with amazement and admiration of her knowledge about a machine that'd had him flummoxed for days past.

'Where-hevver did ee learn all bout that ?' he blurted out.

'Just by watching my Dad.' She smiled at him as she primed the carburettor with petrol. 'I saw him do this job lots of times. Tell you what, you can give it a swing with the starting handle. You'll be better at that than I am.'

Joe obediently went to the front of the tractor thinking that he wouldn't have been surprised if her last remark was not entirely true. He took hold of the handle and turned the engine over once, twice, three times. At the fourth turn he got a promise from two of its four cylinders, but at the fifth he almost went around with the starting handle when, like some hibernating beast rudely awakened, the recently docile machine suddenly roared into life.

With one hand on the throttle lever Violet May looked towards Joe and laughed happily at the sight of his face. He stood there, eyes open wide and cap askew, grinning from ear to ear, looking first at the tractor and then to this slip of a girl who had accomplished in a few minutes what he had been trying to do for days. He could scarcely believe it.

'We'll give it a couple of minutes to warm up,' she shouted above the noise. 'Then we'll see how it acts with the vaporising oil.'

Joe signalled that he understood, and after a short while she reached towards the two-way tap and slowly turned it from petrol to TVO. This was the real testing time and as the fuel changed through the carburettor from one to the other, the engine faltered just for a brief moment, then picked up again and ran on in a most satisfying way. And just at that very minute, as if on cue, the three adults emerged from the kitchen door.

'Us wuz wonderin what wuz gwain on out yer,' said Tom. 'Cawd beggar my britches, you got that ol' thing

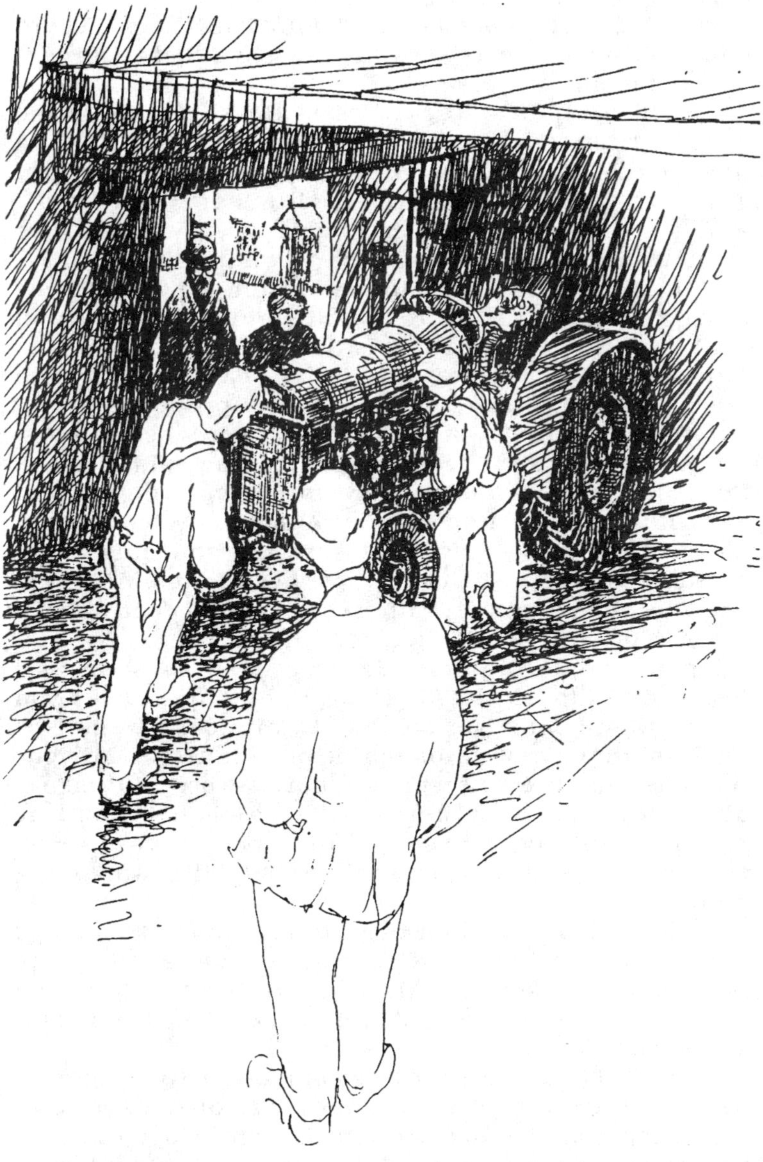

started up ! 'Ow did ee manage t' do that?'

Joe looked a little sheepishly at his father. 'Well,' he said. 'Twad'n me that done it zackly. T'was Violet May who knawed what to do.'

At this Mr. Short laughed long and loud. 'There you are, what did I tell you,' he chuckled. 'Didn't I say she might surprise you?'

'My dear soul an' days,' cried Bess. 'Seems to me there's a fair day's work done already. Well come on now. I think tis time us 'ad a bite to eat. Be you gwain stay fer a bit o' dinner, Mr. Short? I'm 'fraid I ant 'ad time to get much ready, what with all the excitement, but you'm welcome to what us've got.'

'Thank you, no,' said the man from the Ministry. 'I have a lengthy report to put in to Head Office and that will take some time, so I really must get on.' Turning to the girl he said, 'I shall call on you when I'm in this area, but if you have any problems at all, don't hesitate to get in touch. You know where I am.'

'It's very kind of you, Mr. Short,' she said. 'I think I'm going to like it here very much, but there's just one thing. If you find any letters for me, could you please send them on? I feel sure my dad must have written to me, but he can't have been told where I am and I've moved to a few different places recently.'

'Yes of course,' replied Mr. Short kindly. 'In fact I'll make some inquiries for you, and as soon as I hear anything at all, I'll come right out and let you know. Now I must be off, but in any case I shall be back in about a week or ten days. Meantime, do your best, as I'm sure you will. Try not to worry and above all, enjoy your stay here.' As he took her hand he confided quietly, 'These are nice people you know. Bye bye now.' And with that he set off towards the gate.

Violet May gave him a grateful smile and turned back to where Bess was standing, who called out to her husband, 'Tom, see Mr. Short out to the gate. You knaw what 'appened las' time....TOM! LOOK OUT!!' she shrieked.

But Tom was already in command of the situation as a sudden flurry of feathers, vicious claws and menacing beak headed straight for the rear end of the departing visitor. His stick, this time aimed with deadly accuracy, landed with a thud on the back of the old rooster, and the bird, with a painful squawk, leapt into the air, fell to the ground and lay still, its feet pointing to the sky.

Mr. Short turned quickly at the sound of the commotion and looked first at Tom, then to the prostrate bird. No one spoke as Tom stepped forward, seized it by the legs and carried it over to Bess. 'Jus' right fer Sund'y dinner,' he said. 'Wonder if Mr. Short 'd like t' come out and 'elp us t' ate 'n.' But as he looked around to offer his invitation to their visitor, he saw that he was already in his car and starting up the engine. Turning back to Bess, he said, 'Aw well, nice fresh rooster, maid. What shall I do with 'n?'

'Stick 'n in the dairy fer now,' said Bess. 'I'll see to 'n later on, but tis time us all 'ad somethin' to eat, sech as there is to be 'ad. Come on, my dear,' she said to Violet May, 'I'm sorry that 'ad to 'appen on your first day yer, but the ol' devil've bin askin' fer it fer ages.'

'Oh that's alright,' said the girl. 'I know these things have to happen.' But she couldn't help feeling sorry for the poor old rooster. He was such a fine looking bird with a magnificent set of tail feathers, the like of which you would have to travel the whole of Devon to see again — and she wasn't looking forward much to their next Sunday dinner.

With the body of the rooster deposited on the dairy floor, Bess found enough meat pie left over to provide everyone with something to eat and promised that something special would appear at supper time to celebrate this special day. So, having had a morsel or two washed down with a mug of tea, Tom thought it was about time something got done around the place.

'Won't get nowhere sittin' in yer,' he declared. 'Joe, you and me'll see if us c'n get a cartload or two o' dung out to Ten Acres. The maid c'n stay in yer with mother till tis time to get the cows in. Then praps 'er c'n come down and 'elp with the milkin.'

'Wha' bout usin the tractor now we c'n start 'n up?' asked Joe. 'We could itch up that trailer that come with 'n, with the towin bar. Twould be a good chance to see 'ow 'e works.'

'Aise,' agreed Tom. 'Twill be a might quicker than

fetchin the 'osses in. Slip along now. I'll go and get the prongs.'

Joe followed his father out through the back door, but as he got to the dairy, he suddenly stopped, for someone or something inside seemed to be having a terrible row with one of the milking pails. He opened the door and saw that the rooster, instead of being very dead, was still very much alive and doing its best to extract revenge from the first thing it saw on recovering consciousness — its own reflection in the side of the milking pail, which happened to be a shiny new one that Tom had brought home from Newton Market only a few days earlier.

Due most likely to shock from the ordeal it had just gone through, the bird had lost all of its beautiful set of tail feathers. They were lying around all over the dairy floor, leaving the rooster with an undignified bare backside. Joe went in and picked up the squawking old bird, pinning its wings to its side, and carried it back into the kitchen, where he thought his mother would have some idea as to its future, but it was Violet May who took the somewhat confused rooster from Joe's hands and cradled it in her arms.

'Oh my goodness me,' she cooed, smoothing its chest. 'You're not dead after all, and we're not going to eat you up are we? Oh no, no, no,' to which the rooster responded with a comfortable sounding gurgle, obviously pleased to be fussed over in this way, rather than being concussed by flying walking sticks.

'Well, ' said Bess. 'I'm sure I don' knaw what father'll say, but I s'pose us better put'n back with the fowls.'

'But he's lost all his tail feathers,' said the girl. 'The chickens will all laugh at him with no tail feathers, won't they?'

'I don' knaw nort about that,' said Bess, looking at Joe who, in turn, was looking at Violet May, not knowing whether to laugh or not. To him, all animals including roosters were there for one reason, and that was to supply man's needs. But here was someone who saw things differently, and he wasn't sure what to make of it.

'Couldn't we make him a little pair of trousers to

put on, just until his feathers grow again?' asked Violet May'

That did it ! Joe couldn't hold back any longer and burst out laughing. 'I c'n just see that one chasin' a hen across the yard on one leg,' he chortled 'and tryin' to undo his fly buttons with th'other one!'

'Joe Dryfield!' shouted his mother. 'Don't you dare to come in yer with that sort o' talk. Get on out t' yer dung spreadin'. Go on, this minute!' And picking up the biggest ladle she could lay her hands on, she chased him through the passage and out of the back door.

When she came back into the kitchen, flushed and breathless, Joe could still be heard guffawing down across the yard, and as Violet May looked at Bess, and Bess looked back at Violet May, without another word they both put their hands to their faces and were consumed with fits of uncontrollable laughter.

'Oh isn't he lovely,' said Violet May at last. 'I'm sure I'm going to like him ever so much.'

'My dear soul an' days.' The words came from a softer and more thoughtful Bess as she looked into the eyes of the girl, and what thoughts did she have in her mind? Well, she was a mother, and she had a son who was just about grown up.... but this was early days. She'd work on it perhaps, later.

'Come on my dear,' she said, getting back to the job in hand. 'Give me a hand with some teddies and greens. There's a nice bit o' pork outside in the meat safe. I'll stick that in the oven and twill be just about right be time the work's all finished. Shove that ol' rooster outside the back door and let 'n find his own way back to the fowls.'

And so Violet May came to Stoney Downe Farm. She followed Joe around almost everywhere, getting to know the whereabouts of this and that, and soon fell into a routine which consisted mainly of 'milkin' in the mornin', feedin', milkin' in the evenin', feedin' but she loved the work and the involvement with the animals and couldn't think of anywhere else she would rather be. The Dryfields were, as Mr. Short had said, very nice people and in no time she felt very much at home there. She helped Bess around the house whenever she could and the two got on extremely well, but as a Land Army Girl her duties were meant to be outside, and that was where she spent most of her time.

Tom was now able to make an earlier start with the horses, hauling cartloads of dung out to the fields, replenishing the loft with hay from the ricks and working down some of the ground that Joe was now ploughing up like mad with the revitalised tractor.

And what of the old rooster? Well, very quickly, he grew a brand new set of tail feathers which equalled the magnificence of the ones he'd had before, and pretty soon he was up to his old tricks of chasing any stranger that he didn't like the look of. Except that now he chased with an odd difference. When coming to within two or three feet of his quarry he would stop short, flatten himself on the ground with wings spread out, then lift his head so that he could see backwards and upwards. Having in this way satisfied himself that no missiles were heading in his direction, he would then amble off back to his hens happy in the belief that he had once again successfully protected his territory.

But he'd certainly taken a liking to Violet May, presumably because of the tender loving care she had administered to him on the day of the near fatal episode in his life when he had been earmarked to grace the Sunday dinner table stuffed with sage and onions, for whenever he saw her in the yard he would sashay towards her in a comical sideways fashion, and anyone witnessing this would swear that he had a smile — or rather, a toothless leer — on his face, but of course there had to be an added factor. He'd learned that this particular human being always carried a certain amount of his favourite food in her pocket.

5

The days went by quick enough for everyone at Stoney Downe farm and it was some two and a half weeks after Violet May's arrival when, at the supper table on a Saturday evening, Bess reminded them all that the morrow was the second Sunday in the month and that she.... 'wuz gwain Chapel come rain or shine — so all you party better way get finished up early if you want any tay becuz by ten to six I sh'll be off out th' road. In fact, twouldn' be a bad idea if all of ee didn' come and shaw a bit o' respect t' the Lord, specially you, Joe Dryfield !'

Now, what exactly was the nature of Joe's sins no one seemed to know, least of all Joe, but perhaps Bess had something else in mind because, turning to Violet May, she said smilingly,

'What about you comin', dear? Twould be a change for ee t' get away fer a hour or two, and you might see one 'r two of yer Land Army friends. Joe c'n drive us in far's the village. Whether 'e comes in Chapel 'r no, is up to 'e.'

'I wouldn't mind going,' said Violet May. 'It would be a change, as you say. I used to go with my dad sometimes when he was at home.'

'I s'pose I could drive ee in,' Joe said. 'Twould be somethin to do, but us'll have t' milk a bit earlier so's us c'n get claned up in time. I don' knaw 'bout Father though. I spect e'll want t' stay 'ome and keep a eye on things, won' ee, Dad?'

'Aise,' Tom answered, 'there's three cows due to

calve any time now, so somebody ought t' be yer, just in case.' Then, winking a mischievous eye at Joe, he added, 'I'm fraid Pottles Cross Chapel will have t' carry on without me fer once.'

'Huh,' sniffed Bess disdainfully. 'When was the last time you put your nawse inside of Chapel door, Tom Dryfield? I reck'n us'll 'ave black snaw next time you do.'

'Waddee mean! I was in there last Harvest,' protested Tom. 'Took two sheaves o' barley in fer the decoratin, and a bag o' teddies, and two swedes. Tha's a sight more than a lot've folks done I might tell ee.'

'I knaw that,' replied Bess. 'But still, twouldn' hurt ee to come a bit more offen.'

'Don' ee worry my dear,' said Tom. 'I dare say you'll say a prayer fer me, won' ee, maid?'

'Well I s'pose if I don't, nobody else will,' replied Bess,

And everyone laughed, and that was the end of that.

And so the next day just the usual Sunday duties were carried out. Tom, whatever else anyone might say about him was a firm believer in having one day of rest if it was at all possible. On Sundays what usually had to be done got done, and nothing more. This day was no exception so the work was restricted to just milking and feeding. As Joe had suggested the previous day, the afternoon milking was started a bit earlier and this this meant they were finished in plenty of time to get all spruced up for the trip to Pottles Cross Chapel. All except Tom, who hadn't been seen since tea time.

'I spect he's out lookin' at they tha's due,' said Joe. 'I reck'n e'll be back in a minute.'

'Tid'n much odds,' said Bess. 'e idn comin t' Chapel anyway, so us might as well get ready.' And this they did, with Bess looking just so in her navy blue coat and hat to match, and Joe with his good suit on, covered by a well-worn mackintosh which, having not yet been relegated to every day use about the farm, was at least free from any dung splashes.

Violet May, as pretty as a picture, had on the clothes she was wearing on the day she arrived

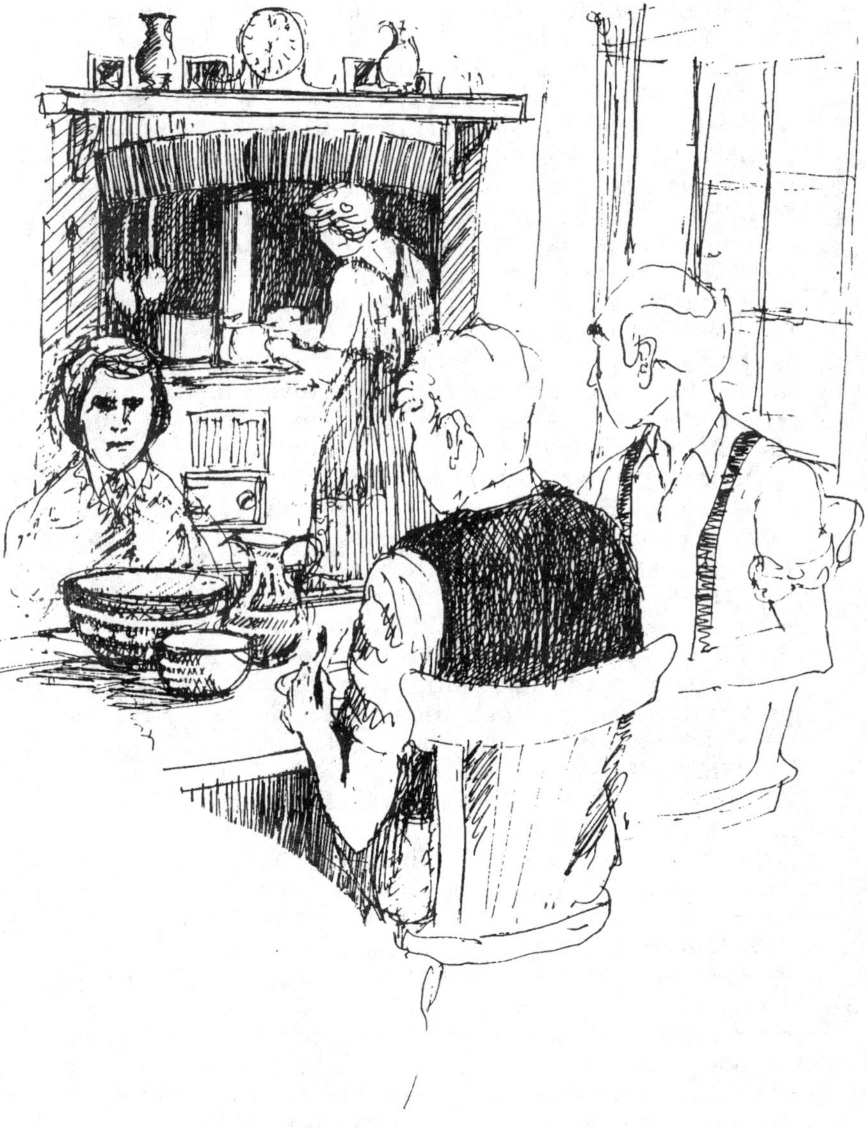

at Stoney Downe, the green pullover and the brown corduroys, knee length socks and brown shoes. As the weather was somewhat inclement, she had also put on her short great-coat and, with her hat perched just at the right angle, she looked....well...

'You'm lookin' 'andsome dear,' Bess confided in her ear, then out loud to Joe, she said, 'Joe, don' ee think 'er looks 'andsome? C'mon, tell the truth.'

Joe, forced to answer his mother looked everywhere except at the girl, grinned and said, 'Well aise, I s'pose,' then blushed right to his ears.

But it made Violet May smile happily and say, 'You look very nice too Joe,' which probably from anyone else would have made him feel worse than ever, only, somehow it didn't, and he had yet to find out why that was and why it was that he liked being in the company of this young lady.

The three of them went out the back door and made their way across the yard towards the barn, where the old Austin waited. As Joe reached to open the car door, a voice called out behind them.

'I hope you wad'n thinkin of gwain without me.'

For a moment, no one could speak, for there was Tom dressed in his very best suit — the one he kept for weddings and funerals, and other special occasions. He had even found a clean shirt to put on, with a tie as well. His mackintosh hung loosely on his shoulders and on his head sat a bowler, a hand-me-down from a relative long since gone, which was probably as old as Tom himself. On his feet were his best black boots, shining as bright as new.

'What be ee all starin' at?' he asked. 'Be us gwain Chapel or no?' and taking Bess by the arm, he steered her towards the car.

'Come on Mother,' he continued, 'You an' me'll sit in the back and they two youngsters c'n go in the front. Joe c'n drive and us'll keep eye on 'em t' see they behave in the proper manner.'

For once Bess couldn't think of very much to say, except, 'Tom Dryfield, you'm a one fer surprises, sure 'nough.' Then, as she realised that she was feeling rather pleased with her husband she added, 'but tis a pleasant one to say the least. How did ee manage t' dress up like that without me knawin.'

'I'll tell ee one day,' said Tom with a smile, 'but c'mon now, else us shan't get there in time.' And off they went in the old car, chugging along the road to Pottles Cross.

On arriving at the village, Joe stopped a short distance from the Chapel entrance, leaving them with but a few yards to walk to the door. Some people had already gone inside and taken their seats and a little group approaching from the opposite direction had someone with them who was dressed very much in the same manner as Violet May, and Tom was quick to spot them. They were a family who farmed on the other side of the parish from the Dryfields, but they knew each other quite well.

'Looks like John Galworth got a Land Army Maid,' observed Tom quietly to Bess.

'Aise I noticed that,' replied she, and with a sidelong glance at Violet May, added, 'er idn so perty as ours though.' Which remark caused Tom to shake his head and chuckle quietly.

Violet May, who was walking slightly ahead with Joe, had also seen the Land Army Girl and recognised her as being someone who she had been particularly friendly with, when staying at the hostel in Newton Waybrook.

As they met, near the steps that led up to the Chapel door, both families and the two girls greeted each other. 'Tom, Mrs. Dryfield,' said John Galworth, nodding his head, 'and Joe. Not a bad evenin fer time of the year?'

'Aise, 'ow be ee John, Mrs. Galworth?' replied Tom. 'Nice t' see ee. I see you'm like us, got a new addition to the family. Well, we find ours is a good help all round the place. Fits in well, and got a good pair of hands, don' ee knaw?'

'Well aise, tha's right Tom. Us be findin the same. Takes the strain off Missus a bit, but course 'er ant bin keepin too well just lately, what wi' one thing an' 'nother.'

'Hello, Polly,' Violet May smiled at her friend. 'Are you alright?'

'Yes, I'm fine thanks, Vi.,'she replied. 'I'm settled in pretty well. Are you getting on alright?'

'Oh yes, coudn't be better, with a really nice family too.'

And there were introductions all round, with both families taking part in friendly chatter until Bess said they ought to be getting inside, otherwise 'Praichur'll be startin' up without us.'

Inside the Chapel the people were gradually quietening down in anticipation of the preacher's opening sentences. The Dryfields and Galworths sat in one row near the back, with their girls between them. The Chapel was almost full, the time exactly half past six and the congregation fell silent as the preacher stepped up into the pulpit. He paused for a moment, moved his notes around, put his hands to his mouth as he cleared his throat, then began to speak.

'My friends, I bring a Christian Welcome on this Sunday evening in the name of the Lord Jesus, to all who have come to worship in His House. May we feel His presence now in the time that we have, and as we leave at the end let us be able to surely say that it was good to be here. Praise the Lord now with hearts and voices as we sing our first hymn, number 519. 'Stand up, stand up for Jesus. Ye soldiers of the Cross.'

Mrs. Cherry, the organist, signalled to the organ blower for some wind, and began to play the first two lines of this lively and lovely old hymn to get the congregation started. Not that there was any need to, because everyone knew it off by heart, but the idea was to get them all going in the right key.

This is not to say that the congregation was in any way lacking in musicality. Far from it. In the beautiful chords and phrases that lay within those well-loved hymns was the power to extract from these country people the most sensitive and well-tried harmonies. There was no choir, and therefore no choir practice, but depending on voice range each sang as he or she wanted to, which meant that most of the people sang the tune, with some of the men able to sing 'second', while others with lower voices would follow, perhaps without realising it, the bass notes of the organ. No one could argue with the end result. It was a sound that was good and full, and everyone felt lifted.

That is, as long as the organ blower could keep up with the organist. He was an elderly man, called Charlie Cooper, who had lived in the village all his life and, although before retirement, had worked for the Parish Council digging ditches and paring hedges and that kind of thing, he had recently begun to suffer some breathing problems. Funnily enough, this was a malady he shared with the organ, whose bellows were well past their best and sadly in need of repair. Against this, Mrs. Cherry, who was also the village school mistress, always delighted in getting everything she could out of the organ, especially with the tune she was now playing, which required pulling out all the stops, and consequently meant that poor Charlie, in his position at the lever behind the organ, had it all to do to keep up with the good lady.

He was beginning to lose patience with her and muttering things to himself, like, '...this's th' last time er'll caitch me pumpin th' bleddy thing fer 'er.'

But he had to keep going, because his own reputation was at stake, and all those people were singing away and the more they sang the louder Mrs. Cherry played.

As Charlie pumped as hard as he could, the words of verse three did nothing to help him in his time of need.

"Stand up, stand up for Jesus, Stand in His strength alone. The arm of flesh will fail you, You dare not trust your own...."

Struggling for breath and panting heavily, he could only think to himself 'they'll never zing nort truer th'n that.'

And in the fourth and last verse, "Stand up, stand up for Jesus, ...the strife will not be long...." two or three people in the front row swore they heard him say 'Thank Gawd fer that!'

Fortunately for Charlie, the rest of the hymns chosen by the preacher were of a more moderate and slower tempo, and so he was able to cope with the rest of the service fairly easily.

Towards the rear of the Chapel, Violet May, wedged between Polly and the Dryfields, was thoroughly enjoying the service, listening to every word as the preacher prayed for all those who were in danger and far from home, echoing her own prayers for her father. Then, the prayers for peace came.... 'that nation shall not rise against nation.... that they should forget the steps already trod and onward surge Thy way, when victor's wreaths and monarch's gems shall blend in common dust.'

As the preacher's words resounded through the Chapel she raised her eyes to the beautiful stained glass window at the opposite side of the room, which depicted Jesus surrounded by children. Outside, a wintry moon struggled to rise in a frosted sky, sending its rays earthwards, seeking it seemed, the Chapel and its window, and as it did the face of the Master appeared to slowly become alive with the light. Her eyes were transfixed on the scene and she scarcely heard the preacher announce the final hymn.

'O, thou great Friend to all the sons of men. Who once did come in humblest guise below....'

It was a favourite hymn and she somehow could remember the words. 'We look to thee; Thy truth is still the light which guides the nations, groping on their way....'

The light of the moon was now fully behind the stained glass window, shining through the face of Jesus in a way that only Violet May could see, and in that fleeting moment it was as if He smiled at her and she was unable to take her eyes away from the scene. Then the moon moved slowly on, taking its rays from the Chapel, but she had seen something, perhaps a Vision even, which told her that her dearest wish would come true. Now she was sure that her father was safe, and she would see him again, perhaps soon.

'Yes, Thou art still the Life; Thou art the Way the holiest know; Light, Life, and Way of Heaven....' The congregation sang the lovely hymn to its end, and then the preacher said the Grace, and the service was over.

Mrs. Cherry began to play something suitable as a 'voluntary' and the people got ready to leave. Tom and Joe went out ahead but Bess lingered a little. She wasn't going to miss the chance of showing off her new charge to the other ladies present. After all, these opportunities didn't come very often.

Mrs. Cherry presently emerged from behind the organ screen and she too was brought into the introductions. Not that she needed any persuasion, because she was always actively engaged in all the social 'goings on' in the village and wanted to know everything about Violet May and her friend Polly, and Bess and Mrs. Galworth were right there to supply all the information they could.

'I do hope you hear from your father soon dear,' she said to Violet May. 'It must be so worrying for you. I do know what it's like. I have three sons in the armed forces myself although thankfully they are still in England at the moment. But you must both come to our Village Hall next Saturday. We are having a Social evening with some food, whatever the rations will allow, and there will be some dancing too if we can get Bert Holley with his accordion, and Stanley Millbrook as well. He's got a kettledrum you know, and of course I shall be able to assist them on the piano. It's going to be great fun. Do try and come.'

'Oh well, I don't know,' said Violet May, looking at Bess and then at Polly. 'It's quite a long way in for us, and by the time we finish milking....'

'Aw get out, maid,' interrupted Bess. 'You and Joe c'n finish up early fer once, and it won't take ee long to come in cross the fields. Might as well enjoy yourself whilst you'm able to,' and turning to Mrs. Cherry she said, 'I reck'n you'll see they two in yer anyway, though I don' knaw bout the other young lady.'

'I'm sure it can be arranged,' said Mrs. Galworth, not wishing to outdone. 'We shall bring Polly in ourselves.' She felt rather pleased with herself, thinking that having said that, she was now a point or two up on Bess, but of course Bess had other things on her mind regarding Violet May and Joe, and wasn't put out by Mrs. Galworth's remark.

'Well there tis then, Mrs. Cherry,' she said amiably. 'Looks like you'm gwain 'ave two 'r three customers anyway. Now us better way get on I s'pose. Father and Joe be waitin patiently I shouldn wonder. See ee all next Chapel Sunday if us be livin and spared.' And, holding Violet May by the arm, she headed for the door.

'Wait a minute,' said Mrs. Galworth. 'We're coming

too. Come on, Polly, and good-night everybody.'

Outside the Chapel the menfolk stood around and talked of what they knew most about and as the women came out of the door, they solemnly said their 'Goodnights' and went their separate ways.

Now Tom was at the wheel of the old car as they drove back through the lanes to Stoney Downe. Joe was at his side, Bess and Violet May sat in the back.

'Wad'n a bad Service tonight,' said Tom, as he eased the old Austin along the road.

'Aise,' said Joe. 'Aise,' said Bess. 'What did you think of it, maid? Be ee glad you went?'

'Oh yes,' answered the girl, 'I wouldn't have missed it for anything.' Her thoughts were still full of seeing the moon shining through the beautiful stained glass window, and remained convinced that it had brought a special message just for her.

'The ol' praichur seemed to knaw what 'e wuz tellin' bout I thought,' Bess carried on. 'But anyway, the next thing us got to think of is what us be gwain do about this yer Social that Mrs. Cherry was on upon. The trouble is you see, my dear, us can't run the car as us'd like to, due to the blumin' ol' petrol rationin. Father needs most of what us get fer gwain Market, so us got to be a bit careful 'ow us use the ol' thing.'

'Well I can understand that,' said Violet May. 'But I don't really mind not going, and anyway, perhaps Joe won't feel like going either.'

'Get out do, course 'e will,' replied Bess. 'Come Saturday e'll be keen as mustard, don't you fret. I'll make sure o' that. Tidn' all that far y' knaw, if you cut down 'cross the fields. Me and Father've done it 'underds of times when us wuz younger. Only thing is, you must wear yer boots in and change into yer dancin' shoes when you get there.'

'I won't mind doing that,' said the girl. 'In fact, I shall look forward to it. Do you know,' she went on, 'this has been a lovely evening for me, and I'm sure there's nowhere else I'd rather be than at Stoney Downe Farm.'

'Well, did ee hear that, Tom?' Bess said. 'My dear soul an' days, I do believe the young maid's yer t' stay.'

'Aise,' replied Tom, as he turned the car into the yard. 'I 'eard what the maid said, and er's very welcome far's I'm concerned. What d'you say Joe?'

But Joe had got out of the car just before it had stopped, so that his father could park closer to the barn wall, and he was standing behind the old Austin near the entrance to the building which now served as temporary accommodation for the three expectant cows, due to become mothers at any time. He listened there in the moonlight with his head to one side.

'Somethin's on in yer Dad,' he said. 'Got any matches? There's a lamp just inside the door.'

Tom was quickly out of the car and so was Violet May. 'Where's the lamp Joe?' he said as he opened the door. 'Alright, I got 'n.' He struck a match and lit the hurricane lantern. Holding it over his head, he cast a practised eye on the straw-covered barn floor. Two of the cows were lying down, while the third was standing slightly apart, a little agitated, although without any doubt fully aware of what was about to happen. Tom thought for a moment as Violet May joined the two men. 'I reck'n us'll have time to change,' he said 'but us better not be too long about it.'

'I'll stay with her till you get back,' Violet May said, her eyes filled with excitement, while Bess, who had seen it all so many times before, elected to go and prepare supper for everyone in the earnest hope that they would get the job over and done with as quick as they could.

'And mind you don't get yer best britches in a mess,' was her parting shot.

'I won't,' Violet May called back as the others walked quickly towards the house, and then turned her attention to the mother-to-be.

For a moment she wondered if she really would be able to handle the situation, but then putting her worries aside, and overcoming an initial trepidation, she began to speak softly to the cow and stroked its neck and back. Slowly, Mother Nature brought into being yet one more of life's little miracles.

Inside the house Bess had raked up the fire in the stove and was getting the table laid for supper. Tom and Joe had changed out of their Sunday clothes and were pulling on their boots.

'Don' ee leave that maid out there too long by 'erself,' said Bess. 'er might not've seen a calve born before, and be fretn'd p'raps.'

'Well I don't allow ther's much to worry bout,' Tom said. 'The ol' cow've bin perty good all along, and probably idn in no hurry.'

'I daresay you'm right Father,' said Joe, but he was on his feet and on the way out to the barn, which caused Tom to look up at Bess with some surprise as he tied his boot lace.

'Now who do ee think e's worried about most,' said he to his wife. 'the cow or the maid?'

'I s'pose tis bound to be one or t'other,' said Bess, smiling to herself.

As Joe reached the barn and looked inside the half open door, his face relaxed and a smile appeared as he took in the scene before him. The cow was up on her feet and Violet May, with coat off and sleeves rolled up, was kneeling on the floor. In front of her lay a bundle of wet brown fur which she was rubbing down with handfuls of straw, aided by the mother who was nibbling at her new calf, stimulating it into activity.

Violet May looked up and smiled as Joe came in. 'It's a little heifer,' she said. 'I've cleared her mouth and nose, and she's breathing fine.'

'Well, good fer you,' said Joe. 'I reck'n us'll make a farmer out of you before us be finished.'

They stood back and gazed at this new addition to the farm, barely five minutes old. 'You watch,' he went on. 'He'll be up on his legs soon, lookin fer a drink.'

'Oh Joe,' she smiled happily at his manner of speech. 'She's not a *he*, she's a *she*. You'll get her mum all confused.'

'Aise well, *he* or *she* looks like e's gettin a bit 'ungry,' replied Joe with a grin as the calf raised its head and attempted to get up on its feet. First the rear legs and then the front, and as the front legs extended, the rear ones collapsed. So it went on two, three, four times, and at each attempt its mother mooed soft encouragement until at last it could stand on all four legs without falling.

'Let 'n go,' said Joe quietly as the calf appeared to be looking for the nourishment area. 'His mother'll shaw 'n which way to go next.' And sure enough, with a bit of help from its mother, the calf found its way to an ample supply of rich, creamy milk.

Violet May could do no more than gaze in wonderment at the scene. The birth had been perfectly simple and uncomplicated, but she had been there and alone when it happened and had not panicked or cried out for help, but had calmly done the things she remembered being taught during her brief training period. She was well pleased with herself.

When Tom's footsteps were heard outside the door, they stood back so that he could see the new arrival. With raised eyebrows, he smiled as he looked at the cow and her calf.

'It all went 'right then, boy,' he said to Joe.

'Better ask Violet May,' replied Joe. 'Twas all over be time I got yer.'

Tom frowned when he heard this, and looked towards the girl. She turned her head away and attempted to hide behind Joe's shoulder, wondering if there was something that she hadn't done. Tom turned his attention back to the cow and walked around it a couple of times looking with an expert's eye, this way and that, then at the calf which had now decided to lie down again.

'You done very well, my dear,' he said at last. 'Don' ee think the maid done well, Joe? Come on now. Tell me straight.'

'Aise I reck'n,' replied Joe, who had a good idea what his father had in mind. 'I think 'er done very well, considerin.'

'Just what I thought meself boy,' said Tom, looking at the girl with a smile, and she with a puzzled expression on her face.

'Now then,' he continued. 'I'll clane up in yer and settle 'em down fer the night. You two go on in and get washed up before supper, and whilst you'm bout it, my 'andsome,' he laid a hand on her shoulder, 'see if you can think up a nice name fer that little one down there.'

Violet May smiled and frowned at the same time.

Both Joe and his father, she felt, were being rather mysterious about something As she and Joe walked across the yard towards the house, she decided to ask him if everything was alright.

'Couldn' be better,' replied Joe.

'Well why does your dad want me to think of a name for the new calf,' she persisted. 'They haven't all got names, all the other calves I mean, have they?'

'No, tha's true,' answered Joe. 'But this is just Dad's way of sayin that e's pleased with ee, tha's all. You see, ' he explained, 'you was by yourself when the ol' cow gived birth, but you stayed with 'n and done everything right, and the cow and calve be both doin' fine and tha's what matters to Father. Now 'e wants you to put your name to 'n and the reason fer that is that fer as long as you bide yer with us, that calve'll belong to you and nuthin' will ever happen to'n unless you say so. 'Course e'll run with the rest of 'em as 'e gets older and come in with the milkin' cows evench'lly, but so long as you stay yer, e's yours.'

She fell silent then as she pondered on what to say next. So many unexpected things seemed to have happened to her since her arrival at Stoney Downe. When they got to the kitchen door she stopped and put her hand on his arm.

'Joe,' she said quietly. 'I think your mum and dad are the two nicest people I've ever met.'

'Couldn' agree with ee more on that,' said Joe with a grin. 'But then, they must think somethin bout you as well, in fact I'm sure of it, else they wouldn' do things fer ee like they do.'

'That's nice to know,' she answered, then suddenly, 'How about you, Joe, are you glad I'm here?'

Joe, taken aback by her straightforward question, looked for the right thing to say. 'Aise, course I be,' he said. 'Come on, le's get in and see what mother've found fer supper,' and as he opened the kitchen door and stood back for her to enter, he gently put his hand on her shoulder and said, 'I hope you won' ever want to go 'way and leave us.'

'Well, that's really nice to know,' she said, and smiled happily.

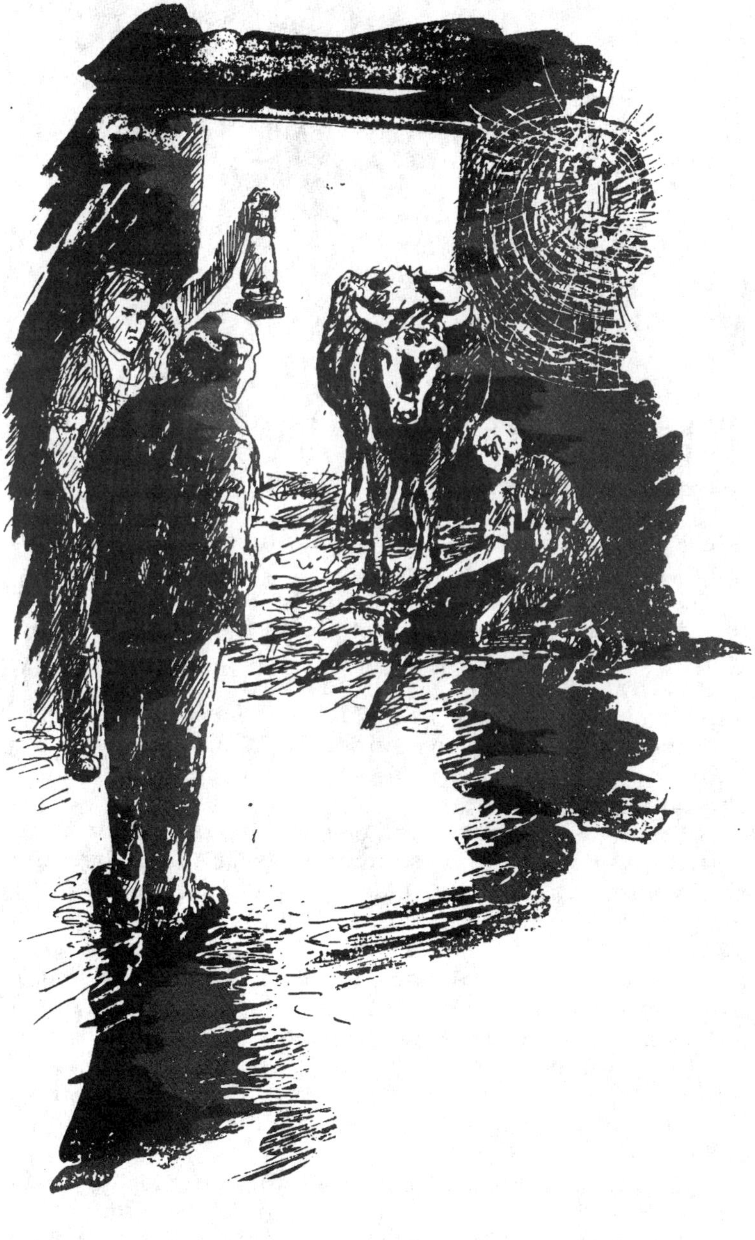

6

Bess welcomed them into the kitchen with a mug of tea and bade them sit down and drink it before they did another thing.

'I'd better wash my hands first,' said Violet May. 'We've got a new little heifer and she's a little beauty, isn't she, Joe?'

'Certainly is,' replied Joe, as he pumped the water for her, and looking at his mother, he said, 'Dad wants Violet May to put a name to 'n.'

'Is that the truth?' queried Bess. 'Do ee mean t' say 'er seen to it by 'erself? My dear soul an' days, tis a brave while since that 'appened. What name 'ave ee thought up fer 'n, my 'andsome, or else you amn thought of one yet?'

'Well I don't know what to say. I've only been here a little while. Perhaps someone else should give the calf a name,' said Violet May.

'No, no, no. That won't do at all.' Bess was adamant. 'Tis always the way o, things in this family, and always wuz, right back to Joe's gran'father's time and before that, I shouldn' wonder. If you bring a calve in the world with no trouble and by yerself, you c'n put a name to 'n and you'll 'ave all the say bout what'll 'appen to 'n, an' that's it an' all about it, so put yer mind to it and see if you c'n think up a name before Tom comes in.'

The girl sat down at the table and rested her head in her hands. She remained silent for a moment or two, and then said quietly, 'My mum's name was

Annie. I think she would be pleased to have a little calf called after her, and I'm sure my dad will be pleased as well.'

'Annie it is then,' said Bess, 'and I don' think you could 'ave a better reason for pickin that name, what say you, Joe?'

'Sounds alright t' me,' answered Joe.

'And it sounds alright t'me as well,' said Bess. 'Now yer comes Father, so le's all 'ave a bite o' supper, then us c'n get up t' baid. If you ask me, t've bin a long ol' day.'

Tom had a fair bit to say at the supper table, praising Violet May for the way she had performed with the cow and calf, and thanked Goodness that Mr. Short had picked out 'somebody with a bit o' sense and not some scatterbrain who didn' knaw a pig's ass from 'is ear-awl.'

'Don' be so crude, Tom Dryfield,' Bess said sharply. 'Remember ther's a young lady present, and you amn been long home from Chapel neither!'

'Sorry, my dear,' said Tom, looking at Violet May with an apologetic smile, but tis good t' 'ave folks around ee with a fair notion of what they'm bout.'

He paused for a moment and drank from his mug of tea. 'D'you knaw,' he went on, 'I can remember the last time I asked somebody to put a name to a calve, and I wonder if that person c'n mind it as well?' He glanced at Joe with raised eyebrows. 'Must be up four, five year ago, wad'n it, boy?'

'Well aise, course twuz.' Bess chimed in before Joe had a chance to say anything. 'You amn fergot, 'ave ee, my 'andsome?'

'No, course I amn fergot,' said Joe, just a little sharply and with some embarrassment. 'I didn' wanta say nort about that now, tha's all.'

'Aw, dear,' laughed Bess. 'Get on with ee, boy, tell the maid all bout it. I'm sure er'd like to 'ear it.'

'Yes, come on Joe.' Violet May was now all interest and encouragement. 'What did you call your calf? Is it still here? Which one is it?'

As the questions came thick and fast, Joe looked at his father and mother, and with a sigh, he said, 'Well if you mus' knaw, mine wuz born with a white flash on 'is face, so tha's what I called 'n — "Flash".

You might not 've noticed it yet, but you'll see it fer certain in th' mornin'. Your Annie got a white flash as well, and tha's what these two be laughin at.' He indicated towards his parents.

'You mean that your calf is Annie's mother then?' asked the girl, and then was startled by the sudden laughter from Tom and Bess.

'No,' shouted Tom with a guffaw. 'Joe's calf is the father of your Annie. You amn seen 'n yet because e's down in the bull field, but I reck'n you will 'fore long. 'E's a proper chap, a real gent long's you treat 'n right, idn that true, mother?'

'If you say so,' smiled Bess, 'though I don' knaw why you'm askin' me. Anyway, p'raps Joe'll make time to take the maid down there and have a look at th' ol' fella one day, but now I think tis time us all turned in. There's another busy day comin'.'

As they rose from the table, Joe and Violet May smiled at each other. 'Do ee still want t' be a farmer?' he asked. 'You c'n see that there's always somethin that you got to be doin.'

'Course I do', she replied. 'I can't think of anything else that I'd ever want to do now, but I want to be up extra early in the morning and have a look at Annie before we start the milking.'

She began to clear the dishes towards the sink, and as she did she gave Joe a sidelong glance.

'I want to make sure that white flash really is on her face,' she said.

Next morning Violet May awoke early and got dressed as quick as she could. Without stopping for the usual cup of tea, she hurried out through the kitchen door into the cold November air. As she crossed the farmyard, almost running towards the barn, she was glad that she had put on an extra jumper under her coat. On reaching the door, however, she was surprised to see that she was not the first one to get there. Tom had beaten her to it. He looked as she came through the door and noticed her surprised and concerned expression.

'Nuthin' to worry 'bout my 'andsome,' he said cheerfully. 'Li'l Annie's doin' fine and so's 'er mother, but tis always best to keep eye on 'em as much as you can fust gwain off. The ol' cow've cleansed 'erself quite well now, and they both shouldn give us any trouble. I parted 'em off from the other two las' night, and now us'll leave 'em where they be so as Annie c'n take most of the buss milk. Then us'll knaw better what to do.'

'I couldn't get out here quick enough this morning,' Violet May said. 'Do you think she ought to have a bit more to eat, now that she's feeding Annie?'

'You c'n give 'er some more cake if you mind to,' said Tom. 'Then er'll get t' knaw ee better, and come t' trust ee, don' ee knaw?'

Violet May pulled out some cattle cake from her pocket and walked quietly in beside the mother. She fed it to the cow and gently stroked her neck. 'I think she trusts me now,' she said as Tom looked on approvingly. 'But I wanted to get a closer look at Annie's face. It's funny I didn't notice her flash last night, but I can see it plain as anything now.'

'That's because er was jus' born then,' explained Tom. 'The ol' cow've clained 'er up a bit over-night, but come on now, my 'andsome, tis a cold ol' mornin and you be shiverin so us better way get indoors and 'ave a hot drink 'fore you and Joe start milkin.'

They both got it from Bess as they walked back into the kitchen. 'What-hevver be ee thinkin' bout, both of ee, gwain outside without a hot drink inside of ee on a cold mornin like this,' she scolded. 'Tis a wonder you don't caitch yer death o' cold. Yer now, I've made ee some kiddly broth. Ate it up quick and drink down a cup o' tay. Twill keep ee gwain till breakfast time. Come on, Tom, there's a bit fer you as well.'

'Well I'm pleased to knaw you ad'n fergot about me,' said Tom with mock concern and winking an eye at Violet May, who was standing next to Bess by the kitchen stove.

The two women looked at each other and grinned. 'What-hevver shall I do with'n? Bess asked, still grinning.

'You'll have to keep him,' said the girl. 'You'll never get another one like him.'

'Aise I s'pose,' said Bess. 'Ther's wiss th'n 'e about I reck'n.'

'Oh, look at the time,' said Violet May as she

pushed down the rest of the broth and swallowed most of her tea. 'I'd better hurry or else Joe will think that I'm not going to help with the milking today.'

Buttoning her coat, she rushed out through the passage to the back door and down towards the shippens.

You could get surprisingly warm even on the coldest of mornings, when sitting on a three-legged stool right up close to a cow that was willing, most of the time, to allow you to pull its teats and relieve it of its milk. They never seemed to mind as long as there was something in the manger for them to chew at. Then, when all the milk was safely in the churns and placed in position on the milk stand to await the arrival of the milk lorry, everyone could relax for a little while and return to the kitchen, where a breakfast was put in front of them which Bess reckoned to be the most important meal of the day. It usually consisted of fried ham or bacon, eggs of course, and lots of fried potato, added to which were thick slices of bread with real home made butter, washed down with huge mugs of tea. So much for war-time food rationing, which made little difference to Bess who had the ability and the resources to conjure up almost anything in the food line. If she wanted butter or cream, she made some. Bread too, and there was always more than enough in the way of vegetables. Meat could be a problem sometimes, but only because someone had to find the time to go out and catch, snare, or shoot some of the wild life of which there was plenty around the farm.

The cows had time to relax as well, after milking. While the family breakfasted and deliberated upon what was to be done for the rest of the day, they chewed at what was left of the hay in the mangers, and at the same time, manufactured a bit more dung. As Violet May's duties were mainly with the cattle, the first thing she did on emerging from the kitchen was to turn the cows out of the shippens and drive them to one of the grass fields close to the farm, where they would stay until the afternoon. In this, she was ably assisted by Ben, the old farm dog, who was looking quite a bit younger since she had given him a good scrub and a rather drastic haircut, and although the poor dog had protested somewhat while the treatment was being administered, Ben had still taken a liking to Violet May, and was never far from her side throughout the day.

Joe's first duty was to 'aive out the dung' from the shippens before starting up his tractor, and Tom helped, before looking at his horses. When Violet May returned from the field with Ben, there were the calves to feed, and pigs as well, before going back to the shippens to spread fresh bedding on the floor and replenishing the mangers with fresh hay from the loft above, in readiness for the cows when they came back for the evening milking and the night's lie in.

On this Monday morning Violet May hurried around doing her usual chores, attempting to gain a little time to spend with her new calf, Annie. She crossed the yard after an hour or so and opened the barn door, and she smiled as she saw that mother and daughter were evidently doing very well, with Annie guzzling away at an ample supply of her mother's milk, who in turn, was contentedly chewing at something or other but at the same time adopting a protective attitude over her offspring. However, she allowed Violet May to come in beside her to empty her pockets of cattle cake into the makeshift manger which Tom had fixed up in the corner, and then permitted a little bit of head rubbing and neck patting as she devoured the tasty tit-bits. Violet May wisely decided not to touch the feeding calf though, as her instinct told her that the protective mother might get the wrong idea about her motives, and then who knows what might happen? So she quietly removed herself from their quarters, and out of the barn.

As she secured the door and turned to cross the yard again, she was confronted by a cheerful looking man who greeted her with the time of day and the usual enquiry into her well being.

'I'm quite well thank you,' she replied. 'Mr. Dryfield and Joe have gone out to get some more hay in, but I shouldn't think they'll be very long. Mrs. Dryfield is indoors. Shall I go and call her for you?'

'No tha's alright, my 'andsome, I knaw me way round yer, and the fust thing you c'n do is t'call me

George,' said the man, for it was none other than George Mattford who had come to visit his friends. The first time, in fact, since his and Tom's escapade with their pigs. 'Tom an' me is old chums,' he continued. 'Matter o' fact, us went school same time and bin neighbours all our lives. You mus' be the new Land Army maid I've yer'd tell about, and if you be, I'm plaised to meet ee. What do 'em call ee might I ask? A perty maid like you oughta 'ave a perty name I should think.'

She smilingly held out her hand and took hold of his huge fist. 'My name is Violet May Johnson,' she said. 'They mostly call me Violet May around here, but I can answer to almost anything really.'

'Well make sure they don' call ee late for dinner,' said George, and his little bit of wit brought an even bigger smile to her face.

'George Mattford. I thought you was daid and yer clothes waished!' Bess's voice hailed them from the kitchen door. 'Come on in, there's a cup o' tay in th' pot. You as well, Violet. I dare say you c'n spare a minute or two.'

'I'd better stay here a bit longer, Mam,' she said. 'I can hear the horse and wagon coming,' and turning to George she added, 'I'll help Joe with the hay and tell Mr. Dryfield you're indoors.'

'Righto, my dear,' replied George as he headed for the kitchen, 'but make sure I see ee again 'fore I go, and don' ee work too 'ard. There's anuther day tomorra mind, th't ant bin teched yet.'

She smiled as she watched him disappear through the kitchen door and a minute later Tom and Joe came in through the yard gate with a wagon load of hay drawn by one of the cart horses with Tom at its head. As it approached the shippens, below the loft door, whinnies of welcome came from its partners still in the stable. Tom drew the wagon in close and tied the horse to a hook in the wall.

'You've got a visitor indoors,' said Violet May as Tom went to the rear of the wagon to untie the ropes. 'Shall I help Joe to unload? Then you can go in and see him.'

'Well, alright, my dear, you c'n help Joe if you mind to,' answered Tom. 'But did you say twas a *him*?

I wonder who that is then?'

'A friend of yours called George Mattford,' she informed him. 'He seemed like a nice man.'

'Cawd beggar my shirt, I amn set eyes on George for a brave while,' Tom said, as a vision of a big fat sow briefly appeared before him. 'I hope ther' idn nort wrong. I better way go in an' see what e's on upon. You stay an' 'elp Joe an' us'll see ee dinnertime.'

Turning to Joe she smiled sweetly and said, 'Shall I go up in the loft and pull the hay back Joe?' But she already knew what his answer would be. It was much easier to be up there than down on the wagon throwing the hay upwards to the loft doorway, and Joe was too much of a gentleman to let her do the hard bit.

'Aise, get on up top,' he said with a grin, 'else you might'n 'ave strength to ate yer dinner.'

'Aw you be a lovely boy, Joe,' she said with a mischievous attempt at the dialect, and then climbed the rickety stairway to the loft.

7

When Tom entered the kitchen his friend George Mattford was sitting at the table with a mug of tea before him.

'How be knackin' vor, my ol' beauty,' said the visitor. 'I amn seen ee fer days.'

'Days!' repeated Tom. 'You mean weeks don' ee? Us ant seen you since, well, you knaw when. Mus' be four, five weeks ago, wad'n it Mother?' He turned to Bess to verify the time lapse.

'Aw aise you, tis easy that, if not a bit longer,' said Bess. 'Come on now George, you ought to be made tell what you bin up to.'

'Well to tell ee th' truth,' said George, after swallowing his tea, 'I bin clainin up me ol' place up there to try and make it look a bit tidy. And I've 'ad the ol' Ministry man out t' see about producin' somethin extra from they fields o' mine, but tis like I told'n, I'm only there by meself, and I got 'nough t' think about wi' th' pigs an' fowls, so I don' knaw what ee wants me t' do I'm sure.'

'Aise, I see what you mean,' said Tom, with Bess nodding her head in agreement. 'Some o' these yer office people oughta come out and try farm work fer a day or two. I reck'n they'd soon tell a different tale.'

Tom's remarks were wholeheartedly agreed with by those present, and then Bess began to set the table for the midday meal. 'I 'spect they two will be in soon fer somethin t' ate,' she said, referring to Violet May and Joe. 'What about you, George, be you gwain stop fer a bit o' dinner? Ther's plenty yer, and you knaw you'm welcome.'

'Well, I don' mind if I do, thankee,' replied George. 'I ant got nort spoilin up 'ome.'

At this last remark Tom looked at George thoughtfully and wondered what, if anything, was on his friend's mind, for he knew him well enough to sense that there had to be something. It was unlike George to visit Stoney Downe in the middle of the day. It will all come out in due course, he thought to himself.

'What else 've ee bin bout since us seen ee last?' Tom's question was to try to get to the bottom of things.

'I bin lookin round fer another boar pig to take the place of that ol' saddleback don' ee knaw,' replied George. 'Took it in me mind to ride out and see ol' Josh Sandy one afternoon las' week, las Tuesd'y, I b'lieve. Aise tha's right, twas a week ago tomorra. He keeps several pigs out there, and I thought that 'e might 'ave a one that would suit. Folks do say that e's a bit rough and I der'say 'e is, but when it comes t' pigs, 'e knaws what e's tellin about.'

'You don' mean 'e out there top of West Moor do ee George?' asked Bess.

'Aise, that's 'e,' answered George. 'I knaw tis awful rough out there but 'e idn a bad sort of chap to deal with. But you 'ardly ever see his missus. Always, stays indoors when anybody comes callin, and they still got that ol' maaze boy livin there, though e's a good boy to work they say.'

'What about the boar pig?' asked Tom. 'Did ol' Josh 'ave a one there or no?'

'No, nothing much wuth lookin at,' said George. 'But I'll tell ee what 'e did 'ave.'

'Aw, wha's that then George,' prompted Tom, while Bess looked on expectantly.

'A Land Army maid.' George watched the faces of his two friends and waited for the roof to lift.

'What!' shouted Tom. 'A Land Army maid?' While Bess threw her hands up in the air and said, 'My dear soul an' days, why-hevver would they put a Land Army maid out there in that ol' place? Now come on, George. This idn another one o' your funny stories comin out, is it?'

'No, tis truth,' said George. 'I seen 'er there with me own eyes. Party bout thirty year old or so, p'raps a bit more, but, matter o'fact, tidn' zackly true t' say there's a Land Army maid out there *now* — t'would be more like it if I was to say that there *was* a Land Army Maid out there last Tuesd'y.'

Tom and Bess glanced at each other, and then back to George to await the rest of the story.

'I think what I best way do,' continued George, 'is to tell ee the story as I seen it 'appen. Seems like, when the maid fust went there to work, 'er brought 'er push-bike along as well, so whenever ol' Josh sent 'er out to the fields t' look about the sheep or the bullocks, or bring the cows in fer milkin and things like that, 'er always jumped on this yer push bike. Well, las' Tuesd'y when I was stood in the yard talkin to Josh about thase yer pigs, who should come wobblin in through the gate on the bike was the poor ol' maaze boy. Cawd, ol' Josh perty near fell over back'ards when 'e seed'n.

"Yer,' he shouted, "what be you doin on that maid's bike?"

"Well I asked 'er if I could 'ave a ride on'n," said the ol' boy, "an 'er said I could – so yer I be!"

"Aise, well 'er wouldn' up and give ee 'er push bike, jus' like that," says Josh. You shoulda come affway 'ome , then gone back t' where 'er wuz to, 'an let 'er 'ave th' bike back again so's 'er could ride'n 'ome,"

"There id'n no sense t' that," says th'ol' boy. "If I wuz aff-way 'ome, there id'n no sense to go back t' where 'er wuz to. If I'd a'done that, I'd 'ad t' walk 'ome meself. I bent maaze y'knaw!"

By this time Bess and Tom were convinced that this had to be another one of George's funny stories and began to laugh out loud.

'George,' said Tom between guffaws, 'you'm a proper bleddy cough-drop you be,' and laughed more than ever.

'Every word I'm tellin ee is true as I'm sittin yer at this table,' insisted George, 'Poor ol' Josh give'd the boy a funny kind of look, then ee looked at me in the same sort of way, and then back to the boy again. That was when I felt awful sorry for the poor ol' chap,

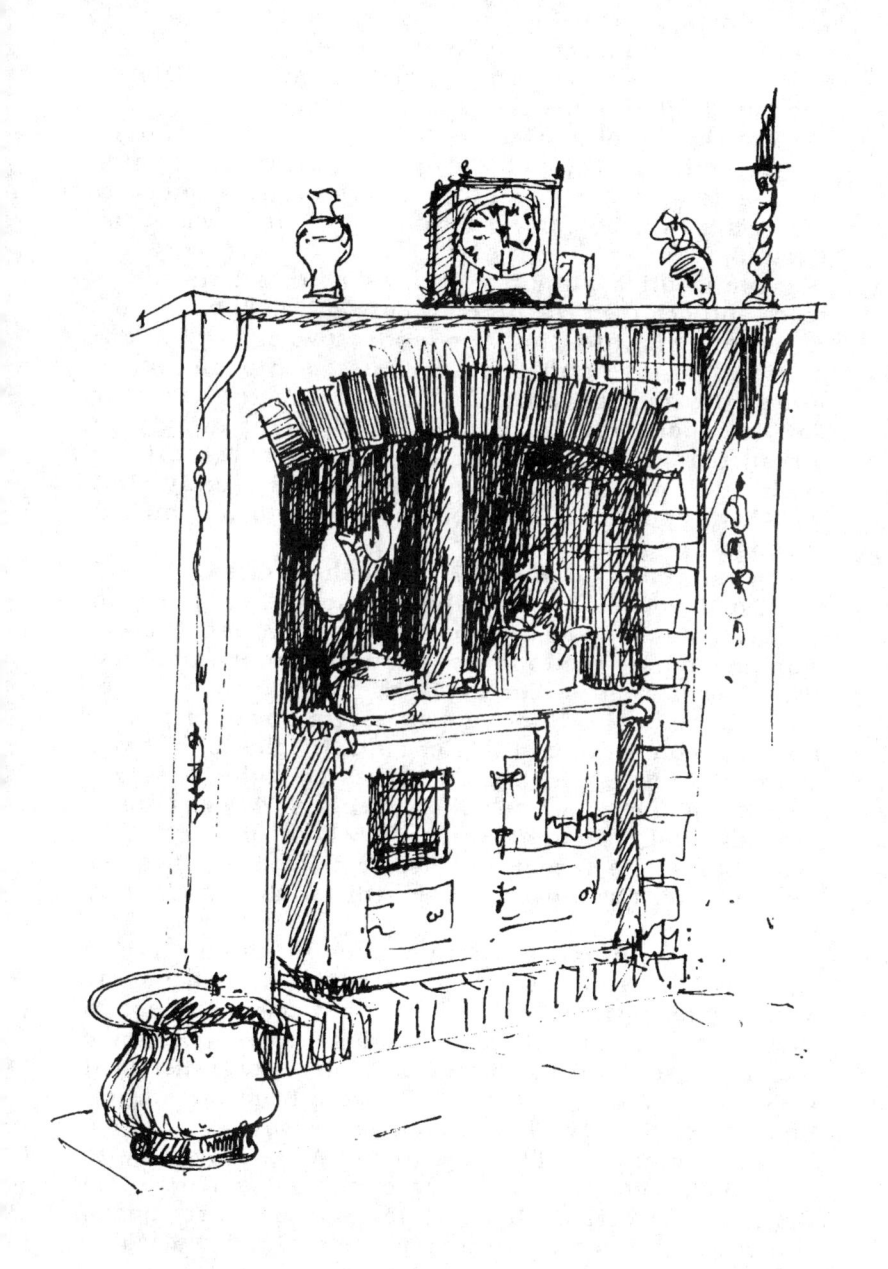

havin' to bring up the boy like ee is. And then all this t' see to in front of me, don' ee knaw? Tid'n as if ee gets much help from 'is missus neither.'

'What happened to the maid?' asked Tom. 'Did ee see anything of 'er before you left, or no?'

'Aw aise,' replied George. 'After a minute 'r two 'er come stridin in through th' gate a'puffin and pantin with a face red's a beetroot. I thought t' meself, "there's gwain be some ructions now" an' I wadn far wrong.'

"You'm all a bunch o' loonies in this house," 'er said, and grabbed the bike away from the boy.

'Then 'er said that 'er wadn gwain stay there another minute and that 'er must've bin out of 'er mind to come there in the first place, and then 'er run'd indoors and come'd out nearly right away with 'er suitcase and tied 'n on the back of 'er bike. I reck'n 'er must've ad'n packed up all ready, but whether 'r no, 'er jumped on the bike and was off out through the gate.

"What about th' milkin'?" ol' Josh shouted.'

"Do it yourself," 'er 'ollered back, then rawd off towards Newton. And then, all of a sudden the old woman come an' stood there in the doorway. Fust time I ever seen 'er in daylight. Old black coat on, face white's a sheet and 'air all 'angin down. "I told ee no good would come of it," 'er said. "I told ee, but you wouldn listen to me. Well it serves ee right, it serves ee right." Then 'er turned round and went back indoors, and I thought to meself, "Poor ol' Josh, tidn much of a life fer ee out there with they two fer certain, and t'would be worse still fer the Land Army maid".'

At this point, George's tale came to an end due to the sudden arrival of Mr. Short, the man from the Ministry of Agriculture. As Tom answered the door to his knock, he explained that some correspondence had been sent to his office for Violet May, and as it seemed obvious that the letters were from her father, he had decided to deliver them right away.

'As it happens, I've had to come out this way to see a neighbour of yours,' he explained to Tom. 'But I'm a little worried about Violet May because among the letters there is an Army Field Card, which is normally sent to next of kin. In this case the Field Card states that her father has been wounded and taken from the battle front to a base hospital. Now, just how badly he has been hurt, we don't know, but no doubt the letters will contain much more information. We can only hope that his condition is not terribly serious.'

Tom was just about to invite Mr. Short into the kitchen when Joe came up from the shippens. 'Is Mam there?' he asked with a worried look. 'Violet May've got some letters from 'er father, and er's a bit upset about 'em.'

At Tom's call Bess came hurrying along the passage to the kitchen door. She gave a quick 'Hello' to Mr. Short and demanded to know what was wrong.

'Slip down to the cow shippen will ee?' said Tom. 'The maid 've 'ad some letters from 'er daddy. Seems like e've bin hurt in the fightin an' Joe says er's a might upset over it.'

Without another word Bess left the three men at the door and walked quickly towards the shippens. Tom turned back to Mr. Short and said, 'Be ee comin in fer a minute? I dare say us'll find ee a cup o' tay. In fact you c'n stop fer a bit o' dinner if you mind to.'

'Thank you kindly, Mr. Dryfield,' replied Mr. Short. 'A cup of tea would be most welcome, but I really ought not to stay too long.'

'Well come on in anyway,' said Tom, and led the way into the kitchen.

'Ah, good day to you, Mr. Mattford,' said Mr. Short when he saw George sitting at the table. 'I hadn't expected to see you here. As a matter of fact, I was on my way up to your place to let you have our decision on your application.'

'Aw, well um, ah, ther's no 'urry, uh, any time'll do,' said George, who appeared to be somewhat ill at ease at the sight of the visitor. A fact that did not go unnoticed by Tom and caused him to give his friend a puzzled sidelong glance.

'Well I may as well tell you now, as it will save me a bit of time and petrol,' Mr. Short persisted. 'I'm afraid the Ministry cannot send you a specific member of our work force as you have requested, for reasons which I believe have already been pointed out to you. I'm very sorry, but that's how the matter stands at the moment.'

'Aise, well o'course I do see your side of it.' George was unable to hide an expression of disappointment, which again, did not go unnoticed by Tom. 'I'll think about it,' he went on. 'P'raps I'll get anuther notion on what I c'n do.'

Mr. Short nodded his head and finished the cup of tea that Tom had poured for him. 'Now I really must be going,' he said. 'Thank you for your kind offer of a meal ,Mr. Dryfield, and I do hope things will turn out well for young Violet May. Perhaps I should see her before I leave, but I hesitate to do so as I don't think I would be of much help. However, I am sure your good lady will be a pillar of strength to her at this time.' With that, he hurried through the passage and out of the kitchen door.

'Huh!' snorted George. 'He's about as much 'elp as a one legged milkin stool.'.

'Aise, I reck'n you'm right there, George,' Tom agreed with his friend. 'But somethin tells me that you got more t' say about what's 'appened to ee since us seen ee last. You ben't in no trouble, be ee?'

George's face gradually eased into a smile, and then he chuckled. 'No, I ben't in no trouble,' he said. 'But I will tell ee what I got on me mind. As a matter o' fact, tha's what I've come t' see ee fer, because I got t' talk t' somebody, and you and Bess be the only folks that I want t' tell it to.'

8

As Bess entered the cow shippen she saw that Violet May was sitting on a milking stool just inside the door. Her eyes were filled with tears and her father's letters lying on the floor beside her.

'What is it, my 'andsome?' she asked gently. 'Is it bad news?'

'No, Mam,' answered Violet May, and leant back against the wall with her hands clasped, as though resting. With tears still in her eyes, she sighed and said, 'I'm glad I'm here with all of you. You're all so good to me, and I don't think I could take this if I didn't have you to turn to.'

'That's alright my dear, you 'ave a good cry if you want to. Let it all come out, you knaw you'm with friends yer, more th'n friends I might tell ee. Us all love ee, tha's fer certain, and none of us wants t' see ee unhappy. Now, do ee want t' tell me wha's happened?'

'I'm not unhappy, Mam,' said the girl, dabbing her eyes. 'That's why I feel so silly. You see I'm so happy to have heard from my dad, although he says that he's been hurt. Quite badly I should think, because he's been taken back to a Base Hospital. All these letters have come from there, so he must have been there for a good while, but at least I know that he isn't in any danger. He says that he is able to walk around a little bit every day, but I mustn't worry, and not to write back to him because, do you know what, Mam? He thinks he's going to be sent home again.

Isn't that wonderful news? I'm so relieved and happy about it all, I just couldn't help crying. You don't think I'm silly, do you?'

'I should say not!' said Bess, who had to dab her own eyes with her hankie after listening to what the girl had to say. 'I'm sure us'll all be very happy and relieved, same as you be my love. I'm 'fraid us 'ardly knaw ther's a war on, livin' out yer, till somethin like this comes up, but come on now, le's get in and 'ave a bit o' dinner 'fore they men ate it all, then you c'n sit yerself down and rest fer a bit. You've had enough t' put up with fer one day.'

'Oh no, I don't want to rest,' said Violet May. 'There's too much to do, what with the milking and feeding and there's Annie to see to now as well. I'll just nip upstairs and wash my face, and I'll be alright.'

She got to her feet and turned towards Bess. 'You know,' she said, 'I always thought he'd come home sometime, but after the Chapel service yesterday I was never more sure of it. Now, I've got all his letters and he might even be on his way home this very minute. Don't worry about me now, Mam. I'm over the shock of hearing from him and I know that he's more or less in one piece. That's all that matters until I see him again.'

Bess had to admire the girl, and the strength she obviously possessed and was able to call upon in these early years of her life. She could go far, Bess thought, but please, not away from Stoney Downe!

'It's lovely news fer ee, my 'andsome,' she said. 'Well mostly, anyway, but if us don' make haste and get indoors, that dinner won't be wuth aitin'.'

'Wait a minute, I've just thought of something,' cried Violet May. 'All these letters were sent to my aunt in Pevensey — well she's my dad's aunt really — but she's got a bit old and wouldn't know where I've been sent. All she knows is that I'm in the Land Army and most likely gave the letters back to the postman, and he's managed to get them sent on somehow. But how will my dad know where to find me when he comes home?'

'I reck'n e'll use the same "somehow" as the postman,' said Bess with a chuckle. 'Now don' ee worry. If e's smart enough t'ave a maid like you, he won' 'ave no trouble findin ee. Now 'ere comes Joe lookin fer ee.'

'Tis alright boy,' she went on, turning her attention to him. 'Violet May 'ad some worryin news of 'er daddy but us've talked it through and p'raps tid'n so bad as us thought twas. Anyway, us be comin in fer dinner, tha's if ther's any left.'

'Aw aise,' said Joe with some relief in his voice, and looking at Violet May he added, 'Be ee sure you'm alright now? You could stay indoors this aft'noon if you mind to. I c'n see t' things out yer.'

'There now,' chimed in Bess, 'The dear of'n is worried about ee maid, bless 'is 'eart.'

His mother's words caused his neck and ears to colour up considerably, but Violet May gave way to a feeling of pleasure and smiled at Joe's concern for her.

'No, I'll be fine now, Joe,' she said, thanks all the same. 'I suppose it was a lot of startling news coming all at once after a long period of no news at all, but I've got over it now,' and slipping one arm through Joe's and the other into Bess's, she said 'Come on, you must be starving!'

When they entered the kitchen, it was George's voice that welcomed them in.

'Yer they be at last,' he said. 'Come on, Bess, Tom and me c'n 'ardly spake fer lack of food.'

'Well I der'say you done yer share of chin-waggin, George Mattford,' was Bess's reply. 'I just hope you've saved somethin fer me to listen to, tha's all.'

'Aw I reck'n I'm liable t' think of a thing or two,' replied George. 'Wha's 'appened to the young maid? Is everything alright with 'er now? Tom was sayin the ol' Ministry man brought 'er out some bad news.'

'Well as it turned out, twad'n so bad as us thought,' said Bess, 'though tis bad enough really,' and she went to explain quickly what had happened. 'Er's gone upstairs to freshen up a bit 'cos er've bin a bit upset, but er'll be back down in a minute or two.'

'Be ee sure er's alright now, mother?' asked Tom anxiously.

'Aw aise,' replied Bess. 'Twas a shock fer the poor cheel first, but er's made of good stuff and will come round again perty quick I reck'n. Er's comin down the stairs now so mind what you 'm sayin.'

Bess had no need to worry about that as far as George was concerned. On the darkest of days he could charm the hind leg off a donkey, and as Violet May came into the kitchen he sang out his greeting.

'Ah, there you be, my little ray o' sunshine. I wondered when I was gwain see ee again. Come over yer and sit by me. Now listen, my 'andsome, if these folks ben't treatin ee proper, you come up to my place. You'll be alright up there I c'n promise ee.'

'Take no notice of 'e,' said Tom, as Violet May took her seat at the table. 'Even they ol' pigs up there don' spake to 'n if they can 'elp it. Do you knaw, 'e came 'ome one night, the worse fer drink, fall'd down in the pig's 'ouse, and went t' slape, and all 'is ol' pigs got up and walked out!'

'How did *you* knaw that Tom Dryfield?' cried Bess. 'I s'pose you was there with 'n. That wouldn' have surprised me, one bit.'

The good-natured banter was carried for several minutes and pretty soon it had its desired effect on Violet May who was, by this time, smiling happily, although she had a notion that it was all put on for her benefit.

'You know,' she said, as she finished her meal, 'I like working here, but if Joe and me don't hurry up and do some work, we shall both get the sack.'

'And a bag t' put 'n in I reck'n,' said Joe, who had also shared in the laughter caused by their favourite visitor.'

'Well ther's nort much spoilin,' Tom said, 'so you two might as well go and get the cows in, and get the milkin done a bit early.'

'Will you be coming to visit us again soon?' Violet May asked George as she and Joe rose from the table.

'Aise I reck'n,' answered he. 'I've always found it a good place to come to.'

'My dad's going to be so pleased to meet all of you when he comes home,' she said. 'It may not be very long now.' Then she quickly turned and disappeared out through the passage towards the kitchen door, followed by Joe.

'Poor maid,' said Bess. 'It've shook 'er up a bit,

hearin from 'er daddy like that.'

'They seem to get on brave, 'er and Joe,' remarked George. 'Do ee think anything'll come of it or no?'

'Well,' said Bess. 'I wouldn' see nort wrong in it, and I don' think Tom would neither, would ee, my 'andsome?'

'Aw no, not at all,' replied Tom. 'Er've settled in very well yer, and got a good understandin of the bullocks, and I do fancy that er've woke the ol' boy up a bit. 'E's a lot perkier these days, and they work very well together I've noticed, but anyway George, you'd started to tell me about somethin else before us got interrupted by Mr. Short comin in. Now, be ee in a 'urry t ' get 'ome or've ee got time t'stay and tell us wha's on yer mind?'

To Bess's questioning gaze, Tom informed her that George hadn't quite finished the tale which had caused her so much laughter before the arrival of the man from the Ministry, and there was more to follow. 'And I should like to knaw the rest of it,' he said.

'Well I got time to tell it to ee if you got time to listen,' replied George. 'In fact when you've 'eard all the story, I'd appreciate to knaw your opinions on it.'

'Sounds a bit mysterious,' remarked Bess as she pulled up a chair.

'No, tidn really,' said George. 'Tis perty straightforward, but I've knawed you folks fer a long time and you'm the only ones that I want t ' tell it to. Tis like this 'ere, you see. When that Land Army maid jumped on 'er bike and left ol' Josh Sandy standin there in the yard, I took it that 'er was gwain ride all the way back to Newton Waybrook, you knaw, back to where their hostel is to. I didn' think no more about it then, but ol' Josh was shoutin at the boy, so I thought I best way get on home out of it, so I jumped in me ol' van and set off out th' rawd.

'Well I adn got more'n a mile'n 'aff when it suddenly come on to rain. Cawd twas fair chuckin it down, like it do sometimes out on the moor, and twuz comin in a bit dark as well. Then I seen this 'ere Land Army maid shelterin under a tree, perty near wet through by the looks of it, and not lookin very 'appy neither, so I thought I better way stop and see if 'er wanted a lift so far. Well, I couldn' leave 'er there like that, could I?'

'I should say not,' said Bess, who was getting quite wrapped up in George's story. 'How could anybody leave a maid out in the middle o' nowhere like that in the pourin' rain.'

'Tha's zackly what I thought,' said George. 'Anyway, I got out o' me van and asked 'er where 'er was off to.

"It don' look like I'm goin very far, does it" 'er said, and then, when I looked, I seen that 'er wadn only wet through to the skin, but 'er 'ad a flat tyre as well.'

'So you finished up givin 'er a lift all the way t' Newton I s'pose,' said Tom. 'That'd be just like you George, usin up yer petrol ration fer somebody else.'

'No, twadn like that Tom, cos I 'ardly 'ad enough petrol to get 'ome,' said George. 'I knawed there wuz about half a gallon in a can 'ome in the shed, but that would've only got me s'far as Bert Cowley's garage, and you knaw 'e won't serve nobody after six o'clock.'

'Well what ever did ee do then, George?' asked Bess, who was now getting very interested in the outcome.

'Well course, I 'ad t' put it to 'er straight,' said George. "Look 'ere," I said to 'er, "Seems t' me you ant got much choice. You either got t' go back and make yer peace with ol' Josh, or else you c'n come 'ome with me and I'll get ee in to Newton in the mornin. Only other thing you c'n do is bide yer by yourself, and I shouldn' think you'd want t' do that."

'Be you gwain tell us that you took 'er 'ome with ee, fer the night?' asked Tom, giving George a quizzical look.

'Aise, tha's just what I done,' answered George. 'But not 'fore I told 'er what the situation was up at my place. I told 'er that I lived by meself and then I told 'er 'ow I'd lost Mary nearly three year ago, and then I told 'er that if 'er didn' 'urry up and dry 'er clothes 'er'd caitch 'er death o' cold. And in the end I told 'er that I was just a 'ard workin' farmer and nort else, hopin that 'er would get my meanin, you understand me, Tom?'

'Aise, aise, course I do,' replied Tom. 'But what did

'er say bout that?'

'Well 'er thought about it fer a minute'r two, then decided to come 'ome with me. "There don't seem to be anything else I can do," 'er said. "Least I'll be able to dry out a bit." But 'er definately wadn gwain back to ol' Josh Sandy's place and couldn understand why anybody was ever sent there at all. Anyway I shoved 'er bike and 'er case in the van and 'er jumped in the front and us come away 'ome, but I couldn 'elp feelin sorry for the maid.'

'Yes o' course, tha's quite understandable,' said Bess. 'But what 'appened when you got indoors, cos the maid had t' take all 'er wet clothes off, didn' 'er?'

'Wait a minute, Mother,' Tom cut in. 'Leave George tell it his own way. 'E may not want t' mention anything of a personal nature.'

'Well I knaw that,' replied Bess, smarting just a little at Tom's rebuke. 'I jus' wondered, tha's all.'

'Aw I don' mind tellin ee,' said George. 'I wuz a bit worried about it meself fust gwain off, but then, I got too many memories of Mary in that 'ouse t' think about ort that wadn proper. Anyway, I 'aived a few logs on the fire and with a drop of oil, 'e wuz soon blazin up the chimley. Then I went out t' the kitchen and lit up the ol' Primus. I had a bit o' stew left over from dinner time which I wuz keepin fer next day, so I put that on and warmed it up. I 'ad plenty o' bread and some butter and be time that wuz ready, the maid 'ad got some dry clothes out of 'er suitcase and put they on. I s'pose t'would be what you might call 'er Sund'y Best really, but I'm beggered if 'er didn' look a lot differ'nt.'

'Whaddee mean, "differ'nt"?' asked Bess, who couldn't resist the question in spite of Tom's restraining look.

'Well, you knaw,' said George, 'Differ'nt. When they there Land Army maids be dressed up in their Land Army clothes they all look the same, but when they got their own Sund'y clothes on, they look differ'nt, and this one looked a lot differ'nt. Tha's all I c'n tell ee.'

'Aise, aise, I c'n see yer meanin', even if Mother can't,' said Tom. 'But what us would both like to knaw, that is, if you think you c'n tell us... is... well you knaw what I'm gettin at George. You bin livin on yer own up there fer the past three years and.... and....'

'Tom, I knaw what you'm tryin t' say and I understand yer meanin,' said George, 'but I told ee just now, there's too many memories of Mary up there fer me t' think of anything that idn right, and I'll tell ee the honest truth, 'er and me sat in the armchairs all through the night. I 'ad plenty o' fire wood indoors as it 'appened, so I kept a good blaze gwain and us just talked, tha's all. 'Er told me all 'bout 'erself and how 'er comed t' be in the Land Army, which 'er joined cos 'er man wuz called up in the Navy.'

'Aw, 'er's a married woman then,' observed Bess coolly, but her expression of coollness disappeared when George went on to explain that the lady in question was now a widow, because the ship her husband was on had been sunk by a German U-Boat, and he was one of several of the crew that would not come home again.

'Oh, 'ow dreadful for the poor woman,' said Bess. 'I tell ee, this yer ol' war's a terrible thing. Us don' knaw nort about it 'ardly, livin out yer, do us Tom?'

'No, tha's quite true,' declared Tom. 'You'm quite right about that, my dear.'

George was coming to the end of his story. 'Us both sot there be the fire and talked a lot and slaped a bit, an' 'fore us knawed it 'ardly, twas nigh on daybreak, so I turned to and made a pot o' tay.'

"You make yerself at 'ome," I said to 'er. "If you'm 'ungry, ther's plenty of eggs in the cubberd and some bacon in the safe outside the back door. I'm gwain out t' see to the pigs and fowls," and off I went. 'Er didn' say much except to give me 'er thanks, but when I got back, I wondered fer a minute if I wuz in the right 'ouse! The table wuz all laid up with a bit o' clane newspaper and there wuz eggs and bacon fryin', and fresh cut bread 'n butter on a plate. I tell ee straight, tis a brave while since I've 'ad that sort of treatment.'

"I waited fer you to come in," 'er said. "Tis all ready, and I made a fresh pot of tay." 'Well I ben't gwain tell ee no lies. Twas a proper job, and I told 'er so too!'

'I dare say you did George,' remarked Bess. 'Sounds t' me as if you wuz gettin a bit spoilt.'

'Didn' do'n no harm if 'e wuz,' spoke up Tom, 'but you didn' bide there all day did ee? Cos you had to get 'er back to Newton Waybrook some'ow.'

'Tha's right, I did, Tom,' said George. 'But not before 'er waished up all the dishes and put everything away, just like Mary used to and, well, I 'ad to stop and think then. Twouldn' be a bad idea if 'er could stay yer, and elp me, same way as 'er wuz doin' at ol' Josh Sandy's place. Anyway I didn' say ort to 'er about it then, cos 'er wuz packin up 'er suitcase and 'er said 'er thought that 'er ought to be gettin back to Newton so I put 'er bike and suitcase in the van and off us went.'

'Well I got a drop more petrol from Bert Cowley's garage on the way, and 'e looked a bit 'ard when 'e seen I 'ad a lady sittin in the front, but I didn' let on to 'e what twas all 'bout. Anyway, bit fu'ther on, I asked 'er what 'er would think if I went to the Ministry people in Newton and asked they if 'er could be transferred up t' my place. Well they bin on to me a time 'r two now t' see if I c'n get a bit more out of they fields o' mine, and I thought it might take the sting out of the fact that er'd walked out of ol' Josh Sandy's place.'

"I would certainly give it some thought myself," 'er said to me, "but I don't think the Ministry would agree to it because there's only you living there, and they would not see that as a desirable situation to put one Land Army girl in."

'Well, 'course not,' exclaimed Bess. 'That would never do, that'd never do at all, would it, Tom?'

'No, I s'pose not,' replied Tom looking at George. 'But somethin tells me that e've took a fancy t' this yer maid. Now, be I right or wrong George? You c'n tell us boy. You'm among friends 'ere y'knaw.'

'Well, whether 'r no, after I dropped 'er off at the hostel, I told 'er I wuz gwain try anyway, and see what the Ministry would say.' George had carefully avoided Tom's question, but knew he hadn't fooled anybody so he added a little sheepishly, 'Aise, I s'pose I 'ave took a bit of a shine to 'er. Tha's why I wuz a mite disappointed when thicky fella Mr. Short said me application wuz turned down... well there tis, now you knaw the lot of it and you'm both as wise as I be. I got t' thank ee fer listenin, and I hope I amn kept ee from yer work, Tom, but I felt like I 'ad t' tell ee all about it. Like I said before, you'm the only folks that I feel I c'n talk to.'

He got to his feet and eased himself out from behind the table. 'Lot of 'ungry mouths t' feed up 'ome,' he said. 'better way get on I s'pose...'

'George.' Bess spoke his name quietly. 'This yer Land Army maid you bin tellin us about. C'n ee tell us what 'er name is?'

'Aise I reck'n,' he said, 'though I can't think why I didn' mention it before. Branstone, tha's what tis. Kathy Branstone. Comes from up North Devon. Somewhere 'andy t' Bideford I think.'

'Well,' Bess said. 'If by any chance you should be bringin 'er this way, Tom and me would like t' meet 'er, wouldn' us, Tom?

'Tha's quite right, my 'andsome,' replied Tom who, like Bess, could see that their friend of many a long year was in need of just a little moral support. 'You mind it now, George, if you'm passin' and you got the lady with ee, make sure you bring 'er in t' meet us.'

As he spoke, George saw the look of sincerity in Tom's eyes and in Bess's too, and he felt a lot better.

'That I will Tom,' he said. 'That I will, and thank ee.' And with that, he was back to his old tomfoolery. 'Better get on,' he said with a smile. 'I got a hot dinner up 'ome t' warm up!'

'Just hark at'n,' said Bess as George disappeared out through the passage. 'Talk about ancient. But what do ee make of it all? Wouldn' surprise me a bit if George ant found hisself a fresh partner.'

'Twouldn' be a bad thing if George did pick up with somebody,' said Tom thoughtfully. 'And I tell ee this much. If George is 'aff as good at pickin out a wife as 'e is at pickin out his animals in Newton Market, e'll do alright.'

'Well I don't much like the sound of that remark, Tom Dryfield,' said Bess with a snort. 'Anybody'd think you blumin men got yer wives from Newton Waybrook on Market days!'

'No, no, I didn' mean it that way,' said Tom hastily. 'All I'm sayin is that if George picks hisself a new wife, twouldn' be nort else but a good one, tha's all. Anyway, I c'n 'ear the cows comin in across the yard, so I'll slip out and give they two a hand with the milkin.'

As he beat a retreat out through the passage to the kitchen door, Bess smiled to herself. 'I wuz only jokin, y'maaze ol' fule,' she said, thinking he was out of earshot, but the grinning face of her husband appeared again from outside the half open door.

'Aise, I knawed you wuz, my beauty,' he said, then he was gone again.

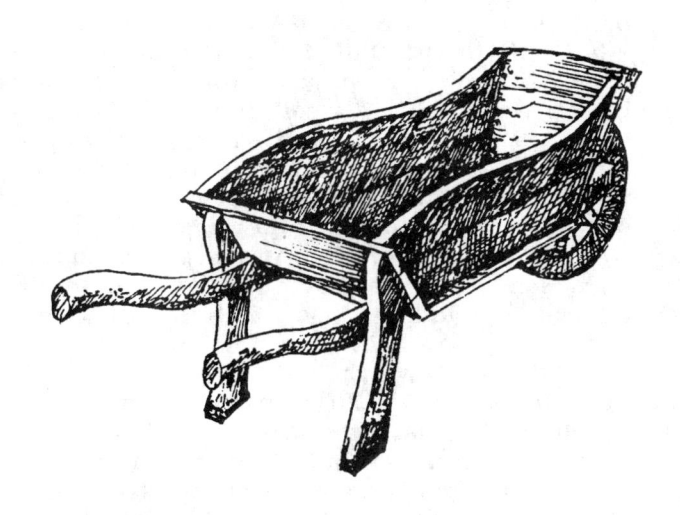

9

As the days came and went, the subject of George Mattford and his problems was gradually replaced by the coming event on Saturday evening in the Village Hall, namely, the Social 'shindig' to which Violet and Joe had been invited by Mrs. Cherry, the Chapel organist and school mistress. Bess, of course, had to be sure that 'her maid' was going to be in with a good chance of being the Belle of the Ball. It didn't matter so much about Joe. He had a pair of grey flannels and a sports coat which were quite reasonable, so all he really needed was a clean shirt, but Violet May's appearance in public was quite a different thing. She would be representing Stoney Downe Farm, or to be more precise, Bess Dryfield of Stoney Downe Farm and Bess was going to present her 'in the proper manner.'

'Le's see now, my 'andsome,' she said to Violet May a couple of evenings prior to the event. 'What be us gwain dress ee up in?'

'I really don't know,' replied the girl. 'I haven't got much in the way of clothes upstairs, but then I've never been to a social evening before. Mind you, we used to have dancing lessons at school, and that was one thing that I really enjoyed doing, and got good marks for,' she added modestly. 'But for all that, I never ever went to any dances. Dad used to say that I was still a bit young. He worried about me a bit I suppose, but he did buy me a dress once, just before he went overseas. I couldn't tell him so at the time, but I didn't like it very much.'

'Oh, why wuz that, my dear?' asked Bess.

'Well I always thought it was too big for me,' she answered. 'That was just like him you know. Whenever he bought any clothes for me he aways said that we had to allow for growing.'

'Very sensible I reck'n, to think o' that,' said Bess. 'You might not've noticed it, gwain round in yer workin clothes nearly all the time, but you've put on a pound or two since you've bin yer with us, so c'mon maid, le's go up and 'ave a look at this yer dress.' And off they went, up to Violet May's bedroom.

'I've got to admit, you're right about me putting on weight,' said the girl as she went through the clothes that were hanging in the wardrobe. 'There isn't a lot here, and what there is will have to be replaced soon, if I can find enough clothing coupons.'

'Where's that dress your daddy bought fer ee?' asked Bess.

'Still in the suitcase, folded up,' was the reply. 'I'll show it to you, but I'm not very sure about it really.' Kneeling down, she pulled the case from under the bed.

'Twon't 'urt to 'ave a look at 'n maid,' said Bess, and added with a smile, 'You ben't zackly spoilt fer choice, be ee?'

'No, I suppose not, Mam.'

Violet May had to agree as she pulled the hidden garment out from under a pile of old letters and photographs, and held it in front of her for Bess's inspection.

'Don' look too bad t' me,' was her first remark. 'Course, e'll need ironin but us c'n soon do that. Tell ee what, slip 'n on a minute so's I c'n see 'n proper.'

As Violet May changed out of her work clothes and into the dress, Bess couldn't help but say to her, 'Aise, you've put on a pound or two sure enough, but at least tis all gwain on in the right places. In fact my 'andsome, you'm gettin to be a fine maid, I must say.'

The girl smiled happily. 'That's your rabbit stew and dumplings,' she said. 'But what about the dress, do you think it could've shrunk? It certainly seems to fit me now, much better than the last time I put it on.'

'Well now you c'n see what yer daddy meant when he said that you 'ad to allow fer grawin,' said Bess. 'And the way you'm grawin you'll 'ave all the young men in the village chasin ee next Saturd'y night!'

'I don't want any young men chasing me, Mam,' said the girl. 'I shall be with Joe, and as long as he's happy with the way I look, that's all I shall be worried about.'

Her frankness took Bess a little by surprise, but she smiled and kept her thoughts to herself.

'Seems to me,' she said, 'what you want now is somethin' t' put around yer neck, like a silk scarf, if you got one. Tis rather a perty frock with all these yer little red flowers all over'n, but e's just a trifle big in the neck. If you 'ad a scarf you could put on, p'raps a blue colour one, that would just about finish it off.'

'There's this one,' said Violet May, reaching into her suitcase again. 'It was my Mother's, but Dad gave it to me to keep, as a sort of remembrance I suppose. Do you think it will match? I'm not very good at dressing up, but then, I haven't really had much practise. I can't remember the last time I went to a party, or anything like that.'

'You'm none the wiss fer that maid,' said Bess as Violet May tied the scarf around her neck.

'Now that is a perty light blue,' Bess continued, 'and it suits the dress beautiful. You'm gwain look perty as a picture, and us'll all be plaised with ee I'm sure.'

Her eyes, at that moment, had been drawn towards the suitcase on the bed. 'Tell me now,' she said, 'You got one or two photygraphs there I see, 'ave ee got any of your folks at 'ome?'

'Yes, I have got some,' said the girl. 'There aren't many, but Dad gave them to me to keep before he went away, probably so as I wouldn't forget that I had a family. Not that I ever could. Look, this is my dad, working in our garden at Eastbourne, and here's one of me when I was at school, and look at this one. It was taken by one of those beach photographers when we were walking along the sea front one day.'

Bess took the photos one by one and studied them all with a great deal of interest. The last one, taken by the beach photographer, interested her rather more than the rest of them. It showed Violet May as a gangling schoolgirl clutching her mother's hand, who in turn, had her other arm linked to her husband's. All three were smiling happily. These were, after all, happier pre-war days, but it was the dress her mother was wearing that intrigued Bess.

Although the photo was in black and white, she could see quite clearly that it was identical to the one Violet May had on at this very minute, and not only that, her mother wore a scarf around her neck which could easily have been a light blue one. It wasn't the same dress of course. Too many years had gone by since that photograph was taken, but as Bess studied the image of Violet May's mother and then looked up at the girl standing there wearing the dress and scarf, it was as though she was seeing one and the same person.

'My dear soul an' days, you do favour yer mammy, don'ee, my 'andsome,' said Bess at last, which brought a smile to the girl's face.

'Do you really think so?' she asked.

'Aise I do,' answered Bess. 'You look zackly like 'er with that dress on, and I reck'n your daddy will think the same as me when he comes back 'ome again. Anyway, tidn gwain be very long before tis Saturday night so I reck'n us'll settle fer what you got on there. C'mon now, le's get down and see if us can find a bit o' supper.'

Saturday was indeed soon upon them and the day's chores were carried out as usual. Violet May's calf, Annie, had graduated from the makeshift pen in the barn to the space between the shippens, so that her mother could return to the herd and help to increase the amount of milk which was sent to the milk factory every day, but just for the time being, a little milk would be left for Annie to suckle.

The other two cows that occupied the barn had also become mothers and provided the farm with two more calves, but they had chosen a more convenient time to perform Natures miracles, when there was plenty of help around. It all made extra work for Violet May though, and when the day's work was done she wasn't too sure whether she wanted to go to Mrs. Cherry's Social or not, and said as much to Bess.

'I think I'd just as soon stay home with you Mam,' she said. 'There's a nice fire and Joe says it will be a bit frosty tonight.'

'Aw get out do,' answered Bess. 'Twill do ee good to get away from the farm for a while. You take and go. You'm sure t 'see some of yer Land Army friends there I reck'n. Besides, Joe's lookin' forward to goin' and I sh'll feel 'appier if 'e got you along with'n.'

'Oh well, if you put it that way,' said the girl with a smile, 'I'll go upstairs and get ready. I wouldn't want to let Joe down.'

'Tha's a good maid,' said Bess. 'Now look. Tis a longish ol' walk in across the fields, so I should put on yer big coat and wear yer rubber boots. You c'n carr' yer dancin shoes one in each pocket. Now be ee sure you've 'ad enough t'ate?'

'Yes thanks, Mam,' said Violet May. There was something awfully good about being on the receiving end of Bess's fussing.

'I wonder where Joe is,' she went on. 'I haven't seen him since he finished his tea.'

'Upstairs titivatin 'isself up I reck'n,' answered Bess. 'He might'n look like much when e's yer about the farm, but 'e don' look so bad when e's dressed up proper and ther's somethin on in Pottles Cross Village that 'e wants t' go to. And 'e knaws 'ow t' put one foot before t'other one as well when it comes t' dancin, so you better way keep yer eye on 'n cos e'll 'ave all the village maidens runnin after 'n.'

'Will he now,' replied Violet May with mock concern, and then added mischieviously 'Well don'ee worry. I shall see that 'e gets 'ome safe and sound, my beauty.' Which caused Bess so much amusement that she just had to say, 'Oh my dear soul an' days, whatever next !'

At last Violet May and Joe were ready for their journey to the Social Evening at Pottles Cross. She with the flowery dress and silk scarf, and he in his sports coat and flannels, clean shirt, tie and pullover. Both of them had on their big coats and rubber boots, and both of them had their best shoes in their pockets. After saying farewell to Bess and Tom, they set out across the yard towards the farm gate where, instead of going to the right as they would have done if travelling by car, Joe steered the girl to the left. They walked past the orchard for some fifty yards or so before turning to the right along a somewhat unused track. Another hundred yards and they came to an even narrower path to the right again.

Although she had been at Stoney Downe for some weeks now, this was the first time she had been in this particular area of the farm so she clung on to Joe's coat sleeve while he explained that 'this'll take us down 'cross two fields t' the river, then tidn all that far in t' the village.'

There was a full moon in the evening sky and the crispness of the air intensified as they progressed along the track. A million stars twinkled and welcomed the night, and Violet May saw for the first time what appeared to be an old derelict barn with a thatched roof. As they got closer she could see that it wasn't a barn at all, but an old cottage in which someone must be living, because there were curtains at the windows, although the place was in darkness.

'Tha's old Johnny Crickett's 'ouse,' said Joe, as if anticipating her question. 'But 'e don' live there now.'

'Who's Johnny Crickett?' she asked. 'And why doesn't he live there any more?'

'Well, 'e worked fer us fer years,' explained Joe. 'Twuz right back in Granfer's time when 'e first came yer. I've 'eard father tell about it a few times. Nobody knawed where 'e came from but 'e turned up yer one day lookin' fer a job. Granfer took a likin to 'n and took 'n on.'

'Did he live in this cottage all the time then?' Violet May wanted to know.

'No, 'e lived in the farm at first,' said Joe. 'Then 'e met a maid from the village and after a while they wanted t' get married, but 'fore they did, 'e asked Granfer if 'e'd let'n build somewhere to live. Well, 'e wuz a good chap t' work and Granfer didn' want t' lose 'n, so between both of 'em they built up this place yer. That must've bin perty near sixty year ago, cos 'e wuz well past seventy when he died.'

'What about his wife and family?' was the girl's next question.

'They never 'ad no children,' replied Joe, 'and 'e lost his missus eight or nine year ago. Mother looked after 'n as much as 'er could when 'e 'ad to give up work, and one of us always brought'n out a cooked dinner on Sund'ys, but in the end they 'ad t' take in t' hospital becos 'e just couldn' do nort fer hisself.'

Violet May said nothing then for a while, but thought what a sad ending that was for the old man.

'Do you think they were happy living here Joe?' she inquired at last.

'Wadn no doubt about that,' replied Joe. 'But you must ask mother, 'er knaws more bout it than I do. Mind out now, us got t' go through this gate yer.'

And so they went on down across the two fields to the river, which they followed then across another field until they could see the outline of some of the buildings of the village. No lights were visible because this was wartime, and there were rigid blackout laws in force. Anyone daring to show the smallest chink of light, which could possibly be of some help to passing enemy aircraft, would incur the wrath of the village Constabulary in the shape of Police Constable Percy Southcombe. Percy wore the letters 'W.R.' upon the collar of his policeman's tunic, which meant that he was a War Reserve called back from retirement so that a younger man could go off to the battlefront. But even though he had been retired for some time, Percy was by no means past his best, as one or two errant villagers had found out to their cost. And as a result, he was held in high esteem by all the law abiding folk.

As Violet May and Joe came towards the end of their short cut across the fields, they could hear the merry sound of Bert Holley's accordion and Stan Millbrook's kettledrum, and yes, Mrs. Cherry was there as well, doing her best to keep up with them on the old piano.

'Sounds like they've started already,' observed Joe, as they rounded the corner towards the village hall entrance. 'Still,' he added, 'Us ben't all that late, and in any case I never like t' be too early, cos you'm only standin around gawpin at one 'nuther.'

Violet May smiled and remarked that the night was young and there would be plenty of time to get into the swing of things. Then they were at the door, and Joe was delving into his pocket for the admission

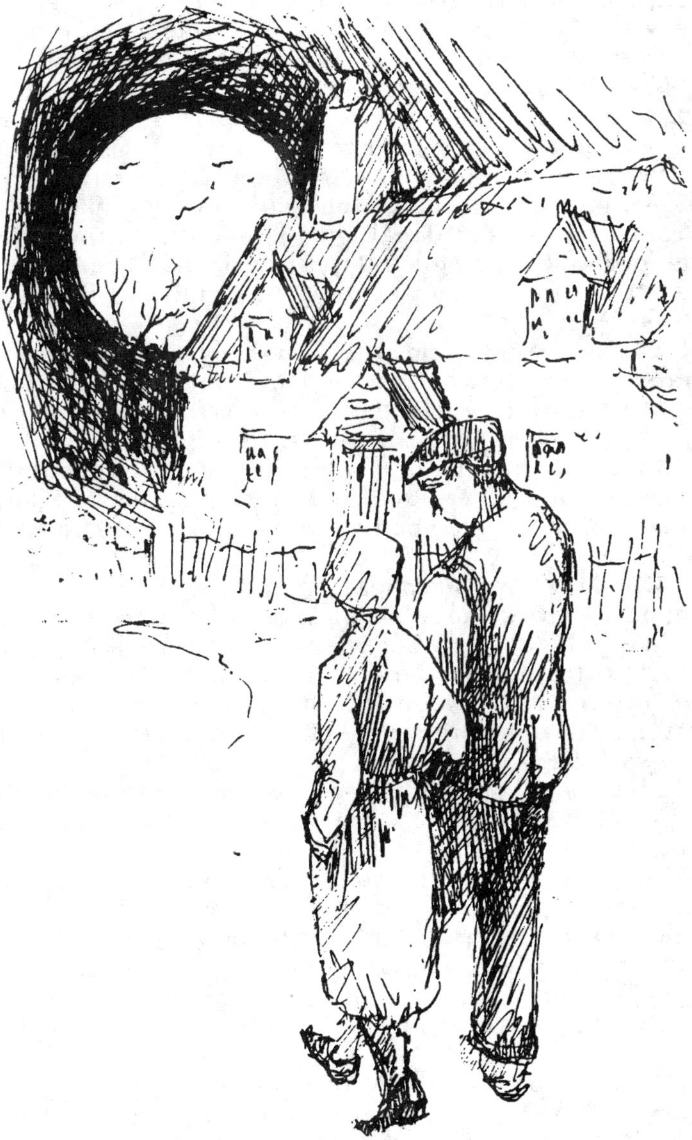

fee — one shilling each — which he paid to the treasurer, an elderly, and rather mild mannered man called Charles Smythen. He almost always worked in close collaboration with Mrs. Cherry in the social activities of the village and one was rarely seen without the other. He was also a churchwarden, and he knew everybody pretty well.

'Nice to see you've come to support us, young Joe,' he said. 'It's quite a long way in from Stoney Downe, but we're glad to see you. Mum and Dad keeping well I hope, and this is the young lady who is staying with you now, is it?' And looking at Violet May through his old spectacles, he added 'Mrs. Cherry has been telling me all about you, my dear. Come right in now and join in the fun.'

After showing them where to hang their coats and change their footwear, he added 'You'll find a couple of your Land Army friends in there somewhere.'

'Thank you,' she said, smiling sweetly, and followed Joe into the hall where it was all happening.

'Nosey ol' beggar,' Joe said quietly to her. 'e knaws everything bout everybody, and what 'e don' knaw, e'll ask.'

'Oh, he seems harmless enough,' Violet May said. 'I expect there's worse people than him around.'

Then she spotted her friend Polly across the room sitting with another girl whom she remembered from the hostel in Newton Waybrook. 'Look Joe,' she caught his arm, 'there's Polly, and I believe that's Rita with her.'

'Aise,' said Joe. 'Well you go on over and talk to 'em fer a minute and I'll see what they got on the food table.'

'Alright, I won't be long,' she said, and walked across the room to where the girls were sitting. They greeted each other warmly, Rita making the remark that she hardly recognised Violet May because she seemed to have put on quite a bit of weight. She then asked, 'Who's the good looking fella that brought you in?'

'That's Joe,' Violet May said with a smile. 'His mum and dad own Stoney Downe Farm where I am. Honestly, I couldn't wish to be in a better place. They treat me just as if I was one of the family, but look, we'll talk again later. I think Joe is getting something from the food table so I'd better go and see what it is. I'll see you both a bit later on.' And off she tripped across the room to where Joe had put a little refreshment on a plate for them both, with two glasses of cordial to wash it down.

'Lucky her,' remarked Rita, as she and Polly watched her cross the floor. 'I wouldn't be surprised if she really does become one of the family before she's much older. Just look at the way they're looking at each other.'

'Well she is a very nice girl, and she's had quite a lot to put up with since her father was called up,' answered Polly. 'Good luck to her, I say.'

The conversation ended there as the voice of Mrs. Cherry was suddenly heard by one and all.

'Come along now everyone,' she said. 'As you have already heard, the musicians are in fine form this evening and we are now going to play the Valeta. Now, I want you all to join in with this one, so come along. It doesn't matter if you're not quite sure how it goes. Just get up on your feet and have a try. I'm sure you'll soon get the hang of it.'

There was a sudden clatter as Stan Millbrook attempted to play a 'roll' on his kettledrum to start things going, which was followed by the wheezy notes from Bert Holley's ancient squeeze-box as he tried gamely to get his harmony in order. Fortunately for them both, Mrs. Cherry at the piano had her music in front of her, and with her foot hard down on the loud pedal, she was able to keep them both going in the right direction, with the result being a not too far removed rendering of this lovely old dance tune.

Joe looked at Violet May and grinned. 'Do ee fancy 'avin a go at this one?' he asked her.

'Yes please,' she replied. 'But I'm warning you, I was taught how to do this dance when I was at school, so you'd better be as good as your mum said you were.'

Joe laughed at this and grabbed her hand. 'Mother talks too much,' he said. 'Come on, shaw us all 'ow good you be.'

And then, as the trio up on the stage battled their way through the familiar chords of the well known music, the dancers carried out the equally well known steps around the floor. There was no doubt about it. Bess was right when she said that Joe 'knaws 'ow t' put one foot before t'other when it comes to dancin.' Back home on the farm with his hob-nail boots on he seemed to clutter and clump all around the place, but not so here on the dance floor. With his best shoes on, which he liked to keep for these occasions, he was as light as a feather and Violet May could well see why Bess had warned her, laughingly of course, that she had better keep an eye on him.

She had a feeling that they were being watched by some of the village 'maids', but she wasn't at all concerned about that. Like most young ladies, she loved dancing, even though there hadn't been much opportunity to take part in any of it since leaving school, but here, at this very minute, she found that she could follow Joe quite easily, matching him step for step, remembering the sequence without any trouble at all.

As they moved around the dance floor she caught herself thinking that, although she lived in the same house and worked quite a lot alongside him, this was the first time she had got this close to Joe. What did it matter if the whole roomful of people were staring at them, and a goodly number of them actually were! She knew that she was being a good if not perfect partner for him, but best of all, the look on Joe's face told her that he knew it too.

But the people were not really staring. They were only looking, some admiring perhaps, and some maybe a little envious. Whatever it was, it didn't stop the evening progressing through a fox-trot followed by a quick-step, a barn dance, a waltz and eventually the Paul Jones. She danced her way through all of them with Joe except the last one, when of course everyone had to change partners at least half a dozen times, but it didn't matter. When it was over they were back together again and everyone was happy, and she, with the flowery dress and the pale blue scarf and the 'good looking fella' and the stars in her eyes, perhaps happiest of them all. Her troubles, for the moment at any rate, were forgotten.

Between all the activities of the evening Joe had been introduced to Polly and Rita by Violet May and they were all a little amused when Polly reminded them that it was the second time inside a week that she had met Joe, as they had met on the previous Sunday outside the Chapel. Joe, in turn, had introduced Violet May to some of his friends there present, who were mostly farmer's sons like himself. One of them, Ashley Woodstock, farmed with his father just to the north of the village about a mile or so away. He was a year or two older than Joe and had recently got married to the daughter of the local butcher. The Dryfields and the Woodstocks always got on well with each other, doing the odd deal with bullocks and pigs, and as a result some considerable respect existed between the two families.

'I like the looks of yer young lady, Joe,' Ashley nodded towards Violet May who had now rejoined Polly and Rita. 'ow long 'ave ee knawed 'er?'

'Aw, must be couple o' months 'r more I s'pose,' replied Joe, 'somethin like that, but er's a Land Army maid really. Bin sent out t' help us whilst the war's on. Father's plaised with 'er I b'lieve, and Mother's delighted. Somebody of 'er own sort 'er can talk to I reck'n.'

'And what about you, boy?' said Ashley. 'I noticed 'er makes ee a perty little partner on the dance floor, didn' you, Jen?' He turned towards Jenny, his bride of about seven months who had just returned from the food table.

'Yes, I must say she's very pretty, and a nice dancer too,' replied Jenny, 'but you mustn't ask Joe too many questions, Ash, you'll embarrass him.

'Aw, get out do, Joe don' mind do ee boy,' Ashley went on. 'Tell ee what, Joe, ther's a lot to be said fer married life. Me and Jen c'n recommaind it, can't us maid?' And he gave her a playful nudge as he spoke, which caused her to hide her head behind his shoulder and flush with pleasure. 'Ash! Don't be so rude,' she said.

Joe grinned at them both and said that he hadn't thought much about it as yet, but in any case he had to save up some money first, and then the subject was suddenly put to one side as Mrs. Cherry commanded the attention of everyone to announce that there would be one more quickstep, followed by the last waltz.

'Time, I'm afraid, has overtaken us,' she said, 'and I know that some of you have quite a long walk to get home, but it has been absolutely marvellous to see so many people here this evening, and as a result, we will be able to send a sizeable donation to the Comforts for Christmas Fund for the Armed Forces.'

'So that's what twas all in aid of,' remarked Joe, as the applause died down. 'I never knawed that, did you, Ash?'

'Well I b'lieve I did 'ear somethin about it,' answered Ashley. 'But lookee 'fore there by the door. Looks t' me like some o' they there Armed Forces Mrs. Cherry was tellin' about!'

As the music began once again, Joe looked across to where Ashley had indicated and watched two soldiers stagger in. They were rather untidy with their battle dress jackets undone and hats on the back of their heads, and it was reasonable to assume that they had spent the last couple of hours and probably most of their money in the public house on the other side of the village green. His face took on a slightly worried expression as the two made a bee-line to where Polly, Rita and Violet May were sitting, and he became even more worried when the taller one pulled Violet May to her feet and was attempting to dance with her. She was obviously very uncomfortable with the situation and looked towards Joe for some help.

Ashley said, 'I think us better keep eye on they two, Joe,' but Joe was already moving because now the soldier was trying to dance his way out of the room, taking Violet May with him. On reaching the door, however, she was suddenly able to break lose from his grasp and as she did, he half turned and found himself confronted by Joe.

'Now what th' hell be you tryin t' do?' An angry Joe fired the question at the inebriated gatecrasher.

'You keep yer big nose out of it,' snarled the soldier, and then, without warning, he threw a vicious right hook to Joe's face. Now Joe, it has to be said, had little or no idea of pugilistic expertise and apart from a few rough and tumbles while still at school, had never been in a fight in his life, but if you have been born on a farm, and been alive for twenty years or so, you will have definitely learnt something about the art of survival. For instance, Joe could hold a sick cow's head back by its horns so that his father could give it a 'drench' or medication. He knew how to hold a horse's hind leg so that it couldn't kick when its shoe needed tightening, and he could also upend a sheep and sit it on its backside at shearing time, several times a day in fact. And he knew how to single out one pig from the rest of them in the sty by grabbing its back legs and pulling it out backwards. He had instinctively managed to avoid the full force of the right hook by raising his left arm, but there was enough steam in the blow to throw him off balance and sit him on the floor, and it was then, as he saw two khaki clad legs coming towards, him that he thought about pigs.

In two moves he was back on his feet and by the time he was standing up he had a khaki leg under each arm, and the rest of the soldier had hit the floor with a painful thud. Not wishing to cause too much furore inside the dance hall, and to the great amusement of Ashley Woodstock, he retreated with some alacrity out through the doorway, dragging his opponent with him. Incredibly, so quick was their combined exit, most of the dancers hadn't realised what had happened, but Joe in his hurry had pulled the blackout curtain down, causing a great shaft of light to shine out into the night. He continued out over the doorstep, giving his man a painful bump on the head on the way, and finished up dumping him into a puddle of icy water outside.

They were closely followed by the other soldier who seemed to have formed an alliance with Ashley, by way of having his arm held tightly behind his back, and amongst others taking an interest in the proceedings from the open doorway could be seen the anxious faces of the three Land Army girls.

'You alright, Joe?' shouted Ashley. 'This one's decided not t' interfere, so 'e tells me.'

'Aise, I'm alright Ash,' answered Joe, who had now stepped back from the trouble-making soldier to allow him to get out of the puddle. The fracas, however, had to suddenly end there, not only because the soldier had all the fight bumped out of him, but also because of the appearance of the Pottles Cross 'Chief of Police', Constable Percy Southcombe.

'What'n th' hell's goin' on 'ere?' he demanded to know as he surveyed the scene, and turning towards the doorway he shouted 'Somebody black that light out 'fore us get half the German Luffwaff over the top of us. Now then, Ashley Woodstock, what be you doin' with that chap's arm, and wuss this other one bin doin sittin in that puddle? Come on now. I want some answers yer.'

'Well these two 've come out of the pub and busted in on the Social,' Ashley started to explain.

'Yes well what be ee all doin out yer with the blackout curtain all knacked down and 'e over there sat in the puddle?' Constable Southcombe pointed to the doorway with one hand and to the dripping wet soldier with the other.

'Well 'e and 'is mate started to annoy the Land Army maids,' replied Ashley, 'and then 'e upset Joe's young lady.'

'Joe?' queried the constable, 'Joe who?'

'You knaw,' Ashley explained. 'Joe Dryfield from out Stoney Downe.'

'Aw aise,' The policeman swung his torch around until its light rested on the figure of Joe standing near the puddle.

'Hullo, Joe,' he said. 'Didn' see twas you standin there. I amn seen you in the village fer a brave while, 'ow's mother and father, alright?'

'Not too bad thanks, Mr. Southcombe,' answered Joe respectfully. 'Keepin up perty well, considerin.'

'Glad t' hear it boy, glad t' hear it,' said Percy, his stern attitude having vanished for the moment. Well, once in a while, weather permitting, he would feel it to be his duty, since Stoney Downe Farm came just inside his jurisdiction, to cycle out there and, well, show the folks that he was 'on the job' so to speak. Of course he knew that he would always be invited into the kitchen for a cup of tea and a generous slice of cake, Bess being the sort of lady that she was. And he never went home without something in a bag, a brace of rabbits and a swede perhaps, and at least half a dozen eggs.

'You've got a young lady now, did I hear Ashley say?'

'Well tis our new Land Army girl really,' explained Joe, and went on to tell how Mrs. Cherry had invited them to the Social after Chapel the previous Sunday.

'Aise, now look 'ere boy,' said Percy. 'I'll talk to ee again in a minute, so don' go 'way. I'm goin to have a little word with these two rascals,' and putting his stern attitude back on, he commanded them to stand before him.

'Now let's have a look at yer pay books,' he said, 'and us'll see who you be.' He copied their names and numbers into his note book, and asked them where they were stationed.

'Burley Camp,' answered one, sullenly.

'Burley Camp?' repeated Percy. 'Well you got better than six miles to walk, so if you get a move on you might just get back before midnight, unless you'd like me to telephone the Red Caps to come and give ee a lift....?' This offer was immediately refused by the two since Red Caps were invariably bad news to soldiers who weren't behaving themselves, and Percy, as an old sweat from the first World War, knew it.

'Well you best get on yer way then,' he said, handing them back their pay books. 'And don't think you've got away with anything, because I sh'll be sending a full report to yer Commanding Officer first thing Monday morning.' Whether he did or not would remain to be seen. If it was a nice day, Monday, he might decide to ride his bike out to Stoney Downe Farm instead.

He watched the two errant soldiers take the road out of the village towards Burley Camp, then turned back to Joe and Ashley, who by this time had been joined by the three Land Army girls and Jenny. Violet May, everyone was glad to see, had just about recovered from her upset and was more concerned with the mark on Joe's cheek, under his left eye.

'He'll 'ave a bit of a shiner in the mornin',' remarked Percy after giving the injury the once-over under the light of his torch. 'But I c'n see e's in good 'ands, and I reck'n 'e'll be as right as rain in a couple o' days.'

'What I can't understand,' said Joe, 'is why 'e wanted t' drag Violet May outside. Us was all enjoyin ourselves in the dance.'

Constable Southcombe looked thoughtfully at them all for a moment, then took Joe by the arm.

'Come over 'ere fer a minute boy,' he said quietly, and led him a short distance away from the rest.

'Joe,' he kept his voice down so no one else could hear. 'If you don' knaw the answer to that question by now, tis about time you did.'

But it wasn't that Joe didn't know the answer. He just hadn't thought of it, that's all. In his mind there couldn't be anyone in the whole wide world who would want to harm an innocent girl like Violet May. Pure, happy, young and lovely Violet May, whose very life he had been entrusted with this evening.

As the thought came to him of what might have been had he not been there close by, a terrible anger began to grow inside. He looked along the road that led out of the village, the direction the two soldiers had taken as they set about returning to Burley Camp, and became more and more outraged. He didn't stop to ask himself why he was so outraged, and wouldn't need to be told either, because his anger had unlocked something inside of him which he hadn't realised was there. The only thing he could think of doing at that moment was to catch up with he that called himself a soldier and tear him up into little pieces for daring to lay a hand on his girl! Yes, that was it. She was *his* girl and nobody else's and nothing in the whole world was going to change that now. He clenched his teeth and his fists and took a step towards the disappearing miscreants.

'Forget it, Joe.' He felt the restraining hand of Constable Southcombe on his arm. 'You got the best of the big one yer, when you was matched even, but two of 'em in the dark, tha's a different story. You wouldn't come out of that so well, so leave 'em be. They two'll 'ave plenty to answer for when they get back to camp, you take it from me!'

Joe gradually relaxed and found himself agreeing that what Percy was saying was good advice. His job now would be to make sure that he got Violet May safely back to the farm, and that was going to take up most of the next hour.

'You won't see they two back again, Joe,' Percy continued. 'Now go on back to yer young lady and pick up yer coats and get away 'omewards.' Then looking towards the doorway he spotted Mrs. Cherry heading in his direction, followed by the ever faithful Mr. Smythen.

'Aw hell!' he muttered half to himself, 'I s'pose they two'll want to knaw the ins and outs of a cat's ass' He turned back to Joe. 'Never mind. I'll deal with they. You get on now, and remember me to yer mum and dad. Tell 'em I'll be out to see 'em, maybe Monday aft'noon.'

'I'll tell 'em, Mr. Southcombe,' replied Joe. 'You'll be welcome I reck'n.'

'I'm sure o' that boy,' said Percy. 'I'm sure o' that.' Then he turned towards the two people approaching him to face another session of explanations.

'Mr. Southcombe, what on earth has been happening out here?' Mrs. Cherry demanded.

'Now don' ee take on,' said Percy, quietly. 'Us've got it all under control and tis mostly sorted out....'

'But hardly anyone was aware of anything untoward until the end of the dancing,' she said.

'Well you c'n thank Ashley Woodstock and young Joe Dryfield fer that,' said Percy. 'Twas they that got the two trouble makers outside, quick as a flash, where they couldn' do no harm, and that's when I came on the scene.'

'A most disgraceful display of loutish behaviour, I must say,' put in Mr. Smythen, who had decided it was time for him to say something, and he received a nod of approval from Mrs. Cherry for his effort.

'P'raps it was,' said Percy, 'p'raps it was. But you got to bear in mind certain things. These is funny ol' times us be livin in, where young men be uprooted from their homes and chucked in together all of a heap in the armed forces, and you'm bound to get some who'll take a bit longer than others to settle down to it.'

'Yes, yes, of course.' Mrs. Cherry was suddenly reminded that she herself had three sons called to the colours, the oldest of which had survived the rigours and turmoil of the Dunkirk evacuation, and who could say what else was in store for all of them before this war was over. 'But,' she went on, 'we try our best to help them, and it does seem very unkind when this sort of thing happens.'

'I quite agree,' said Mr. Smythen, patting her arm, 'It is most unkind.'

'Well I wouldn' want to be seen takin' sides,' said Percy. 'But I'm sure you read the papers and hear a lot o' people clammerin for the "Second Front" to start, and when that happens — and you can bet yer boots that it will happen — we sh'll all be thankful fer these young chaps who will be thrawed into the thick of it, and tis gwain cost a lot of 'em their lives, make no mistake bout that.

'Jus' the same, there was no need for they two rascals to bust into the dance and try to kick up a rumpus. Good job somebody was there to stop it 'fore it really got started.'

'Yes, I do see your point, Mr. Southcombe.' Mrs. Cherry was a little more subdued now, and Mr. Smythen was nodding his head sympathetically. 'But,' she continued, 'someone said they came all the way from Burley Camp. Is that true?'

'Yes it is,' said Percy. 'Goodness knaws how they found their way all out here, but my guess is that they won't get back before midnight, and tha's a serious matter in the army. They two'll be put on a fizzer — er, on a charge I mean — and no doubt be confined to barracks and on fatigues for a week, so it'll all catch up with 'em one way or 'nother.'

'Yes, I see what you mean, and I'm sure that you have ascertained the situation correctly, Mr. Southcombe.' Mrs. Cherry was now sure that justice would be done and was satisfied with that.

'As you have intimated, it could have been a lot worse and we must be thankful that it wasn't. We are, of course, grateful for your presence and for the way you have handled things and wish you a very Good Night.' Turning to her companion she said, 'Come along, Mr. Smythen. We must close up the Village Hall and make our way homewards also.'

§

Joe looked at Violet May closely and asked, 'Be you alright again now?'

'Yes, honestly, I feel fine again now, Joe.' His genuine concern for her well being pleased her, perhaps a little more than she would care to admit right at that moment.

'Cawd, I wouldn've had that happen to ee fer anything. Be ee sure you'm alright really?'

'Yes really, Joe. I'm fine, but what about you, are you alright yourself?'

'Well I've bin worse,' he grinned. 'Shouldn' want to do this every day though.' He put his hand up to his face and added, 'Us better get our coats and boots. Tis time us made our way 'ome I reck'n.'

'Yes, alright, Joe,' she replied. 'Polly and Rita are still waiting for Mr. Galworth to pick them up and your friend Ashley and his wife will be going soon.'

The masked headlights of the Galworth's car then appeared and a few minutes later Violet May and Joe, suitably booted and coated and with shoes in their pockets, set off across the field beside the river.

'What did the policeman want to talk to you about?' she asked as they made their way across the field.

'Aw nuthin much,' answered Joe. 'He just gived me some good advice, tha's all, and said 'e might be out t' see Mam and Dad.'

'Do you know what I've just thought of, Joe?' she asked him as they progressed along their way.

'No, wha's that?' queried Joe.

'We missed the last waltz,' she said. 'The best dance of the evening, and we missed it.'

Joe laughed quietly. 'Well you can't 'ave it all ways,' he said. 'Come on, I reck'n Mother's waitin up with some supper fer us.'

He took her hand and led her along quickly beside the river and then up across the two steeper fields which presently brought them to the gate close to Johnny Crickett's cottage. They paused there to rest for a moment and looked back towards the place from whence they had travelled.

The moon was high and the sky clear, and at the bottom of the valley, the river reflected the night and resembled a piece of ribbon slowly moving in the breeze. There was silence, until an owl 'to-whit-to-wooed' in a nearby tree, and then, farther down by the hedgerow, a rabbit squealed as it fell prey to a night marauder, causing her to shudder and instinctively stand closer to him.

'Nuthin t' worry about,' he assured her softly, and placed a protective arm around her. He felt good, and so did she, and neither wanted this moment to end.

Looking up at him there by the light of the moon, she said, 'Joe, I can't tell you how sorry I am about what happened at the dance. I was so frightened, especially when that awful man hit you.' Putting her hand gently to his face, she asked, 'Does it still hurt very much?'

'No,' he said. 'Not any more.'

They stood close to each other by the gate for some minutes then without speaking, quietly enjoying their own company in the silence of the night. Love was getting near to them, but not so near that they really knew of it. Perhaps they would know tomorrow, or the day after. It didn't matter. They were young, and it wasn't going to leave them now.

It was cold where they stood and he felt her shiver against him. 'Come on,' he said. 'We better way get indoors. Don' want t' caitch a cold and I reck'n Mother's lookin out fer us.'

She followed him through the gate then, and arm in arm they walked along the track which would take them past old Johnny Crickett's cottage. She paused there for a moment, and rested an arm on the picket fence, and thought how sad life could be when after so many happy years in a place that must have been so full of love... now, what would become of it? They continued on past the orchard gate and then the familiar shape of the farmhouse came in sight. As he reached to open the yard gate, she spoke again.

'Joe, will you take me to any more dances in the village, after what happened tonight?'

'Aw course I will,' replied Joe. 'But ther's one thing I bin thinkin about....' He seemed hesitant, as though looking for the right words.

'What is it, Joe?' she prompted him.

'Well, there's somethin else,' he was struggling a bit. 'Tis what Constable Southcombe said when 'e wuz talkin to me outside the village hall. I said I wuz goin to tell you all bout it later. But p'raps tidn the right time to say anything....'

'Anything about what, Joe, what is it you're trying to say?' she asked.

'Well Constable Southcombe and Ashley wuz sayin.... well they wuz sayin that you wuz my young lady, but you and me 'ave never spoke of it, and, well, look, if I'm gwain take ee to any more dances, I want ee to be my girl, and I want everybody to knaw that you are my girl. Then p'raps us won't miss any more last waltzes.'

And then, in the middle of the lane by the farm gate, he asked her, quietly and sincerely.

'Do you think you would like to be my girl?'

'Joe Dryfield,' she said, taking his arm. 'I've been your girl from the very first day I walked through this gate, ever since the poor old rooster lost his tail feathers and you laughed at me because I wanted to put a pair of trousers on him. I liked you then, and I told your Mum I did, so you better not do anything to make me change my mind.'

'Tidn likely I'll do that,' said Joe. 'But what did Mother say when you told 'er?'

'I'll give you one guess,' said Violet May, and they both laughed happily as they said together :

'Oh my dear soul an' days.'

As a matter of fact, when they got indoors and related the whole of the evening's proceedings to Bess and Tom, she said it again — at least four times, but added 'that twas lucky that Constable Southcombe wuz there 'andy t' take charge of th' ol' bizzness, else Goodness knaws what might've 'appened.'

'Ow is th' ol' Percy?' queried Tom from his chair by the fire. 'Tis a brave while since 'e wuz out this way. Must be due fer another visit I should think.'

'Matter o' fact 'e did say somethin' about comin' out t' see you and Mam,' said Joe. 'Mond'y aft'noon, I think 'e said, if the weather keeps fine.'

'Mm,' said Tom. 'I better slip up and 'ave a word

with George in the mornin'.

He still had in mind his old sow and George's old boar. In some mysterious way, Percy might have heard that they'd been got rid of, and he and George ought to be armed with some ready answers.

§

It so happened that on the Monday afternoon, Constable Percy Southcombe was seen cycling up the road, in a northerly direction towards Stoney Downe Farm. Bess had spotted him from the bedroom window whilst tidying up and had shouted to Tom, who was in the yard and who, in turn shouted to Joe and bade him jump on the pony and slip up to George Mattford's place and ask him to drop by 'casual like' within the next hour.

'You c'n bring the cows in on th' way back,' he added, 'ready fer th' milkin.'

Tom decided that it was then time for him to go indoors, and on the way, he diverted to the cellar where he filled two large jugs with cider and carried them up to the kitchen, placing them on the floor by the side of the dresser. He sat himself down at the table and was about to pick up an old newspaper when he heard Bess welcoming in the Pottles Cross policeman.

'Go right in, Percy,' she was saying. 'You knaw the way. I'll be in to make a cup o'tay in a minute, I spect you c'n drink one, but I must take in me bit o' washin first. Tom's already in there I b'lieve.'

'Alright my dear, I'll find me way in,' said Percy. And seconds later the tall figure of the policeman entered the kitchen. He greeted Tom with the time of day and Tom said 'Hullo Perc, come in and take the weight off yer feet. Sit down over 'ere, boy,' indicating a chair.

Percy sat down and placed his helmet on the table. 'Some ol' ride that is,' he said, 'from Pottles Cross out t' your place, but I thought twas bout time I come out and seen ee.'

'Aise, well you knaw you'm always welcome,' said Tom, 'and it gives us a chance to thank ee fer lookin after the boy like you did Saturday night.'

'Aw, tha's alright, Tom,' said Percy. 'But young Joe didn' need much help. He and Ashley Woodstock had the situation under control in no time. Matter of fact, just between you and me, I stood there and watched 'em fer a minute or two before I stepped in. I thought the boy handled hisself perty well and was a bit unfortunate to get that bruise on 'is face. Th' other chap caught'n when 'e wasn't lookin I reck'n.'

'P'raps 'e did,' said Tom, 'but 'e'll soon get over it. e've 'ad wiss th'n that yer bout the farm, but 'course, twas the maid 'e wuz worried about most.'

'Yes,' said Percy. 'Perty little maid too. Living out yer with ee, so I understand?'

'Aise tha's right,' replied Tom, 'er comes from the Land Army, but a very good maid to work. Gets on well with everything and everybody. Us ant got no complaints at all with 'er.'

They were interrupted by Bess then, who came into the kitchen carrying a clothes basket full of their clean laundry.

'I'll get the kettle on now,' she said, 'and us'll 'ave a cup o' tay.' Then, turning to Tom she said 'I just seen George out by the gate talkin to Joe, so I dare say e'll be in fer a drink o' somethin.'

'Aw aise,' said Tom. 'I seed 'n go by early on and I thought then that e'd very likely call in on his way back.'

Turning to Percy he said, 'Do ee fancy a drop o' cider instead of tay Perc? I brought a jugful up from the cellar and I knaw you'm partial to 'alf a glass now and then.'

'Don't mind if I do, Tom.'

Perc was more than partial to half a glass, and not just 'now and then', and if Tom had *tried* to time things to happen on cue, he couldn't have done it better because at that moment George Mattford walked in through the back door.

'Just in time, George,' he said. 'Never mind about the tay, Mother, us be all gwain 'ave a drop o' this instead.' And picking up one of the jugs, he filled three glasses, and the three men drank heartily.

'Nice t' see ee Perc,' said George, who had hardly had time to sit down, let alone greet the Dryfield's guest before having a glass of cider thrust into his hand. 'What brings ee out this way, anything important?'

'No-o, not really I s'pose,' said Percy. 'Tis all in the line of duty y'knaw, and I have to make sure you party be all be'aving yourselves.' He smiled at them, and the two farmers grinned back and laughed, a little bit on the weak side.

'Just my fun,' Percy added, to which the laughter became a little stronger.

'Have another glass of cider,' said Tom.

'I don't mind if I do Tom,' said the policeman. Whereupon Tom refilled all three glasses which didn't seem to stay filled for very long.

'Tell ee what,' said Percy, 'I'm glad to see you down 'ere George. I had intended to cycle up to your place, just to say I'd been up there you knaw, but you've saved me a journey.'

'Well I'm plaised to've bin some 'elp to ee,' said George. 'Me and Tom always reck'n to stay on the right side of the law, don' us, Tom?'

'We certainly do, George,' said Tom. Then he said to Bess 'Did ee find that cardboard box I asked ee to get?'

'Aw aise, 'e's out in the dairy,' replied Bess. 'I'll go and see to it now.'

Tom turned to the policeman. 'Drop more cider, Perc?'

'I will if you don't mind, Tom,' said Percy. 'C'yaw, tha's a butiful drop o' stuff, butiful,' he said. Whereupon Tom refilled all three glasses.

'Ere, I'll 'ave to take it a bit steady,' said Percy. 'Don' ferget I got t' ride me bike 'ome, and besides ther's one or two inquiries that I must see to.' He paused, then said, 'While I think of it, I can't say that I noticed that ol' sow of yours in the yard today. You still got'n I spose?'

But before anything else could be said about that, Bess was at Percy's elbow with the cardboard box.

'I've put ee in a nice rabbit, my dear,' she said, 'And a dozen eggs. Do ee think Missus could manage a nice bit o' belly pork?'

'Aw aise I should think so, thank ee,' said Percy. 'Tha's lovely. Thankee very much I'm sure.' And he turned back to Tom who was filling up three more glasses with cider.

'Now then, Tom' he said. 'This yer ol' sow. I ben't quite sure what you said. Is 'e still in your posseshun or no?'

'I'm 'fraid,' said Tom. 'The answer is no. I'm 'fraid e's daid.'

'Daid?' asked Percy. 'What the hell did'n die of?'

'Twas natural causes,' answered Tom. 'But t'be more exzact, the cause of his death wuz heart-fellyer. Id'n that true George?' he turned to George for verification.

'True as I'm yer sittin at this table,' said George.

'Heart-fellyer,' repeated Percy. 'Tha's the first time I ever 'eard of a pig that died of heart-fellyer.'

'Ave another glass of cider, Perc.'

'Aise, thank ee, Tom,' said Percy, taking another swig. 'Hang on a minute. I better put some o'this down in me note book. Now, where exzackly was the deceased ol' sow when 'e suffered this yer fatal attack?'

'Well, I better way let George tell ee that part of it seein' as 'ow it 'appened on his premises,' said Tom, 'otherwise I would be speakin fer George, and that may not be quite right.'

'Yes alright, Tom,' said Percy, 'I reck'n you'm right. Tis up t' George t' say 'ow a thing like this could happen seein' twas on his premises. So 'ow did it happen, George?'

He looked at George and waited.

'Well', said George, 'like Tom said, it 'appened up t' my place. Tom brought 'e's ol' sow up fer my ol' boar t'serve. I thought there must've bin somethin wrong with th'ol' sow, cos 'e'd only bin up there three days before, and then I seed th' ol' boar wuz makin 'ard work of it and takin too long bout it, and then dammee if the poor ol' thing didn' suddenly fall off Tom's ol' sow and died right there in front of us.'

'Wait a minute,' said Percy. 'I thought it was Tom's ol' sow that died up at your place.'

'Aise well that wus afterwards,' said George. 'My ol' boar died first.'

'Well what did ee die of then?' asked Percy.

'Heart fellyer,' said George, with a face as flat as a

frying pan.

'Percy threw his pencil down on the table. 'Ow be I gwain make a report out about this,' he said. 'I s'pose you'm gwain tell me that your ol' sow wuz so frustrated th't that wuz what brought on his fatal attack of heart fellyer.'

'Exzackly what us thought,' said Tom. 'That ol' sow pranced around George's yard angry as a bull dog, then runned up to the poor ol' boar an' dropped down daid as a rag right there beside 'n!'

'Well why didn' ee call the vet out?' Percy wanted to know.

'What for?' asked George. 'Us didn' want a bleddy vet t' tell us they wuz daid, and they wadn no good t' nodody so us 'ad t' dig a hole and bury 'em. Besides, us would 've bin a laughin stock if anything'd got out about it all. Us got our reputations to keep up y'knaw.'

'Will ee 'ave another glass o' cider Perc.?' asked Tom.

'Aise, don't mind if I do, Tom,' said Percy.

The policeman was now having some difficulty in seeing his note book, let alone able to write anything in it, and just at that minute Bess came back with the cardboard box and said, 'I found ee a bit o' fresh cream, my 'andsome. Tis in a jam jar, and I put some fresh butter in as well. Now do ee think you c'n manage t' carr' it 'ome?'

'Aw, thankee, tha's lovely. Thankee very much Missus. Aw aise, I'll carr' that 'ome alright. Now look, Tom, and you too, George, can ee give me some idea of when all this took place? I ought t' 'ave the date of the occurrence if you c'n remember it.' He fumbled around in his note book and managed to find the page he had started writing on.

'Aise, I c'n remember it as if twas yes'day,' said Tom. 'Twas August Bank Holiday, wadn it, George?' And as George duly confirmed that it was indeed August Bank Holiday, Percy laboriously entered the date in his note book.

'Cawd, you two be a perty fine pair, if ever there was one,' said Percy. 'I think I better way get on home. Me Missus'll wonder where I've got to.'

The two farmers followed the Pottles Cross

Policeman out to his bike and helped him to tie the cardboard box on the carrier, then walked as far as the gate and watched him wobble his way down the lane into the early evening, back towards the village.

'Us ought to report 'e, fer bein drunk in charge of a vehicle,' George said.

'Come on George,' said Tom with a grin 'Le's see if Bess got a bit of supper gwain.'

§

Police Constable Percy Southcombe had quite a job getting himself, his bicycle and the cardboard box and its contents back to the Police House in Pottles Cross. Several times en route he almost wobbled into the hedge — on both sides of the road — and pushing his bike up the hills caused him to puff and pant rather alarmingly, but he was able to recover fairly quickly on the downhill sections and eventually he arrived at his house, safe and sound.

He put his bicycle in the shed at the back, untied the cardboard box on the carrier and took it indoors. As the place was in darkness, he guessed his wife was not at home. She'd be out somewhere, he reck'ned, doing something or other for the war effort, so having first made sure the blackout curtains were in place, he then lit the oil lamp, raked the fire which was still smouldering in the stove and took off his uniform jacket, hanging it behind the kitchen door.

The *Morning News* was there on the table, so he picked it up and sat in his armchair by the fire intending to have a quiet read for ten minutes or so. In less than two, he was sound asleep.

He was awakened with a start some considerable time later, by the sound of the front door being unlocked, and then Mrs. Southcombe came in from her war effort activities. He arose from his chair and they greeted each other fondly.

'Had a good day dear?' she asked. 'I was expecting you home for tea, but I guessed you must have been held up somewhere.'

'Well I had to go out to Stoney Downe,' he said. 'There wuz a couple o' things out there that I bin meanin to see into fer some time. Took me a bit longer th'n I thought.'

'I don't suppose you've had anything to eat, or did they out Stoney Downe feed you up with something?' she said.

'No, they didn', as a matter of fact,' said Percy. 'Bit unusual fer they, but they put somethin in a cardboard box for us. Tis there on the table.'

'Oh lovely,' said Mrs. Southcombe as she examined the contents. 'Good gracious. You would never think there was a war on out there would you. Look, why don't I cook you up something nice for supper? It's not a good idea to go too long without eating. Could you manage two fried eggs dear?

'Well aise, I believe I could my 'andsome,' said Percy, who had suddenly realised that it had been some time since he'd had a bite of anything, and as the aroma from the frying pan began to waft in his direction, he moved over and switched on the wireless set. It was getting on for nine o'clock, and he thought there just might be some news worth listening to.

There was a little while to go before the news would start, and an orchestra was playing a selection from something which was unmistakably Gilbert and Sullivan.

Mrs. Southcombe's voice came from the kitchen again. 'I'll put in a thin slice of the belly pork, Percy, and some of these mushrooms. It'll go down nice with a slice of bread and a bit of this lovely fresh butter.'

Percy smiled as he pictured the faces of the two farmers he'd had to deal with earlier in the day. He reached into the pocket of his uniform jacket and pulled out his note book, and thumbing through the pages he came to the last two that he had written on.

'Crafty ol' devils,' he said to himself. 'who ever 'eard of two pigs, on th' job, both dyin of heartfellyer? And on August Bank Holiday too! 'Ow th' hell c'n I put in a report like that!'

He ripped the pages out of his note book and threw them on the fire, just as his wife brought in a heaping plateful of food and put it in front of him. And a man on the wireless was singing something about a policeman's lot not being a happy one.

As he picked up his knife and fork, he chuckled quietly, and said, 'Sometimes tidn too bad.'

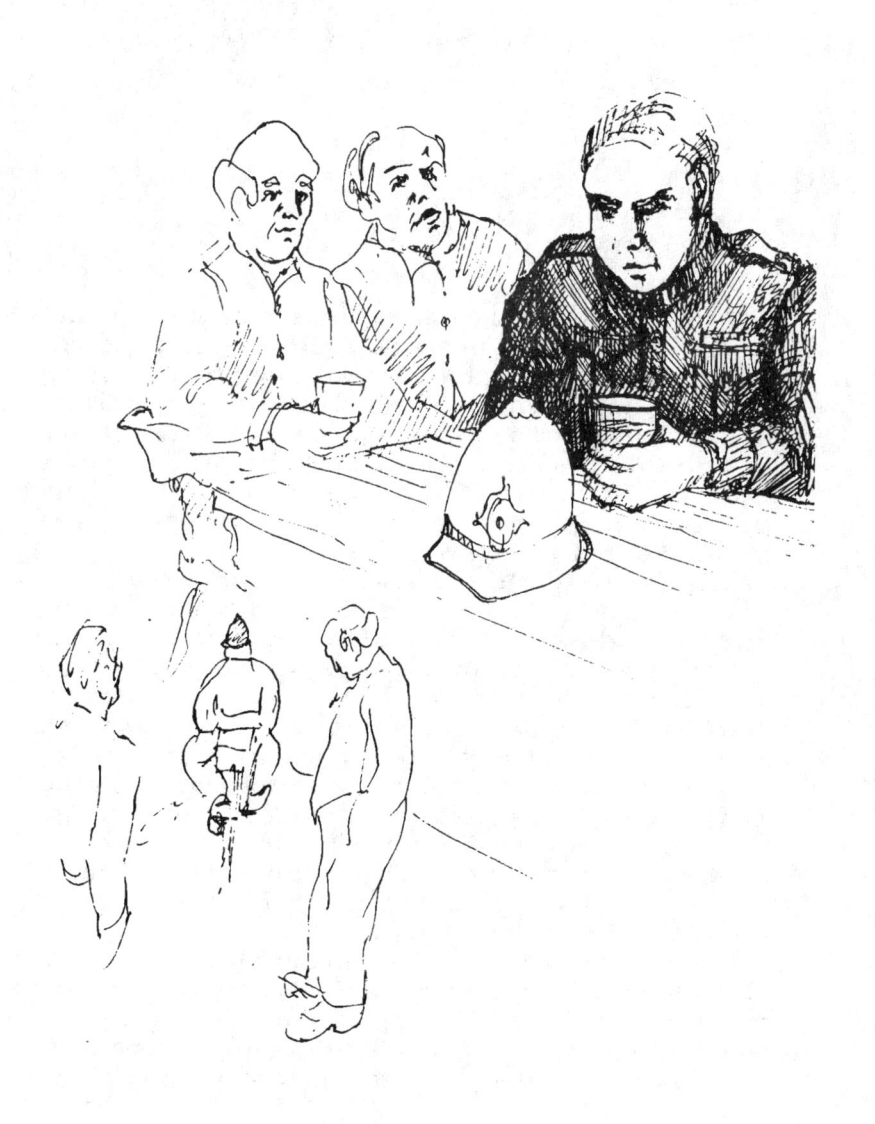

10

George Mattford rose a bit earlier than usual and set about his work with some haste. It was Market Day again at Newton Waybrook and he had a definite reason to go there, having not yet availed himself of another boar pig to replace the one recently disposed of. That, however, was perhaps more the excuse than the reason, the latter being that he might be fortunate enough to bump into a certain Kathy Branstone.

Ever since that evening when he had rescued her from the storm after leaving old Josh Sandy's place, he'd found that he just couldn't get her out of his mind. He was pretty sure that he wasn't going to find a boar pig in the Market, but at least the thought didn't make him feel quite so guilty about using up some of his valuable Petrol coupons unnecessarily.

Farther down the road at Stoney Downe Farm, Tom Dryfield was also preparing to motor off to Newton Market, his interest being to see if he could pick out another one, or perhaps two, in-calve heifers. He had got part way through eating his breakfast when he was joined by Violet May.

'Do you think you'll have time to pick up some oil and a filter for the tractor?' she asked him, as she sat down at the table. 'I've written out all the details you'll need, and it's something that ought to be done fairly soon, now that Joe's doing so much work with it.'

'Aise, I reck'n so, my 'andsome,' Tom said, taking

the piece of paper from her and studying the details. 'I dare say I c'n get all that from th' agents in Market, an' you'm quite right, tis just as well to look after the ol' thing, now that 'e's runnin' proper.'

At that moment, Joe came into the kitchen with the news that one of the cows was 'rummagin' and what did his father think he should do about it.

'Well I shan't have time to see about that this mornin,' said Tom. 'You and the maid will 'ave to 'tend to it. Which one is it, the Guernsey or the Devon?'

'Guernsey,' answered Joe, giving Violet May a sidelong glance. He was thinking she may not have experienced this task before.

'Thought twould be one or the other,' said his father. 'Well, pair 'em up and take 'em down after breakfast. Violet c'n saddle up the pony if 'er minds to, and you c'n go vor 'aid of 'em.'

The custom, when having to drive a cow for any distance along a road, which in this case was to visit the bull, was to pair it up with another one, since a cow always travelled a lot better if it had company. Tom had noted the slightly worried look on Joe's face, so he added, 'The maid c'n stay up by the gate with the pony whilst you'm down in the field. Now I must get on, else I shan't get nothing done. Mother's upstairs I b'lieve. 'Bess!' he called up the stairway, 'I'm on me way now. Violet and Joe be in fer breakfast.' With that he was gone, and a few minutes later the old car could be heard chugging away towards Newton Waybrook.

'Huh, Maister's in a 'urry this morning I notice,' said Bess as she appeared from upstairs. 'Always the same Market days. Never got time fer nothin. Us won't see 'n again till supper time, and if 'e meets up with George Mattford twill be later still.'

She went on with the business of preparing breakfast for the two of them, chatting away, and enquired as to what they would be doing before dinner. She made little of it, however, when Joe told her what had to be done. It was, after all, a common occurrence. It happened all the time. If it didn't there wouldn't be any farms or farmers.

'Mind you don't stand too close,' was all she said

to Violet May with a smile.

Sixteen miles away at Newton Waybrook, George Mattford had stopped his van a short distance from the Market entrance and walked back towards the main shopping centre. As usual, quite a lot of people were in town, it being Market Day, and he noticed several farmers arriving for the Market itself, one of whom was Tom Dryfield, rattling along in his old Austin Six. They waved to each other as they passed, and no doubt they'd meet up sometime later, most likely in the Market House Inn, close by.

Right now though he had other things on his mind, mostly in the shape of Kathy Branstone, and he wondered how he could get in touch with her. He didn't even know if she was still at the hostel, but guessed it doubtful that she had been sent to another farm after walking out on old Josh Sandy. He wandered up and down the main street and in and out of Woolworth's, but there was no sign of her so he turned back towards the Market. He'd try again later, he decided, and cursed himself for not making a definite arrangement when he'd last seen her.

Making his way around the various pens, he eventually came to the pigs, but even though he tried to capture some interest in them, he knew without looking that he wasn't buying today. The crowd jostled for position around him as they waited for the auctioneer, and then someone nudged his arm and a voice he immediately recognised said, 'Thought I'd find you up this end.'

He turned quickly and suddenly the day seemed to take on a new meaning, as if a weight had been lifted from his shoulders.

'Hullo Kathy,' he said. 'I've been up the main street, thinkin I might bump in to ee. You'm still in the Land Army I notice.'

'Well yes,' she smiled, and looked pleased to see him, 'but I don't know for how much longer.' The crowd was building up now, and getting noisier. 'Are you buying anything today?' she asked.

'No,' he answered. 'Ther's nothin 'ere that interests me today 'cept you. May as well be straight about it, and I'd like to go somewhere so's us c'n have a talk. Now tis gettin on fer dinner time, so us could either go in the cafe over the road or visit the Market House fer a drink and a pasty. That is, if you got the time to spare,' he added.

'The Market House sounds best to me,' she said. 'It may not be so crowded.'

So they made their way out of the Market and over to the Inn, where George selected a table that wasn't too close to the bar. Kathy sat down while he went to get something to drink and a couple of warm pasties. There were quite a lot of people in town by this time, no doubt taking advantage of Market Day bargains, and one or two servicemen could be seen walking around with wives or girl friends, enjoying a few days leave. Yesterday the sight of them would have filled her with envy and sadness, remembering the little time spent with her sailor husband who, tragically, would not be coming home again, but today that feeling wasn't quite so much in evidence, and the reason for it was, at this very minute, putting food and drink on the table in front of her.

'Hope this'll be alright fer ee,' said George. 'It don' seem much t' give a lady fer a meal, but p'raps you'll 'low me t' make a better job of it anuther time. And not too far ahead,' he added quickly.

She smiled and said it was fine. 'I'm still being fed at the hostel, at least till tomorrow,' she said. 'After that, I don't know.'

'What do ee mean by that?' George asked.

'Well it's the big day,' she replied. 'I have to stand before a committee to explain why I didn't stay at that old Sandy's place out on the moors. Honestly, how anyone could be expected to work there I'll never know. Old Josh wasn't so bad, but his wife and that boy must have come straight out of the stone age.'

'I s'pose you'll tell 'em all that won't ee?' said George. 'Surely they'll want t' knaw your side of it.'

'I'm not counting on that,' she said, and there was anger in her voice. 'You know yourself, George, what that place is like. Nobody should have been sent out there, but they had to pick me, didn't they. As if I haven't had enough to put up with already, and now I've got to suffer this, but you can't tell these Ministry people anything. They won't admit to being wrong, but they are, and well they know it. Blinkin' jumped up little so and so's. If it wasn't for the war, the only place you'd see them is in the dole queue.'

He gazed at her across the table and liked her all the more for the spirit that she undoubtedly possessed. 'Eat yer pasty,' he said, 'fore 'e gets cold.'

She smiled back and said, 'Yes alright George, I suppose I shouldn't talk to you about it like this, but I've got a good idea what their decision is going to be. They won't give me the boot before I've told them what I think of 'em though. What have I got to lose? I've lost enough already through this blasted war, so I'm not going to be kicked around by little people like them!'

It flashed across George's mind that if those 'little people' she mentioned 'knawed what they wuz in fer' the following morning, they might well put the proceedings off to some future date. What, he asked her then, did she think their decision would be, assuming that what she was expecting actually happened.

'Oh they'll probably give me a letter of dismissal or something like that, and I suppose travel expenses back to Bideford,' she replied. 'Then, I think I would have to re-register at the Labour Exchange. After that, I don't know. You can be sent anywhere these days. Might even be to a munitions factory.'

He watched her without speaking for a few moments as she ate her pasty. Then he said,

'Kathy, I hope I'm not goin t' say a lot of wrong things to ee now, but I don't want this to be the last time that I shall see ee. I've gived it a lot of thought — a lot of thought I might tell ee, and I've put together a couple of ideas that you may think to consider.'

'Oh yes,' she said between mouthfuls. 'Well I'm listening, George. What's the first one?'

'I think the second idea is a lot better than the first one,' said George, 'but t' my way of thinkin, I've got t' put 'em to ee in the right order. So first of all, if you do get dismissed from the Land Army tomorrow mornin, I'll give ee a job out t' my place. Ther's plenty of room out there fer ee t' have board and lodgin's in the proper manner, and you'd still be in a reserved occupation, doin more or less the same job as you be now.'

She looked at him thoughtfully, and had already made up her mind that he was a good man, some years older than herself, but not so many that it mattered. If she accepted, she would be able to 'cock a snook' at those Ministry men in the morning, take their travel expenses and disappear in amongst George Mattford's pigs. It might be ages before they found out where she was.

'What's the second idea, George?' she asked. 'I mean, I like the first one, but can I know what the second one is now, or have I got to wait for that one till later on?'

'No,' said George, after a pause. 'I'll tell'n to ee now. Tis a much better idea as far as I'm concerned, but it got t' follow the first one in every way. Now, I knaw you'm smart enough to see that the Ministry might be able to stop ee, or catch up with ee and try to stick their noses in, so if you do take on the first idea, the second one could follow on any time after, that'd suit ee.'

'Well, go on George,' she said, as he paused again.

'George straightened himself in his chair, and looked directly at her. 'Idea number two,' he said, 'will require me to go to the Registry Office and get a special Licence so that you and me could get married. If you wuz agreeable to that, there wouldn' be nobody in this world that could do a thing about it, least of all they Ministry people. And you,' he added, putting his hand upon hers across the table, 'would make me a very happy man.'

She wasn't really surprised at the content of George's 'idea number two'. Looking down at his big hand covering hers on the table, she thought carefully on what her reply should be. More than twelve months had passed since that terrible letter had arrived to tell her that her husband had been lost at sea, along with who knows how many others. Since that time she had fought hard against the choking sadness and loneliness. Joining the Land Army had been a great help to her because she liked the work involved and found it easy to cope with. Now, it seemed, this episode in her life was coming to an end. But was there another one about to begin? Here was someone offering her an arrangement that would take care of her for the rest of her life and it was certainly not without a good deal of attraction.

She knew that this man had driven all the way into town from his pig farm, not for the Market, but to find her and make his proposal to her. A proposal that was heavily weighted in her favour. She could go out there and work for him with no other demands upon her, and if it didn't work out, well that would be that. But if she liked it well enough, it could be made into a permanent partnership.

'George,' she said at last. 'Do you realise what you're saying? We've only met a couple of times and you hardly know a thing about me. How can you be so sure of something as important as this?'

'Well,' said George. 'I knaw I ant seen much of ee, but I've had plenty of time to think it all out, and I'm bound t' tell ee, Kathy, I amn thought of much else since I seen ee last, and that's a fact. As fer bein sure, well, you'll have t' believe me when I tell ee that I reck'n I knaw a bargain when I see one. I knaw ther's a few years between us, but not enough to make much odds. I've reasoned it all out, maid, and I knaw inside me that everything I've said to ee is nothin' else but right and proper. I've drove sixteen mile to Newton Waybrook today just so's I could see ee and tell it all to ee, and I'm thankful that the Good Lord fixed it up fer me t' do that much. All I c'n do now is to ask ee if you might consider it, and p'raps let me knaw what you think of it.'

Kathy looked across the table and saw the sincerity in his eyes. She was right. He had come all the way into town for one reason only, and that was to see her. But, what of herself? She had no excuse at all for going to the Market, except.... and then she came close to knowing what she was going to do, because the only reason for her being there was the hope that she might bump into him. After all, wasn't that why she had hung around the pig pens, knowing that was where he would most likely be?

At last she spoke. 'I made a snap decision the other day George,' she said, 'when I left old Josh Sandy's place. I don't think I was wrong in what I did, and I don't want you to think that I'm always making snap decisions. But I'm going to make another one

The proposal.

now. I'm going back to the hostel to pack my case and collect my bicycle, and I'd like you to come along with your van and take me out to your place today.'

For a moment George was absolutely lost for words. He had not expected her answer so quickly.

'Kathy,' he said. 'Do ee really mean it?'

'Yes, I really mean it George,' she replied. 'So let's get going before you change your mind.'

'No fear o' that,' said George, pushing his chair back. 'But what about this meetin' you got on tomorrow mornin'?'

'I'll write them a letter,' she said, and looked at him with a smile that he was going to see an awful lot of in their time to come. 'Don't worry about a thing,' she went on. 'I'll tell them I'm getting married. You said it yourself. There isn't much they can do about that!'

'By Cracky,' exploded George as she made for the door. 'I think 'er means it, sure 'nough!'

§

Outside the Market House Inn a wintery sun decided to show some of its warming rays to prove, perhaps, that the world wasn't such a bad place to be in. The crowd of shoppers had decreased considerably as the shopkeepers closed their doors for the midday break, leaving the town quieter. Even the busy Market took on a more restful period as farmers, auctioneers and market officials stopped for some refreshment.

Across the square a bus entered the town, operating its scheduled service from Plymouth, and pulled up on its stop. The driver turned off the engine and clambered down from his cab. By force of habit over many years, he removed his watch from a waistcoat pocket and checked it with the clock in the little tower over the Town Hall entrance, then leant against the radiator and lit a cigarette. To the rear, the conductress stood by the door as her passengers alighted, and then joined the driver at the front for a smoke and a chat.

They had brought several people into town, mostly housewives from the outlying areas en route, who like everyone else, came in the hope of securing a bargain or two on Market Day and perhaps something to put away for Christmas. Last one to get off the bus was a soldier. A stranger, anyone watching might say, for he stood there on the pavement, looking this way and that, seemingly undecided as to which direction to take. He carried the rank of sergeant on the sleeves of his battledress and on both arms above the stripes was the emblem of the British Eighth Army, the Desert Rat. On his head he wore the familiar black beret, fastened upon which was the badge of the Royal Tank Corps. It was the Market that finally took his attention and it was in this direction that he made his way, walking with a pronounced limp.

He walked slowly through the entrance to the Market, looking around, and then stopped by an auctioneer's office where through a half open door he could see a man laboriously adding up figures and trying to eat a large sandwich at the same time. He was unwilling to interrupt the man at his work, but he needed some information and as there was no one else in sight, he waited.

'Something I can do for you, Sergeant?' The auctioneer's clerk called to him after a moment or two from his desk.

'I'm sorry to trouble you,' the sergeant replied, 'but I'm trying to get in touch with a farmer by the name of Dryfield. I was told that he may be in the Market here today. Would you happen to know him?'

'Tom Dryfield from out Stoney Downe? Yes, I know Tom,' said the clerk. He was here only a few minutes ago to pay a bill. Now where was it he said he was going to? I know, he's gone over to the oil store to get something for his tractor. That's where you'll find him I reckon. It's a little way over on this side, just past the corn merchant's office. Tell you what, you'll most likely see his car there. It's an old black Austin Six, at least it would be black if Tom washed the mud off now and again, but if the car's there, Tom won't be far away.'

'Thanks, I'm much obliged to you,' said the sergeant.

'Don't mention it, Sarge',' said the clerk, and went back to his figures and his sandwich.

The sergeant walked the short distance over to the

oil store, just a little quicker now, and sure enough, there was the mud-splattered old Austin parked outside. Almost as soon as he got there, the man he wanted to see came out of the store carrying a drum of oil and a cardboard box, which he packed away in the car boot. As he turned, he met the gaze of the sergeant.

'Mr. Dryfield?'

The sound of his name being called by a complete stranger caught Tom unawares and sent his head in a spin as he tried to think who the heck would know him from the army. He looked at the soldier, frowned, and said 'Well you've got me, boy, but I'm blawed if I knaw who you be.'

'My name is Johnson,' replied the Sergeant. 'I'm trying to find my daughter. I've just come from the Land Army Department office in Plymouth, and they told me that she's....'

'Wait a minute,' interrupted Tom, as he suddenly grasped the situation. 'You must be Violet May's daddy,' and grabbing his hand and shaking it vigorously he said, 'Cawd beggar my shirt, you'm gain be a sight fer sore eyes, I'm damned if you id'n.'

At that moment the sergeant visibly relaxed and leaned back against the wall of the oil store. He took off his hat and Tom could see that he was tired and drawn, and that here was someone who'd had more than his fair share of turmoil, a whole lot more.

'Now then, Mr. Johnson,' Tom spoke again. 'Let me tell ee right away that Violet May is with us at my place, and is very well and lookin as perty as a picture, and what's more, us be all delighted to 'ave the maid there with us. Now, it seems to me that ther's only one thing to do, and that's take ee home to see her right away. But you look as if you could do with a drink and a bite to eat, so do ee think you c'n spare ten minutes or so fer some refreshment? I c'n promise ee this much, your maid is doin fine, and is very happy with us out there to th' farm, and today is goin to be special fer Violet, and I don't need to tell ee why, so what do ee want t' do?'

Sergeant Johnson smiled and gave out a huge sigh of relief. 'Mr. Dryfield, I can't tell you how much I appreciate what you're saying,' he said. 'It's been a long time since I last saw my daughter and I can hardly wait to see her again, but now that I know she's happy and it seems in very good hands, I think I will have that drink and something to eat. To be truthful, I haven't had time for anything since first thing this morning.'

'C'mon then boy,' said Tom. 'Market House will still be open. Us'll get somethin in there to keep us gwain till us get 'ome.'

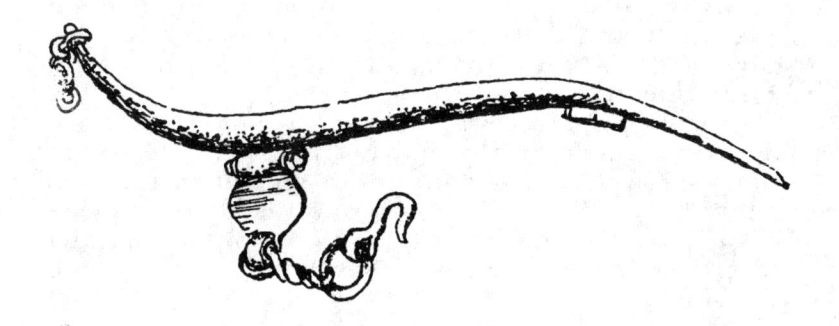

11

Back at Stoney Downe Joe had turned the cows out to field and cleaned out the shippens or, as he so quaintly put it, 'haiv'd the shit out'. These were the days when farmers ran mixed herds, and had not yet arrived at the keeping of one breed. Stoney Downe's herd was made up of several differing breeds and crosses, but there was nothing much wrong with the end product, the milk itself, which was pretty well everything it was supposed to be. The days of fields full of bovine 'look-a-likes' yet several years away into the future.

But two of the cows had been kept tied in when the rest of them ambled out to their field. They were the amorous Guernsey and its neighbour in the next stall. They didn't take too kindly to it and bawled quite a bit, but there was a job to do, which wouldn't take long and soon enough they would be back with the others again.

As soon as the morning chores were completed, Joe brought the pony out of the stable and put bridle and saddle on him. He was almost a full Dartmoor, just under fourteen hands and a gelding, and had been given the name 'Rocky', just like Dartmoor itself. The prospect of seeing something other than the stable for a while obviously pleased him, for his head was up and he was looking all around.

Violet May was a little apprehensive when Joe called her over to mount up. Since her job was almost entirely with the cows and calves, she had not had time to get to know the horses. Not that she didn't want to. Quite the opposite in fact, but they were in Tom's domain and he knew them well, as indeed they knew him well also. Still, she had often thought that she'd be allowed to get close to them one day, and now here it was. She was actually going to ride the pony!

Her apprehension faded however as her natural instinct with animals came to the fore. Standing close to Rocky's head, she allowed him to get to know her by scent and spoke to him quietly, patting him on the neck. Then from her pocket she produced a piece of cattle cake, which he chewed hungrily and looked around for more. He got a couple more pieces and some more pats on the neck, and he knew he had a friend. She wasn't afraid of him now. And he knew that too.

'Ever bin up on a pony before?'

She was hoping Joe wouldn't have asked that question. But he did, so she had to answer it truthfully. 'Does riding a donkey on Eastbourne beach count?' she asked him.

'Aise I s'pose,' said Joe with a laugh. 'But don' let Rocky 'ear you call 'n a donkey. Come on, I'll give ee a leg up.' And almost before she knew it, she was in the saddle with her feet in the stirrups, walking a circuit around the farmyard and feeling on top of the world. Joe watched her for a moment. She was slightly off balance, but he reckoned she'd soon right herself once she had mastered the pony's rhythm. He went into the shippen and turned out the two cows.

It was not far down to where Flash, the bull, father of Annie and many others, resided and carried out his duties. In fact, if you climbed over a hedge at the back of the farmyard you were almost there. But cows don't — or shouldn't — climb over hedges, especially high ones as they all were around Flash's territory, and so the only way in was to travel along the farm lane for about half a mile to a left turn, then two or three hundred yards to another left which was rather a muddy track. This one led for a similar distance to a secure gate, the entrance to the bull's domain. The security of the place was the reason for the bull being kept there. The high hedges and the stout gate, well away from anywhere, made it an ideal situation. Not that Flash was anything but a 'real gent' as Tom liked to refer to him but, as always with bulls, it was better to be safe than sorry. Flash had his own stone-built barn there, which he shared with a family of owls. There was plenty of grass and a fresh running stream, and a visit from Tom every day with hay and feed if it was needed.

It was to this location that Joe led the way. He was followed by the Guernsey and its travelling partner and behind them, playing a very important role, was Ben the dog who made sure that neither of the cows went the wrong way, or rather he would upon a shout from Joe, soon get 'em back again if they decided to wander. Something he seemed to enjoy doing most of all. Last of the group was Violet May up on Rocky, and she kept the whole party going as smooth as she could, and not doing so bad either, having now got the hang of the pony's gait, more or less.

Soon they were at the second turn to the left and now it was easy to see why Tom had suggested that Violet May should ride the pony instead of walking. With his usual forethought he had realised that the track would be particularly muddy at this time of the year and whilst Joe would cope with it well enough, it would be more than a little difficult for the girl, whereas sitting on the pony made things a lot easier for her.

As to the bull's prowess as 'the great lover', suffice it to say that the exercise was carried out to everyone's satisfaction, the Guernsey in particular. The next time we see the little group of people and animals is when they were about half way back towards the farm and they came by an old gentleman standing in a gateway, holding his bicycle. Joe hailed the old man and wished him the time of day, and as Violet May, bringing up the rear, came along, she saw that it was Mr. Smythen the Churchwarden, whom she had last seen at the Village Social.

'Good morning, Mr. Smythen,' she said politely. 'What brings you out this far from Pottles Cross?'

'Oh, good morning my dear,' he said, and in answer to her question, 'Well actually I was looking for some holly with lots of berries to decorate the Church this Christmas. I usually come out at this time of the year and collect as much as I can carry, but tell me, why are you driving only two cows along the road. Have they erred and strayed from the rest, as it were, and you are now returning them to the fold?'

'Oh no,' replied Violet May with simple honesty. 'We've had to take the Guernsey to the bull, because it's her time you know.'

Mr. Smythen frowned. 'Dear me,' he said, with a worried look, and thinking that it was hardly a task for a young lady. 'Isn't that something Mr. Dryfield ought to see to himself?'

'Oh my goodness, no,' said the girl, looking at Mr. Smythen with her eyes full of mischievous innocence. 'It's got to be done by the bull.'

The Churchwarden stared dumbly at her for a moment, his jaw sagging. Then he coughed awkwardly and said, 'Yes, yes, quite so, ahem, quite so. Ah, good day Miss Johnson,' and turning his bicycle around, he jumped on and pedalled quickly back towards Pottles Cross. This year he would have to find his holly elsewhere, though where exactly, he had no idea, but anywhere that wasn't inhabited by such forthright young ladies.

'The ol' man went off a bit quick' remarked Joe, as they arrived back to the field which held all the other cows. 'What did ee say to 'n to make 'n ride off like that?' He laughed loudly when Violet May told him what had transpired. 'Cawd, wait till I tell Father!' he said as he held the gate open to let the Guernsey and its companion in to rejoin the rest of the herd, then walked beside the pony the short distance to the stable, where Violet May dismounted, took off the bridle and saddle and put Rocky into his stall.

'I'll give him a quick rub down, shall I, Joe?' she asked.

'Can if you mind to,' replied Joe. 'Twill be time fer dinner when you've done that I reck'n.'

Thereupon she set to with brush and curry-comb and a song in her heart, giving the pony a good clean, talking to him all the time, telling him what a handsome being he was and she was going to make him even more handsome so that he would be the envy of the whole county.

'What a morning this had been,' she thought to herself happily, and wondered what the rest of the day had in store for her.... Ah! If she did but know.

12

'Come on in 'ere, boy,' said Tom, as he pulled up outside the Market House Inn. 'Us'll get a drink and a bite t' eat, then us c'n make tracks fer home and you'll be seein' that maid o' yours.'

Sergeant Johnson got out of the old Austin and followed Tom into the bar. 'Le's 'ave two glasses of beer and a couple of pasties, Charlie,' Tom called to the barman. 'Us ant got too much time t' spare, so it don' matter if they ben't all that 'ot.'

In due course these arrived and Tom indicated to a vacant table, where the two men sat down. Tom picked up one of the pasties and motioned to his companion to do likewise, explaining as he did that 'ther's plenty of teddies and swede in 'em, but don't say nothin' to nobody if you find a bit of meat 'cos that would've only got there by accident, and by the way, my name is Tom. So what can I call you?'

'Reginald Johnson is my full name,' said the sergeant, reaching across the table. 'Reg for short, and I'm really pleased to meet you, Tom. I came home from North Africa three days ago, and it has taken me until now to find out where my daughter is. She's all I've got you see and I'm very relieved to know that she is alright.'

Tom took the proffered hand and shook it warmly. 'Very glad to meet ee, Reg.' he said. 'And I c'n tell ee now that I couldn wish fer a better maid to be workin on my place. Missus will tell ee the same, and us all like 'er ever so much. You'm lucky to 'ave a maid like her, tha's no mistake.'

'It's been three years since I last saw her,' said Reg. 'Just about left school when I went away, and now she's in her nineteenth year. I keep wondering what she looks like. She'll be pretty, just like her mother was, I should think.'

'Perty as a picture Reg,' said Tom, 'but come on now, boy, drink up and us'll get on our way. Ought to get 'ome by milkin time I should think.' Turning to the barman he said 'Charlie, if you see that neighbour of mine, tell 'n I've gone on 'ome will ee?'

Tom was somewhat taken aback then when Charlie told him that George had been in earlier, accompanied by a lady, and they had left the inn together before dinner.

As he and Reg left and got into the old car, Tom wondered what George was up to. He drove back towards Stoney Downe at his usual leisurely pace, glancing now and again at his passenger who had become a little silent, and then Reg suddenly asked, 'Is it much further to go, Tom?'

'Aw, about eight or nine mile I s'pose,' answered Tom. 'Why do ee ask?'

'It's just occurred to me that I haven't got anywhere to stay tonight,' replied Reg. 'Is there a pub, or anything like that close by, where I can get a bed for the night?'

'My dear chap,' said Tom. 'You can put that right out of yer 'ead. I'll tell ee this much, us've 'ardly 'eard anything else from Violet May, except than about you comin back, and I knaw that 'er and the missus've got it all planned out. Take it from me Reg. You'll be stayin with us on the farm fer as long as you mind to.' He chuckled as he went on, 'Cawd, ther's gain be a lively ol' time of it tonight with 'em, I'm beggered if ther' idn!'

There was just a glimmer of a smile on his face as Reg relaxed. 'This,' he said, 'is the day I've been dreaming about for a long time, and it looks like you and your family are going to make it extra special.'

'Don't think another word about it, Reg,' replied Tom. 'Us be very glad to 'ave the maid yer with us.'

But Reg wasn't altogether listening to Tom. He was

feeling a bit ill at ease. It was all too, well, different he thought, for the want of a better word. He'd been in a war, a bloody horrible war where the battlefields of the desert were littered with the wreckage of tanks, guns, trucks and equipment. And men.

He'd been lucky. He was still alive. Badly wounded, but still alive and back in England, and at this moment not a handful of miles from the only thing he'd got left — his daughter. He had no home of his own to go to. No wife there to welcome him, and precious little to call his own except what he stood up in. But he still had Violet May didn't he? And yet he was worried.

This farmer was going on about how good she was, and how much they thought about her, and had said that she "wuz jus' like one o' the family." Was he going to lose her now?

What did these people know about war? He'd been through it, and now he wanted something back. His home, his job, a sense of purpose, a fair chance, which he and his comrades didn't get in the desert when they had to face a much better equipped enemy. But above all, he wanted to be sure that he was going to get his daughter back.

He came back to earth suddenly, or rather the front seat of the old car, and realised that Tom was still talking.

'....you'd knaw what I mean,' he was saying, 'and you'd see that you'm the most welcome being this side of Christmas. Anyway, Reg, you'm soon goin to find out because us'll be comin up to our yard gate any minute.'

And sure enough, ahead of them in what was left of the late afternoon light, Reg could pick out the shape of the farm buildings amongst the surrounding trees, and a moment or two later Tom was turning the old Austin in through the yard gate. He pulled in beside the barn as usual, and switched off the engine,

From there they could look across to the cow shippens and see Joe, who was hustling the last of the cows in for the evening milking. The two men sat there for a moment, seemingly unwilling to get out.

Tom glanced at his companion and said, 'That's

my boy, Joe, you c'n see, but Violet May is inside I reck'n, tying the cows up. Go on over and see her.'

But Reg remained in his seat, and Tom could see that he was trying hard to keep hold of himself.

'Tom,' he said. 'I wonder if you could go and get her to come over here?'

'Yes, alright, boy.' Tom lifted his hand and patted him on the shoulder. 'You sit tight and stay where you be. I'll send 'er over to ee.'

He got out of the car, walked across and disappeared into the cow shippen. Once inside, he greeted Violet May and Joe and inquired, as was usual, into their well being and was everything alright about the farm, to which Joe replied that it was and had he, his father, had a successful day at the market, and so on.

'Aise, you could say that I had a very good day today,' said Tom.

'Did you manage to get the oil and the filter for the tractor?' Violet May wanted to know.

'Aw aise, I got that,' said Tom. 'Tis in the back of the car, but before you start with the milkin, do a little job fer me, will ee, my 'andsome? I've brought somebody back from Newton Waybrook and he's gain stay with us fer a day or two. Take 'n in t' mother, will ee? I'll be in to explain it to 'er in a minute. He's over there by the car.'

While Joe fixed his father with a quizzical look, Violet May, suspecting nothing, hastened to do the 'Maister's' bidding.

'Right,' she said with a smile, and then cheekily to Joe, 'you can start without me if you want to,' referring to the milking, and set off out of the shippen towards the old Austin.

As she went she couldn't help but wonder who this person might be, and how long he would be staying. Not too long, she hoped, because she and Bess had got it all worked out where her father was going to sleep when he eventually got home and she knew there weren't any more bedrooms in the house. Surely this wasn't going to upset all their plans and why didn't Tom take the man straight indoors when he got back from Market instead of asking her to...?

She suddenly stopped there, right where she was,

and looked back towards the shippen. Tom and Joe were watching from the doorway, illuminated by the hurricane lamps inside. She looked back towards the car again and saw the shadowy figure emerge into the half-light of the early evening. Again she looked back to the shippen doorway and raised her hands to her face. 'It's my Dad!' she whispered to herself. 'He's brought my Dad home!' She turned once more back to the car, then with a cry she ran headlong into her father's arms. 'Dad! Dad!' she cried. 'You've come home, you've come back home! I knew you would come home again,' and they held each other tightly and laughed and sighed.

'I knew you'd be home soon,' she said again, her eyes brimming, 'but why did you stay away for so long?'

'I couldn't get here any quicker sweetheart.' Her father, too, was struggling to stay the tears. 'They wouldn't let me go till now, but here I am and I won't be going away any more.'

'You mean you're home for good, and never going anywhere?' she asked him.

'Only back to hospital for some more treatment, but I think that will be at Plymouth, and that's not far away is it?'

'Oh Dad,' she said happily. She stood back and smiled through her tears. 'Lots of things have happened to me since you went away. I don't know how I'll find the time to tell you all of it.'

'There will be plenty of time,' her father assured her. 'Just let me look at you for a minute. You're certainly not the little girl that you were before I went away. You're quite a grown up young lady now, and you look just like your mum when I first met her. Tell me, sweetheart, do you like it here, on the farm? Are the people here good to you? Do they treat you well?'

'You're going to meet them all now,' said Violet May. 'Then you'll see for yourself, but although I haven't been here long, I feel like it's been forever and I'd never want to leave....' she suddenly gasped and put her hand to her mouth. 'The milking!' she cried. 'I must get back. Come on, Dad. Let me take you indoors, and Bess, that's Mrs. Dryfield, will look after you until we've finished.'

But Tom, in his own particular way, already had the situation in hand. Motioning to Joe to make a start, he had gone indoors to change his clothes and to warn Bess of Reg's arrival. 'Th' maid'll want to be with her Daddy' he had told her, and was on his way out to the shippens when he met Reg and Violet May coming in.

'I'll see to the milkin, my 'andsome,' he said to the girl. 'You take your Daddy indoors and get'n settled in. Mother's makin a cup o' tay. Me and Joe'll see ee all suppertime.' Then he was gone, leaving them both to the tender mercies of Bess, whose greeting was no less in volume than her own ample proportions.

'My dear soul an' days!' she exclaimed, holding out a flour-covered hand to Reg. 'Tis about time you shawed up. That poor maid,ve bin drivin us maaze yer, wonderin where you wuz to. Do ee sit down now, there be the fire, and Violet'll get ee a nice cup o'tay.'

For the next hour Reg was waited on hand and foot by the two women. He was plied with cups of tea and slices of cake, taken upstairs and shown his bedroom, brought down again, but declined more tea and cake because he had seen the meat pie that Bess had put in the oven. Eventually Violet May said she would leave her father there with Bess and go back out to the shippens to help the men finish up, so that they could come in a little earlier for their supper.

'I jus' don't knaw what us'd do without 'er now,' said Bess as the girl went out of the door. 'Nothin's too much trouble to 'er, and nobody tells 'er what to do because 'er jus' gets on and does it. Look at 'er now. Gone out to give the men a hand so's they can come in early.

'Sounds as if she has found herself a good place here,' remarked Reg. 'And I can't tell you what a relief that is to me, but we had a nice house back in Eastbourne before I was called up. It's gone now, furniture and all but I suppose we'll get some compensation eventually, but then we'll have to start again from scratch. Still, I'm luckier than a lot of men. At least I'm alive and been allowed to come home and see my girl. There were plenty of times when I didn't think I was ever going to do that again.'

He paused, then said 'I'm sure I've got an awful lot to thank you and Tom for. She seems to be very happy here with you.'

He wanted to tell of the dreams he'd had over the past three years for himself and his daughter. Dreams that had kept him alive for all those weeks in a military hospital and made the excruciating pain in his body more easy to bear, but he held back from doing so. This didn't seem to be the right time, and anyway, Bess was talking again.

'Well, I'll tell ee this much,' she was saying, 'whatever us do fer that maid, comes back double to us in other ways, and tha's no exaggeration. You wait till you've bin yer two or three days. You'll see it yerself. Tis truth, 'er's a proper ray o' sunshine. Get's on with folks and animals, both the same, even the ol' rooster who'll fly at anybody that comes through the yard will go runnin up to 'er and feed out of 'er 'ands, and not only that, 'er was the only one that knawed what to do with the tractor when 'e wouldn' start up. That wuz the very first day 'er got 'ere. Poor maid 'ardly 'ad time fer a cup o' tay. Told us 'er'd learned all 'bout that from you. Our boy Joe 'd bin tryin fer days to get the ol' thing gwain, then along comes Violet and got 'n started up in no time 'ardly.'

Reg had to smile when he heard Bess going on about Violet May, partly for the way that she put her words together, but mostly because he could see the impression his daughter had obviously made upon this family. His mind went back to the days when he would take Violet May with him to visit farms in Sussex and make repairs to farm machinery.

'Must have been fuel blockage,' he said. 'I was always doing those when I worked on tractors before I was called up, and she watched me do it a few times. She obviously remembered how to clear it. Well, can you imagine that!'

'Aise, well there tis you see,' said Bess. 'I won't tell ee no tales, but twill be a sorry day fer us if 'er ever left Stoney Downe, but there, p'raps neither one of us will be the loser.'

Bess's somewhat profound statement brought a puzzled look to Reg's face, but he was prevented from going farther into the subject by the return of his daughter, accompanied by Tom and Joe. Their work for the day completed, they now busied themselves around the kitchen pump, freshening up prior to attacking the evening meal which Bess was already piling on to the plates.

'Well what do ee think of the maid now, Reg,' was Tom's greeting as they took their places at the table.

'Grown up quite a bit since I last saw her,' said Reg, smiling at his daughter. 'I can see that she is being well looked after, and I'm really most grateful to you folks for that. Perhaps one day I'll be able to do something to repay you for your kindness.'

'My opinion is, you've already done plenty by helpin to protect the country,' Tom said. 'And perty near got killed doin it. And another thing,' he added, 'if it wad'n fer you, us wouldn't 'ave had Violet May to look after, would us?'

There were smiles all around the table at Tom's last remark, and then amidst the rattle of knives and forks on plates, Violet May said, 'You haven't met Joe yet, Dad, not properly, so let me introduce you. Joe, this is Dad, and Dad, this is Joe,' and she added, 'He's the champion wrestler of Pottles Cross!'

Everyone, including Joe, laughed at this. 'Pleased to meet you ,Joe,' said Reg as he reached across the table to shake his hand. 'Is that how you got your black eye?'

'Aw no, not really,' answered Joe. 'I think Violet is tryin to pull me leg a bit bout that.'

Bess then quickly saw the chance to convey to Reg that there could something more than a mere working arrangement between the two young folks.

'He got his black eye fer protectin a certain young lady's honour,' she said, nodding her head meaningfully towards Violet May.

'Mother! Do be quiet,' said Joe, blushing to the roots of his hair, whilst the girl sitting beside him smiled with pleasure and said, 'Well I was glad he was there anyway.' Turning to her father, she told him the story of the incident at Mrs. Cherry's Social Evening and by the time she had finished, Joe was the hero of the day, the flavour of the month, and the colour of the year all wrapped in one, much to his embarrassment.

'I s'pose,' said Tom to Reg, 'Tis a bit early fer ee to think about what you'm gwain do now.?'

'In what way?' asked Reg.

'Well,' Tom was lost for a moment. 'I mean, will ee be stayin around this area or no?'

All eyes were on Reg now. Violet May's more intensely than the others.

'Haven't made up my mind yet.' Reg seemed a little bit caught out. 'Naturally, Violet and me will have to discuss a few things.'

'Aise, aise certainly you will.' Tom said.

'We've got roots in Sussex,' Reg went on, 'And I know my way around up there. I've still got my trade of course. I was an Agricultural Engineer before I was called up, and I can always go back to that and most likely will,' he said.

'I should think there ought to be plenty o' that sort of work round here,' said Joe. 'Anybody with a fair size van and a box o' tools wouldn' have much trouble earnin a livin. Ther's several people with tractors about now, I've noticed.'

Tom had been watching Reg and could see his slightly uncomfortable expression. He was obviously not enjoying this discussion and Tom wisely decided to change the subject.

'Now then, Mother,' he said, turning his attention to Bess. 'A meal such as us've just partaken of ought to be waished down with somethin a bit better th'n a cup o' tay I reck'n, partic'ly as this is somethin of a special occasion, the reason fer which as you all knaw an' c'n see with yer own eyes is sat yer at our table beside of his lovely daughter, who is our Land Army maid. So, if you will all excuse me fer a minute 'r two, I'll nip down the cellar and fetch up a drop o' cider.'

'Well, I thought sure us wus in for a speech there!' exclaimed Bess as Tom left the kitchen. 'He amn made one o' they fer a year or two, an' good job that one didn' last long. Aw well, better get the glasses out I spose, but I hope ther' won't be any thick heads in the mornin.'

Tom was soon back with a huge jug full of cider, and then with glasses charged, he solemnly welcomed on behalf of Bess and Joe, the arrival of Reg and the presence of his daughter, Violet May, who leaned affectionately against her father,.

The men quickly emptied their glasses, but the women drank more slowly. Tom refilled the empty glasses, and the evening wore on with the conversation alternating between the two families and the activities around the farm, especially those which Violet May was involved in, and all the Dryfields were full of praise for the way that she had handled the jobs given her to do. Her father was visibly pleased when told the story of the calf, and why she had named it 'Annie'.

Eventually the subject of the tractor came up, and this time it was Joe who was loud in his praise for the girl 'that got the ol' thing gwain when nobody else knawed what t ' do.'

'We're going to change the oil and filter tomorrow Dad, if we've got time,' she said. 'You could give us a hand if you like, and maybe have a look around it, being as you're the expert.'

'Yes, why not,' said Reg. 'I'll be very glad to do something to help, after all that you've done for me.'

'Never mind bout t'morrow,' Bess said. 'This've bin a long ol' day I'm thinkin, so let's 'ave a bit of supper an' get t' bed, else none of us'll be able t' get up in the mornin.'

At this, Tom looked around the table and said, in the manner of someone who had drunk a little too much cider, 'Did I hear the Lady of the house spake, or wuz that the wind blawin?'

'Just hark at 'n,' she scolded. 'Tryin to make out he've 'ad too much to drink. Get on with ee, y' maaze ol' fool. I've knawed ee to drink two full jugs o' that stuff in one night, you an' George Mattford.'

'Ah well,' corrected Tom. 'That only works out to one jug each of us, my 'andsome.' And, as everyone including Bess, laughed merrily, they all turned their attention to the food being placed in front of them.

So now it was time for bed, and to reflect upon the happenings of the day. Reg watched Violet May as she went about helping Bess to clear the table and put things out ready for the morning. How she had grown, he thought. She had developed from an awkward schoolgirl into a competent and assured young lady, and so much like her mother. He was pleased about that, and thankful to be back with her again.

Still the question of their future would not go away, and he'd have to give that some thought. But hadn't he done so already, in those days and nights, weeks, months, years even, when all those mind-shattering, murderous conflicts in the desert did give him a chance to think about anything? The army, he reckoned, wasn't going to need him for very much longer, and that meant finding somewhere to live as well as getting a job, and that was why his thoughts went back to the only place he knew anything about. Eastbourne and the Sussex Downs.

The cider was having its effect on him now, and he noticed that Bess and his daughter were watching him. He managed a smile and said, 'Bed time for me I think.'

'Aise, you must be weared right out,' Bess said, 'what with all the travellin you've done today. Violet, see your Daddy up to his room. T'won't be long 'fore all of us be fast asleep, and the mornin will be yer soon enough.' And with these words, Stoney Downe said 'Goodnight' and waited for the dawn.

13

Reg awoke in the morning to the sound of rattling milking pails in the dairy, bawling calves impatient for their breakfast, cackling hens in the yard and noisy rooks in the trees. For a moment or two he wondered where on earth he was. Then, as he looked around the bedroom, the events of the day before became clear again. Glancing at his watch, he saw that it was past eight o'clock and an appetising aroma of breakfast cooking was wafting up from the kitchen. He got out of bed and quickly washed his hands and face, using the water left for that purpose in the jug and bowl set, on the dressing table. Feeling much refreshed, he put on trousers shirt and pullover and made his way downstairs.

'Well here 'e is then,' Bess greeted him as he entered the kitchen. 'You've 'ad a good night's rest, for certain.'

'Didn't know a thing until I woke up, about ten minutes ago,' replied Reg. 'That's the best bed I've slept in for a long, long time. I suppose everybody else has done half a day's work by now, haven't they?'

'They'm jus' finishin the milkin I b'lieve,' said Bess. 'Sit down there be the fire and I'll pour ee a cup o' tay. I reck'n you c'n drink one, can't ee? I 'spect they'll be in fer breakfast soon.'

'Thanks very much, Bess.' Reg gratefully took the cup and sat down. 'Just what I need, and the breakfast smells good too. You know it's no wonder Violet

May looks so well, if you eat like this all the time.'

'Well, they work hard for it,' replied Bess, 'so you jus' got t' put the food inside of 'em, else t'wouldn' be no good. But another reason why 'er looks so well is becos 'er's happy and contented. You'm bound to see it Reg, if you ant seen it already. That maid 've found fer 'erself what us be all lookin fer I reck'n, and tidn no bad thing neither.'

Reg frowned and looked at her sideways. What on earth did she mean by that? He would have to give it his consideration later, because just then the back door opened and Violet May and Joe came into the kitchen, having removed their heavy footwear at the door. As Joe went to the water pump, Violet May kissed her father on top of his head.

'Did you sleep well, Dad?' she asked him. 'I looked in just before six, but you were still fast asleep so I didn't disturb you.'

'I should think not,' said he. 'Six o'clock in the morning is the middle of the night to a soldier on leave, I'll have you know!'

She laughed happily and turning to Bess she said, 'I hope he hasn't been telling you stories about me.'

'No, 'course not, my 'andsome,' said Bess. 'Come on now, waish yer hands and ate yer breakfast whilst tis 'ot.'

'Alright, Mam,' she said, and moving to the pump at the sink, she playfully tried to shoulder Joe out of the way saying 'Come on, slow coach, are you going to be there all day?' And Joe responded by dabbing her on both cheeks with his soapy hands, causing them both to laugh like children.

'Now come on the both of ee,' scolded Bess. 'Your breakfast is on the table, so 'urry up and sit down and ate it, 'fore I thraw it out t' the fowls.'

Reg watched them from his chair, a faint smile on his face as they jostled with each other at the table. There was no disputing that some sort of a strong feeling existed between these two, and somehow Eastbourne and the Sussex Downs seemed a little bit farther away.

A few minutes later Tom came in from the yard, washed his hands and took his place at the table. His cheery words of greeting to all those present was followed by each and every one enjoying a hearty breakfast.

When the first meal of the day was over, it was time to deliberate, work-wise, upon what had to be done. The time of the year dictated that nothing much was possible on the land, but the animals had to be fed and watered, same as humans, and just like humans, this followed a more or less regular pattern.

'Put the cows up in Eight Acres this mornin,' Tom said to Violet May. 'Tidn' quite so wet up there, but bring 'em in early after dinner and give 'em a bit extra hay, and a bit o' straw wouldn' hurt 'em if ther's any about up in the loft. Too much ol' wet grass idn no good to 'em. Joe, you knaw what you got t' do. I'm gwain up to see if George is alright. Can't understand why I didn' see 'n in Market yes'day.'

'P'raps Reg would like to go with Violet when 'er takes the cows out,' suggested Bess.

'Yes, come on, Dad,' said the girl. 'It's only a little way, and you can take a stick if you need one.'

'Sounds like a good idea.' Reg was pleased with the suggestion. 'The exercise will do me good, and perhaps when we get back I'll be able to help with that oil change on the tractor.'

It had also occurred to him that he'd have a little time alone with his daughter and perhaps be able to discuss one or two things as to their future.

'Well I'll leave ee to it,' said Tom. 'I shan't stay long up George's. Jus' want t' make sure ther' idn nort wrong with'n, tha's all.' And off he went.

'I don' knaw why 'e should want t' ride all the way up there fer,' remarked Bess. 'But then, George 've been a bit of a mystery man just lately and I s'pose Father wants t' knaw wha's on.'

'Well we'd better get on with it,' said Violet May. 'Are you going to help me to untie the cows, Joe?'

'I b'lieve I usually do,' said Joe with a grin. 'And t' day won't be no differ'nt.'

'Oh my, don't you think he's a lovely chap, Dad?' she said, and grabbing her father's arm, they walked outside and headed towards the shippens. Ten minutes later they were driving the cows out of the yard and up to the eight acre field. Tom had thoughtfully opened the gate for them on his way up to see George, so the cows were able to walk straight into the field, with a little help from Ben, the dog.

'You like living here, don't you?' Reg said to his daughter on the way back to the farmyard.

'Oh yes, I do,' she answered. 'Everybody is good to me, and I like the work and the animals. I'm sure I'll never get tired of it. But what about you Dad? Now that you're home again, and perhaps leaving the army, you will be needing somewhere to live....' She suddenly stopped. 'You won't want to go back to Eastbourne will you?'

Well, there it was. She had put the question to him and he had to answer it.

'Remember what I said last night?' he asked her. 'I told Tom that you and I would have to discuss a few things.'

'Yes, I remember,' she said. 'You told them in the house that you knew your way around at Eastbourne, but I don't think I could ever leave here now and I don't want us to be miles and miles apart again. It wouldn't take you very long to get to know your way around here, would it, Dad? Pottles Cross is a nice little village. Perhaps there's a house or something there that would suit us. I know I'm tied to the farm for the duration, because I'm still in the Land Army, but couldn't you think about staying around here, somewhere close at hand?'

Reg took her hand in his. 'Look, sweetheart,' he said. 'I've still got a good pair of eyes, and I can see how close you are to this family, perhaps extra close to one in particular. Am I right about that?'

She turned towards him, her eyes shining. 'Yes, Dad, I can't be anything but honest about it. They really are lovely people and yes, Joe is a bit special. I think Bess has made up her mind that something will come of it one day, but Joe and me haven't got around to saying anything about it yet.'

'Well you're both a bit young right now,' remarked Reg. 'But I can see that Joe is a hard working boy, and no doubt he knows what lies ahead of him. He'll be running this farm eventually, and that could be a pretty good future for you too if you wanted it that way. In any case, look,' he put his arm around her, 'let's not worry about it all just yet. I've only been home a few days, and we've got the rest of our lives in front of us to make plans. You are still number one in my life, and any plans I make will be made with your happiness in mind. That's a promise.'

She looked up at him. 'Nobody in this whole world could have a Dad as good as you.'

'Come on, girl,' he replied with a grin. 'Let's see how good I am with this old tractor!'

On returning to the farmyard, Violet May left her Dad to do whatever he could with the tractor while she went about her usual chores, and although Joe's tool box was somewhat bereft of the essentials, Reg was able to carry out a considerable amount of routine maintenance. It was good to have the feel of tools in his hands again, and after a while Joe came across the yard and watched as Reg tightened nuts and bolts, checked fan and pulley belts, looked for oil and water leaks and then, wiping his hands with a piece of rag, he pronounced the machine fit for work.

'Pretty good old tractor, that one,' he said to Joe. 'You know there isn't very much that will go wrong with them, but you must keep up with regular oil and filter changes. That's quite important, and of course, keep the fuel supply running clean. Look after that and it will look after you. It's an old saying, but worth remembering.'

'Aise I s'pose,' said Joe. 'Us've never had a tractor before, so there's quite a bit us got to learn about 'em, but I must admit, they'm a good bit quicker than horses fer ploughin and workin ground.'

'And they don't get so tired as horses do,' smiled Reg, 'but once this war is over and things start getting back to normal, I think farmers will go for mechanisation in a big way, and horses will go out of fashion. It's already happening in some parts where they grow a lot of corn. That's where you'll see combine harvesters and balers working, and the same will happen in this county before very long.'

'That'll upset the blacksmiths and horse dealers I reck'n,' Joe suggested.

'Perhaps so,' agreed Reg. 'But there'll always be ponies and hunters to shoe, and blacksmiths will easily turn their hands to other things, like repairing tractors and farm machinery, and even routine maintenance, such as I've just done on this tractor.'

'How's it going, Dad?' Violet May had come across the yard to where her father and Joe were standing.

'Oh alright thanks, my love,' Reg answered. 'The tractor looks fine now and should be trouble free for a while.'

'Thought it would be, after a bit of treatment from the expert,' she said.

Reg smiled. 'Don't know about that,' he said. 'I'm well out of practise, but I suppose it'll all come back soon enough.' Turning to Joe he said, 'I noticed an old bicycle behind the cart over there. It must be yours?'

'Aw aise,' replied Joe, 'e's a few years old now. I used to ride 'n to school and wuz still usin 'n up to bout a year ago, but then 'e got left over there and tha's where e've stayed.'

'Would you mind if I had a look at it Joe? I need to exercise my legs as much as I can and the medical people tell me that riding a bike is a good way of doing it. And it will give me something to do while you're all working.'

'No, I don't mind a bit,' said Joe. 'I don't think ther's much wrong with th' ol' thing, 'cept the tyres is flat and the chain's got a bit rusty, but if you want to 'ave a go at 'n, help yerself.'

'Thanks very much, Joe,' said Reg. 'I shall enjoy doing that, and it might do us both good.' He walked in behind the cart to lift the old bike out and give it a closer look.

At that moment, Tom returned from his visit to George Mattford's place with Rocky, and dismounted at the stable door. He took off the saddle and hung it inside. Violet May walked over and patted the pony's neck.

'Everything alright, my 'andsome?' Tom greeted her.

'Yes thanks,' she replied. 'Want me to give Rocky a rub down?'

'Can if you mind to,' said Tom. 'Then you c'n ride 'n up to eight acres after dinner and bring the cows back in. They'll 've had enough of that ol' wet grass and be glad to fill up with some good hay.'

She felt a thrill of excitement at the thought of

being allowed to ride Rocky again, and hurried to get the brush and curry comb. As she went about the job in hand, Tom turned on his heel and said 'Must go in and see Mother 'bout George. See ee all when you come in fer dinner.' And without any further explanation he marched in through the kitchen door.

'Wonder what tha's all about,' remarked Joe, who had overheard his father's words.

'I'm sure I don't know,' said Violet May. 'We must wait until dinner time to find that out I think.'

'That idn gwain to be very long, the way my stomach's rattlin,' answered Joe with a grin, and looking across to where Reg was already working on the old bicycle, he added 'Your Dad cert'nly knaws what 'e's doin wi' they tools. Looks like I'm in fer a new second 'and bike!'

Violet May laughed at this. 'How can you have both a new and a second hand bike at the same time?' she asked.

'It's just a sayin' said Joe, 'but I reck'n e'll be good as new when your Dad 've finished with 'n.'

'Oh it will,' she said. 'It'll certainly be that alright, but he wants to ride it around a bit himself to get some strength back in his legs. That's what he tells us, but I think there's a bit more to it than that. I'm sure he's got something else on his mind, but I suppose we'll have to wait and see.'

At that moment Bess put her head outside the kitchen door and called them in for the midday meal, so that put an end to any further conversation on the matter for the time being.

'What's the news of George,?' asked Joe. 'Did Father say anything or no?'

'Father says that e's comin down Thursd'y night with his new lady friend,' said Bess, 'and they'm gettin married, if you please, the followin Wens'dy Market day. Special licence job that'll be, in the Register' Office but e'll tell us all bout it Thursd'y.'

The subject of George Mattford and his bride-to-be had a good airing at the kitchen table but as the midday meal came to an end, Reg decided that as he had been on his legs for most of the morning, he'd like to rest and put his feet up for a while, and so Bess sat him in the best armchair by the fire and told him to relax and enjoy himself. However, a half hour of that was enough for him, and he decided to go outside again to see what there was to be done.

There wasn't a great deal wrong with Joe's bike as it happened, but Reg gave it a methodical going over. Both tyres were flat to start with, but off came the wheels and then the tyres and tubes, all to receive a thorough examination inside and out. Two punctures were found in the rear tube and one in the front, but with an ageing puncture outfit which Joe managed to find, effective repairs were successfully carried out. The wheel spindles got adjusted and oiled, and likewise the chain and the brakes of course, and there it was. Joe's bike was once more brought into service.

Reg rode the bike around the farm for a day or so, up the lane and back again and decided that he felt much better, and then announced that he might try going a little farther afield.

Violet May had been watching him carefully, and instinctively knew that her father had something 'up his sleeve'.

'What is it, Dad?' she asked him at last. 'I know you're planning something, and I want to know what it is.'

'Nothing for you to worry about,' he assured her. 'You know I promised you that any plans I make won't interfere with what you want to do.'

'Well don't forget that you're supposed to be in Plymouth on Thursday,' she reminded him,

'I know,' he said. 'I won't forget, but I wanted to go and have a look at Pottles Cross. There's a Post Office there and I want to put some money in the Savings Bank.'

'Why don't I believe him?' she asked herself. 'I'm sure he's up to something.' And then aloud to him — 'That's quite a way, there and back. Do you think you'll make it, with your legs?'

'It would be a lot harder without 'em,' he said, giving her a funny grin.

It wasn't a bad sort of day for the time of the year, and he did make it into the village, taking it along steadily, and he also did go into the Post Office where he bought a stamp for a letter that he'd written.

This was to the hospital authorities at Plymouth, expressing the desire to postpone his previously arranged medical examination for a few days, "due to unforeseen circumstances." And also, whilst in the Post Office, he asked for directions to a Mr. Woodstock's farm, which he understood was not far out from the village, and these directions were duly given to him by the rather pleasant lady behind the counter. Reg, perhaps it ought to be said, still wore his army uniform because that was all that he had to wear, and in such a small community as Pottles Cross, the sight of one of the much-heralded Desert Rats, the emblem of which was still prominently displayed at the top of his sleeves, attracted a fair amount of attention. After posting his letter, he took hold of the handlebars of Joe's bike and walked slowly along in the direction that he had asked for.

The weather had improved somewhat and it felt good to be where he was. He crossed the little stone bridge over the river, and stopped for a while to watch the children in the playground of the village school being shepherded around in some child's intricate game by their school mistress. At the sight of him, a perfect stranger in a uniform, looking over the wall, the children stopped what they were doing and began to giggle, some with their hands covering their mouths. The school mistress, Mrs. Cherry — for it was none other — then came over to the wall and asked him if there was something she could do for him, or did he know any of the children there?

'No, thank you very much, ma'am,' he said politely. 'I'm just on my way to the Woodstock's farm, and I couldn't help but notice the children enjoying themselves.'

'Oh,' said Mrs. Cherry, feeling rather pleased that someone was taking notice of her efforts. 'Really? Do you have some children perhaps?'

'I have a daughter,' replied Reg. 'But she's grown up now, and is in the Land Army. She's out at Stoney Downe with the Dryfield Family.'

'Well, isn't that amazing,' said Mrs. Cherry. 'Of course now I know who you are. You're that young Miss Johnson's father. I met your daughter at the Chapel a couple of weeks ago, and again at the

Village Hall at our Social. We've heard all about you here and I must say that I'm delighted to meet you. Will you be staying long, Mr. Johnson?'

'If things work out, it could be quite a while I think,' said Reg. 'It really depends on the outcome of my meeting with Mr. Woodstock.'

Mrs. Cherry was dying to know the nature of his business with the Woodstock's, but was much too polite to delve into it. However, something else crossed her mind, and she decided to grab the chance of it while it was there.

'It's just occurred to me,' she said. 'I wonder if, after you have finished your business with Mr. Woodstock, you would have time to call into the school for about twenty minutes or so. It's just that we're doing a project in class this term, on "Life in the armed forces", and it would be absolutely marvellous if we could have a real soldier to speak to the children. Do say you will come. It will mean so much to them!'

This was certainly something Reg did not expect. The idea of standing in front of a horde of children was bad enough, but to try and talk to them as well? He wasn't quite sure about that. However, whether it was the challenge, or because of the appealing look on Mrs. Cherry's face, or, what was more likely, the fact that he would have something to tell Violet May and the folks at Stoney Downe, he decided to accept the school mistress's invitation.

'Alright,' he said. 'Thank you for asking me. I'll come back around as soon as I've finished my business with Mr. Woodstock.'

'Wonderful,' cried Mrs. Cherry. 'We shall look forward immensely to seeing you.'

And wouldn't she have something to tell the ladies of the Knitting Circle and the other Women's groups of the village, when next they all met!

It proved to be a good day for Reg. His meeting with Mr. Woodstock was entirely successful and now he had something to take back to his daughter which he knew was going to put her mind at rest, and that gave him considerable satisfaction. No one else at Stoney Downe knew anything about his meeting today and that's how it had to be, because until now he had not been at all sure how things would turn out. No one, that is, except Tom Dryfield, who had started the whole thing going. A chance meeting between Tom and Bradley Woodstock, who owned three properties outside of his farming interests, revealed that one of these properties had become vacant, and did Tom, as an old and trusted friend, happen to know anyone he could recommend?

'You knaw 'ow tis nowadays, Tom,' he had said. 'Ther's all sorts comin in aroun thase yer parts, and I don' want nobody that idn gwain look after the place'. And Tom had replied, 'I may've got the very man fer ee, Brad,' and in due course had put Reg into the picture, explaining that Brad Woodstock was a man of some standing in the Parish, and 'who knows' what it all might lead to. Reg had expressed his thanks to Tom, but asked him not to say anything to anybody until after he'd seen Mr. Woodstock.

Now here he was, walking back towards the school with a secured tenancy in his pocket, and feeling good. He noticed the little village shop was open, even though it was well into the lunch hour, and so he bought himself a pasty which he ate as he slowly went along.

He pushed the bicycle in through the entrance to the school playground and leant it against the wall under the classroom window. Mrs. Cherry greeted him at the door, and said he was just in time. She had assembled all the pupils as soon as the lunch break was over, and she now led him in and stood him in front of the class.

'Children,' she said. 'We are extremely fortunate today. Mr, er I mean Sergeant Johnson is going to talk to us on what it is like to be a soldier. Now I'm going to ask him to speak to you for a little while, and please listen carefully to what he tells you. I shall be asking you questions after he has finished.' She gave a little flourish with her hand and said 'Children — Sergeant Johnson.'

Reg looked down on the sea of faces before him, and wished that he hadn't agreed to come into the school, but, here he was and there was no getting out of it. He had very little idea at all of how he was going to tackle this situation, but tackle it he must.

So he began by telling them that he had been in the army for just over three years. After six weeks infantry training he had been sent to an armoured brigade to learn how to drive. Although he already knew how to drive a car, this was different, because the vehicles he was expected to drive from now on didn't have wheels with rubber tyres on them, but had big heavy iron tracks which you had to steer by using two levers which you held one in each hand. If you wanted to go to the left — you pulled the left hand lever; if you wanted to go to the right — the right hand lever . He went on with a description of the number of guns that were carried, how much ammunition, how many men, and then....then he stopped. And that was because he thought of how many men. How many men he had joined up with. How many men he had sailed across the sea with. How many of them were lost, or how few were lucky enough to come home again. He decided upon another tack.

'I'm sorry,' he said quietly. 'Being in the armed forces can be a very good thing for a young man, as long as there isn't a war on. I would much rather talk to you about peace, but there is still a war on at the moment and I know that too many young men are getting killed or maimed, and every single one of them is a Hero. Make no mistake about that. Every single one. They may not feel very heroic themselves, when they're in the height of battle, but they are there, and the only thing they have to do is to get on with the job they were trained for.

But as you youngsters get older, please try to think about peace, not war. Believe me, it's a much better thing to think about. If you meet anyone from another village or another town or even from another country, don't imagine him, or her, to be a two-headed monster, but perhaps think of them instead as being real nice people, just like I'm sure you yourselves are.'

He went on for another five minutes and then looked at the clock on the classroom wall, and turned to face Mrs. Cherry. 'That's about it I'm afraid, Ma'am,' he said apologetically. 'I haven't got any lights on the bicycle, so I must try and get back before dark.'

'Yes, of course,' replied Mrs. Cherry, 'and thank you very much for coming in. I'm sure you have given the children a great deal to talk about.' Then turning to the class, she commanded them to 'All Stand' and led her guest to the school door.

'One has the impression that you have much to tell us, Mr. Johnson' she said to him.

'I don't know about that,' said Reg. 'I suppose I wasn't prepared to speak to anyone, but if I sat down and thought about it, there's probably an awful lot I could say, but it wouldn't be for the ears of children. That was a problem for me in your classroom. Now if I could show them how to handle tools to carry out repairs on things, any old things, from toys to tractors, and make them useful again, that seems to me to be far better than talking about war.'

'Your point is taken, and well said,' answered Mrs. Cherry. 'I'm sure we will meet again soon. Oh, and by the way. I hope your business with Mr. Woodstock has reached a satisfactory conclusion.'

'Yes, it has thank you, Ma'am. I'm going to live in Amber Cottage, just up the road.'

'Are you really,' she said with a smile. 'How lovely for you.'

She didn't tell him then that Amber Cottage was right next door to her house.

14

By the time Reg got back to Stoney Downe, the cows were in and tied and Violet May and Joe were some way through the evening milking.

'Got a bit of news for you,' he called to his daughter, as she came out of the shippen with a pail almost full of milk.

'Where on earth have you been all day, Dad?' she asked. 'I've been worried sick about you, and what about your dinner? You must be starving. News? What are you talking about about? What news?'

'Here, let me carry that bucket for you, sweetheart,' he said. 'And don't nag. Wait till you hear what I've got to tell you,' and he related the whole day's events to her. 'Not a bad day's work, eh?' he said.

'Oh Dad, that's wonderful news,' she said. 'I've got to forgive you now for staying out all day.'

'Don't make me sound like a naughty boy,' he laughed. 'Now you hurry up and finish milking, and we'll discuss it all when you come in.'

'Well don't forget that George Mattford and his lady friend are coming to visit tonight. You haven't met him yet, but he's an old friend of the family and nice to talk to. I think his lady friend is one of the older Land Army girls but I don't know which one.'

'No doubt we will soon find out,' said Reg. 'Now I'd better go indoors and see Bess. I hope she's got the kettle on.'

'There won't be any doubt about that,' said Violet May.

The evening came and everyone was awaiting the arrival of George and his lady. The day's work had been completed a little earlier, as the cows had been brought in soon after dinner, and all at the farm had 'clained up, proper manner' and were sitting around the table. Bess wondered if Violet May had ever met 'this yer Kathy Branstone' while she was at the Land Army Hostel at Newton Waybrook.

'I can't say I remember her really,' said the girl. 'Several older girls were there at the same time as me, but I couldn't tell you where they were all sent to.' And looking at Joe with a smile, she added 'I lost interest in all of them when I arrived here.'

'You might be able to call 'er 'ome when you see 'er,' suggested Tom, as footsteps were heard crossing the yard.

'That'll be they now,' said Bess, and getting up from the table, she hurried out to the kitchen door to welcome their guests. 'Come on in, come on in.' Her voice could be heard all the way back. 'Go on now, George, you don't 'ave to be told which way to go. You bin comin yer ever since you wuz a boy gwain school. Come on in, my dear, an' welcome. Rest of the family's in sittin down, and they'm dyin to meet ee.'

'That's very nice, I'm sure,' said Kathy, and followed George through the passage into the kitchen.

Tom was on his feet straight away. 'Come and sit over yer, my 'andsome,' he said, offering her his chair. 'George, ther's room fer you as well beside of 'er. Now then, I'll interduce ee to all thuse present... that is, if I c'n mind who they all be!'

'Aw, come on Tom,' said George. 'You amn bin at the cider jug already, 'ave ee?'

'No, not yet George, but don't go 'way, cos ther's plenty yer. Now then....' and he looked around the room, naming everyone starting with his son Joe and then Bess, followed by Reg, to which he added his reason for being there, that being 'his perty little maid' Violet May.

'Oh, I remember you,' said Kathy. 'You're the little maid from Eastbourne, only you're not so little now.

You've put on a bit of weight since I saw you last.'

'Yes, I remember you too, now that I've seen you,' said Violet May, 'and fancy remembering Eastbourne. Isn't that nice, Dad'

'Yes it is,' answered Reg. 'But I think it'll be a while before we see that place again.'

'Are you thinking of staying around here now then?' asked Kathy, and her question was promptly answered by Bess, who explained that 'It looked like Violet May wuz gwain be yer fer a brave while, and her Daddy wuz gwain be close handy as well.'

'Well, you see,' explained Reg. 'I'm expecting to be finished with the army in a week or two and Joe here has given me a notion that I could go back to my old trade as an agricultural engineer, and be of some use to farmers if and when they go mechanised. I'd like to say now though, that I am extremely grateful to all the Dryfield family for the help they have given to me, and Violet May, and particularly to Tom for his help in getting me a place to live, in Pottles Cross.'

Violet May clapped her hands at this from her Dad, and Tom said, 'Aw, twad'n nort, Brad Woodstock asked me if I knawed anybody I could recommained, tha's all.'

'Brad Woodstock?' queried George. 'Well you'll be alright with 'e. Parish Councillor! You won't go far wrong with ol' Brad. Anyway, come on, Tom. You'm a bit slaw pourin up that cider I fancy. A man could be dyin of thirst yer!'

'Aise, well I got two jugfulls up, George, and ther's plenty more where that come from, so come on, Mother, get some glasses out and let's drink hearty.'

So the evening wore on, and by the time they were halfway through the first jug, a very convivial atmosphere reigned inside the Stoney Downe kitchen. It was easy to see that Kathy Branstone was going to make an ideal partner for George as she matched his wit every way, always with a ready answer to his banter, and when Bess and Violet May brought out the meat pie and sandwiches they had prepared earlier, they were, as expected, eaten with gusto. Bess had confided to her young charge beforehand, sort of in an advisory capacity, that you should always 'feed cider when twuz bein' drunk, then you won't get opset stummicks and thick 'aids in the mornin.'

Violet May listened to the wisdom that Bess delivered in her strong dialect. Most days Bess would come out with something. A rhyming couplet, or half a dozen words that she herself had heard and remembered from the utterances of her own forbears long ago.

'Convince a man against his will, he'll keep the same opinion still,' she would say, or,' A forgetful head makes a weary pair of heels.'

There was much, much more, but to get back to the evening and the reason for the presence of George Mattford and his Kathy....

'What I want t' knaw Tom,' he said, speaking with slightly more effort now, 'be you and Bess comin in along with Kathy and me to the Register' Office nex' Wens'dy?'

'Well aise, I reck'n so, id'n us Maid?' Tom still had sense enough to verify his decision with Bess, even though he too had difficulty in picking out his words.

'Don' see how us c'n refuse a offer like that,' smiled Bess. 'Tid'n every day us get invited to a weddin, is it? I der'say Violet and Joe will look after things till us get back again. Don' s'pose t'will take all day, will it?'

'No no, 'course not,' said Kathy. 'But as long as you could come in as well, to stand by me, you know. I haven't got anybody of my own to ask, and I'd like you to be there.'

'If that's the case,' said Bess, 'me and Tom'll be there, don't fret. Violet May and Joe both knaw what they'm bout, and Reg c'n keep eye on 'em. I spect us'll be back just after dinner anyway.'

And that was how it happened for Kathy and George. The following Wednesday came around and Bess and Tom, dressed up in their best clothes, set off in the old Austin to meet them outside the Registry Office in Newton Waybrook, leaving the two youngsters and Reg at home to take care of things. It wasn't altogether a busy time. Joe had one or two jobs to do in the yard, and Violet May had brought the pony out of the stable to give it a little more grooming, prior to going into the kitchen to keep an eye on the stew that Bess had left on the stove. Reg was standing close by, and presently Joe came over to him.

'Do ee think,' he said, then faltered a little, and tried again. 'Do ee think that Violet May, I mean, can ee see whether 'er's happy here with us?'

Reg said, 'I'm sure I've never seen her look so happy, Joe, and I've got you and your mum and dad to thank for that.'

'None of us would want t' see her leave now.' Joe was standing in front of Reg and close to the pony's head, and he had something on his mind which, quite on the spur of the moment, he felt he ought to say to him.

'I've got something that I must ask ee, whilst I've got the chance to,' he began. His voice was strong as he looked straight at Reg, although he had to struggle to find the words.

'What is it Joe?' Reg almost knew what was coming.

'Tis about Violet and me,' said Joe. 'I.... that is, I mean the both of us, well us've got a feelin between us that's brave and strong and... well, I think tis only right t' tell ee, or t' ask ee I mean, if you would give us your permission t' go on fu'ther and.... well, sometime in the future, I'd like to....'

'Joe,' Reg cut in as he could see that Joe was running out of steam. 'Joe, I believe from what I have seen of you and your family that you are a man of honour, and I have no objections at all to you and Violet May forming an association. I've noticed there is something between you both, and I'm not displeased in any way. If she's happy about it, then so am I, because it is her happiness that concerns me, more than anything else.'

Violet May hadn't been doing very much grooming whilst her father and Joe were talking. Rather, she had listened to every word and was a little surprised that Joe had raised the question of their courtship. Surprised, but delighted as she came around from the other side of the pony's head and rested her arm upon Joe's shoulder. She looked at her father with eyes shining as he kissed her on the forehead.

'I think he's a good chap,' he said to her, 'and

I'm pleased that he was man enough to ask my permission first. That's a good sign to me, and I believe that you've got a very good future ahead of you here.'

'I hope so,' she said. 'But he hasn't asked me yet!'

Well, Joe was going to now, but all in good time, just as soon as he could see her alone. After all, that had to be a private thing between the two of them, with no one else around.

It wasn't all that long afterwards, it seemed, that they heard Tom and Bess come trundling back into the yard in the old Austin.

'My dear soul an' days!' cried Bess, as she got out of the car. 'That wuz a bit of a hurry up job. Never seed nort like it. No sooner in there 'fore us wuz out again. Still they two've gone 'ome happy so I s'pose tha's all that matters.'

She walked over to the girl to ask her, 'You been keepin 'n eye on the stew I hope,' and then, quick to see the stars in her eyes, she added, looking at her closely, 'What've you party bin on upon?'

Violet May reached up and whispered in Bess's ear, 'Joe asked Dad if we could go courting,' she said, her voice filled with excitement, 'and he said that we could. Isn't it lovely!'

'Well, if that don't beat all,' replied Bess, with a huge smile. 'I tell ee, it must be caitchin! Come on in now and tell me all bout it. Tis nearly dinner time, and I be ever so pleased and I knaw father will be as well.'

The subject of George and Kathy's wedding had a good airing at the dinner table, but the glances that passed between Violet May and Joe weren't missed by Bess, and she wasn't surprised when they left the table a bit earlier than usual to get back to their afternoon chores.

Outside the stable, the pony waited still and pricked up his ears as he saw the young couple coming towards him. 'Do you think your dad would mind if I took Rocky up for the cows again?' she asked him.

'No, 'course not,' said Joe. 'I'll give ee a hand to saddle 'n up, shall I?'

'If you've got time, Joe. I don't want to do it all

wrong.'

'You couldn' do anything wrong, far's I'm concerned.' Joe took her hand as they reached the stable door. 'I've must ask ee now,' he said earnestly, looking into her eyes, 'If you can think about stayin here with me for the rest of your life, and whenever you think the time is right, p'raps you'll care enough for me to want to get married, because tha's how much I care about you.'

'To stay here at Stoney Downe for ever,' she said quietly, 'is as much as I would ever hope to do. But to be the wife of Joe Dryfield, and be one of the family? That will be a dream come true, Joe. You won't ever change your mind, will you?'

'Tid'n likely,' said Joe quickly. 'I've never wanted anything so much in all me life more than I want you 'ere with me.'

She moved forward then and rested her head on his chest. Two strong arms encircled her, and they were lost in a magical silence.

'This is for always, Joe,' she said at last. 'Do you think you can put up with me for that long?'

'We could have a trial period if you mind to,' he said. 'Like ninety-nine year. Would that suit ee?'

She looked up at him and laughed happily. 'It sounds reasonable,' she said. 'But I must talk it over with my chief adviser.'

'Who the heck is that?' asked Joe with a frown.

'Your mum of course,' she replied. 'Who else could it be?'

'Come on,' laughed Joe. 'Let's get this pony saddled up. I'll go up the loft and thraw some extra hay down while you go an' fetch the cows in.'

'Whatever you say Joe,' she said, smiling at him. And a few minutes later, Rocky was once again carrying her up to the eight acre field, followed by the ever faithful old dog, Ben.

15

Now, what is left to tell of the good folk at Stoney Downe Farm? Nothing more than one might expect, but then again, that could be quite a lot. Depends on who's doing the telling.

George Mattford and his Kathy settled down together on George's smallholding, two miles from Stoney Downe Farm, and were well pleased with their new life. Violet May's father Reg, moved into Amber Cottage at Pottles Cross, after leaving the army with a pension, due to his injuries, and was getting along fairly well doing an odd mechanical job here and there, most of which was courtesy of Bradley Woodstock. And living next door to Mrs. Cherry was not too bad at all... after they had sort of got used to each other, although giving some of the local children piano lessons in her front room on Saturday mornings could be a bit of a trial. Especially when, after struggling through *Oh where, Oh where is my Little Dog gone*, the poor child would have to do it all again, following an order from the teacher who was either upstairs making the bed or out in the back kitchen doing a bit of cooking. 'Octave higher dear!'

Violet May and Joe were now officially engaged, and everyone was happy about that. Life went on at the farm, much as usual, and she had plenty to do with an ever increasing number of calves to look after, and she didn't forget Annie, who was now separated from its mother to come on with all the other followers, but still got special attention from the young lady who had seen her into the world on that Sunday Evening after Chapel. She never missed going to Chapel with Bess if she could help it. Sometimes Joe went as well, but things seemed to get busier about the farm as the year progressed, so he more often stayed home with his father to help keep an eye on things. Bess could drive the old car anyway, and Violet May started to learn as well.

Then it was early summer, and hay making time. Ah! The sweet smell of new mown hay, mingled with the sweat of men and horses. Surpassed only by the corn harvest, a few short weeks away, when the aroma of the cider bottle could be added to the others. George Mattford came to help with the corn, as he always did, but this year he brought Kathy with him and she did a man-sized job. They worked until it was almost dark, but what followed then made everything well worth the effort when all those involved sat down at the Dryfield's table and ate a meal that was fit for kings.

Bess and Violet May had worked it out that a good and reasonable time for a wedding would be soon after the harvest was over, and so plans were made accordingly. It seemed right and proper for the young couple to take over what had been Johnny Crickett's cottage. It had been standing empty there for some time, and strictly speaking, belonged to the farm anyway — it was always thought of as Johnny's because he had helped to build it. What was inside, however, was quite a different matter, and Tom was in the process of getting some legal advice about that. Johnny, it seemed, had not left a will.

However, what had been a Heaven on earth for two people for fifty years or more was going to do the same again, hopefully, for another couple who were on their way to 'jump over the broomstick.'

Now the days were becoming shorter as summer neared its end and autumn leaves began to fall. The folks at Stoney Downe were able to relax a little, although there was still plenty to do. The war progressed into its fourth year, but was hardly noticed by the people at the farm, perhaps because the forthcoming wedding gave them other things to think about. Certainly one could hardly wish to be in more peaceful surroundings as they went on with their everyday chores, remaining untouched by the horrors of enemy bombers.

That was, until the day their attention was attracted by the sound of machine-gun fire, high in the sky, and they watched Pilot Officer Terry Christopher in his Hurricane Fighter shoot down the German Heinkel bomber.

Standing there in the farmyard, they saw quite clearly the enemy's bomb-load leave the aircraft as the German pilot gave the order to jettison, while he struggled to escape back into the clouds. He was unable to do so because the Hurricane's guns had made a mess of his elevator controls, and he was left with just one option, which was to abandon the aircraft and bale out. The folks down below didn't see the parachutes come out of the stricken bomber as at just about the same time its bombs hit the ground less than a mile away, to the south of the farm, causing them to dive for cover down beside the barn wall. Never before had they heard such a thunderous series of explosions, and for a few moments no one could speak.

Then Bess said quietly, 'My dear soul an' days. I hope that id'n down in the field against the copse. Tha's where Joe's workin'.'

'Cawd, beggar my shirt, so tis,' Tom said with some alarm. 'Us better way get down there and see if 'e's alright.' But before he had a chance to get up on his feet, Violet May was running out through the yard gate as fast as her legs would carry her. On she went towards the field down by the copse, scrambling over gates and hedges until, almost breathless, she got to where Joe had been working.

Halfway across the field she could see the tractor with the engine still running, but there was no sign of its driver. With heart pounding, she started to run towards it, and then, as the area to the left came into view, she stopped. Lifting her hands to her face she gasped and stared at the sight that greeted her, for what had been part of a field gently sloping towards the copse that joined it, was now a gaping hole big enough to put two barns full of hay into. Two of the Heinkel's bombs had dropped there. The rest had fallen on the open moorland.

She gave a cry of relief when at last she saw Joe kneeling at the edge of the crater. 'Joe, Joe,' she screamed. 'Joe, are you alright?'

He stood up and grinned at her as she ran towards him. 'You've got blood all over your face,' she said, looking up at him.

'Have I?' said Joe, 'Aw, that id'n nort. I must've caught me head on somethin when I dived under the tractor. Lucky fer me, I wuz down lower side of the field when I heard they bombs comin, and tha's the first thing I thought about doin. Then I drawve halfway up cross the field and walked over to have a look. Killed a few rabbits by the looks o' t, so us ben't gwain starve fer a day 'r two!'

'Joe Dryfield!' she shouted at him. 'Is that all you can think of saying? Dear Lord, thank goodness you're safe...' and as she gave in to the tears of relief and held her head against his chest, she burst out 'Joe, if you don't hurry up and marry me, I'll... I'll...'

Well whatever she was going to do was muffled by her uncontrollable sobbing, but comfort was near in the shape of Bess, who had followed Tom as quick as she could, and when they could see that everyone was apparently in one piece, except for the bump on Joe's head, the tension eased off rapidly.

Three or four times Tom wandered around the crater, giving it a thorough examination and finally decided that he 'didn' knaw what t' do bout that.'

'I shall have to let others look at it,' he said. 'I never would've thought ther' wuz s'much rock as that down under the ol' field. Somebody must've knawed it once 'pon a time though, an' p'raps tha's why they called the farm 'Stoney Downe'. '

'I wonder what become of they German parachuters,' Bess said. 'They must have landed close to the village I reck'n.'

'Home Guard'll pick they up.' said Tom. 'And Percy Southcombe will put a hand to it as well. They'll be havin the time of their life today I'll bet a sovereign! Did ee see which way the ol' bomber went, Joe?'

'No, I didn', 'answered Joe. 'I was down other end of the field under the tractor and I stayed there fer a brave while after the bombs went off. Then I 'eard a bang out over the moor, somewhere handy to Gibbet Hill I should think. I reck'n tha's where 'e finished up to. The ol' fighter plane circled round there a time 'r two before 'e went off back towards Plymouth.'

'Well, us got to be thankful nobody got hurt bad,' said Tom. 'Come on now, let's get back to the 'ouse. Us'll sort that mess out another day, when somebody else 've had a look at it. P'raps there'll be some compensation... I dunnaw.'

Turning to Bess with a sigh, he said 'Come on, my 'andsome, le's all get on back. Do ee think you c'n find us ort to ate fer dinner?'

'Shouldn' be surprised,' answered Bess.

16

It was several days before the family began to recover from the shock of having a piece of real live war practically on their doorstep. Quite a lot of people from the village and surrounding area came out to have a look at the crater in the field down by the copse. Among them was Percy Southcombe, who had to make an official report of course, as well as to call in at the Dryfield's kitchen to enjoy a mug of tea and a large slice of cake. All due respects though, Percy was responsible for capturing two of the German airmen, and had his photograph in the 'Morning News'!

Ministry men also came along to examine the hole in the ground and make assessments, and there was one other gentleman called John Penworthy, who was a very knowledgeable and highly respected person. A local solicitor in fact, with a particular leaning towards farmers and their legal problems. Over the years Tom, and his father before him had good reason to be grateful for the help and advice received from his offices in Newton Waybrook, and after a lengthy examination of Tom's newly acquired hole in the ground, he finally called him to one side and advised him, 'Don't do a thing about it, Tom. Leave it just as it is and don't let anybody talk you into anything without me being present.'

Tom was becoming more and more puzzled by the whole affair.

'Can't make it out,' he said. 'That ol' field always

gived us a reasonable crop, but all we 've got now is a blimmin 'ole in the ground, full o' rocks.'

'Yes, I know that's how it looks right now, Tom,' John Penworthy said, 'but I'm telling you, that field is going to give you a bigger return than you could ever imagine. It's all about mineral rights. Let me look into it for you, and I'll get back to you in a few days. In the meantime, please do nothing at all about it.'

'Well alright, John,' said Tom. 'I think I knaw ee well enough to see that you must be talkin good sense. I'll leave it to ee, and do what you say. You and your family wuz always good friends to us and natur'ly 'nough, us 'd want to be same to you.'

'I know that, Tom' said John Penworthy as they walked back towards the farm. 'I don't think you've got anything to worry about. Quite the reverse, but I'll come back and see you in a few days when I've had a chance to look into it.'

'I could come in and see ee next Market Day if you ben't too busy,' offered Tom.

'That will be fine, Tom,' said John. 'I should have all the information for you by then. I'll look forward to seeing you.' With a cheery wave of his hand, he got into his car and drove back towards town.

Tom waved back as he closed the yard gate, and glanced upwards to the clouds, his thoughts wandering to the enemy bomber and what its deadly cargo had done to Stoney Downe Farm.

Or was he merely concerned about the weather? He pushed his cap to the back of his head, and walked slowly towards the kitchen.

§

Two Saturdays after the bombs dropped in the field at Stoney Downe, a very pretty wedding took place at Pottles Cross Chapel when Violet May Johnson got married to Joseph Thomas Dryfield.

It seemed as if the whole village turned up for the occasion and watched the arrival of the bride, proudly led down the aisle by her father, Ex Sergeant Reginald Johnson, late of the Royal Tank Corps and veteran of the North African Campaign. Practically everyone they knew was there. George Mattford with

Kathy his new wife. Constable Southcombe and his wife. Polly and Rita, the bride's Land Army friends, Ashley Woodstock and his wife Jenny. Ashley had taken on the duties of 'best man'. Then there was Mrs. Cherry of course, who came with her valiant organ blower, Charlie Cooper, and the ever faithful Mr. Smythen. And, by Special Invitation – delivered personally to his offices in Newton Waybrook – Mr Short from the Ministry of Agriculture, who arrived with his wife, but this time without his bowler hat.

After the ceremony was over, everyone including the minister and his wife, made their way the short distance from the Chapel to the Village Hall where a considerable amount of food and drink had been set out upon long trestles covered with long white tablecloths. Where all the food came from was anybody's guess, but Bess Dryfield knew how to "pull all the stops out" where that was concerned, and she had a good bit of help from the ladies of the Chapel as well, who were kept very busy waiting at table, and making tea in the kitchen.

Under the light-hearted, but neat guidance of best man Ashley Woodstock, there followed the usual rituals of toasts and speeches with the bride's father being loud in his praise for the Dryfield family and how they had taken his daughter into their hearts when he was so far away from her. Not to mention how they had given him food and sustenance in his time of need, and how proud he was to know that his daughter would from now on bear the name of Dryfield.

And pretty soon it was Joe's turn, and there were those – who knew him well – who had thought that it was going to be "big awkward Joe, saying about ten words and making a hash of it". But not so.

When Joe got to his feet, he looked all around, and smiled. 'I've bin practising,' he said. 'When I get up from a table, I usually manage to knack somethin over. Tis nearly aways the chair, but as you c'n all see,' he looked behind him and indicated with his hand, 'the chair is still standin up, and that's because I've bin practising.' Then, nodding in the direction of his parents, he continued, 'My mother and father offen told me over the years, that if you want to be any good at ort, you got to practise, and that has always been good advice and I must thank them for it, and also fer all the help they've gived to me all through my life at Stoney Downe.'

He looked at all the faces around the table. Most of them had known him from the time he started going to school, some even before that, but they hadn't seen Joe as he was today. Strong, confident, completely in control, and married to the prettiest maid in the county.

'There's somebody else yer today,' Joe continued. who wuz always tellin me to practise. Practise this and practise that. Didn' matter what you had to do, keep at it, an' in th' end, you'll win, an' I've found out that tis very true, an' for that I must thank Mrs. Cherry, our school teacher, as well as fer playin' they lovely hymns in Chapel.... with th' 'elp of Charlie o' course on th' 'andle.' This caused a ripple of laughter, and Joe continued, 'And fer puttin up with me in school for all they years along with a lot of other kids, some of which be in this room today, all grawed up o' course, like I be.'

He got a good laugh from the people there for his last remark, and he laughed himself, but at the other end of the table a handkerchief was produced from a handbag, where Mrs. Cherry was sitting.

'Most of all,' he continued, now looking very serious, 'most of all, I must thank Mr. Johnson, because he has given me his daughter, who I knaw fer certain was, up to t'day, his most loved an' prized possession. I want him to knaw, that for as long as I'm livin, I will be practisin' to do me very best for her every day, in every way.

The people of Pottles Cross Village and surrounding countryside there in attendance, listened to the words that came from young Joe Dryfield on this, his Wedding Day, and wondered how on earth he was able to think of it all, But hadn't he said so. He'd been practising! And he wasn't finished yet.

'Just one more thing 'fore I sit down,' he said, and looking along the table his eyes rested on the man from the Ministry. 'Mr Short,' he continued, 'I dunnaw any words tha's big enough t' tell ee wha's in our minds, t' shaw ee 'ow us feel. The day you brought

Violet May out t' Stoney Downe is a day us bent likely t' ever forget. I don't want t' think anythin 'bout you *not* bringin' 'er out to us, because if you 'adn this room would be empty now. But instead o' that, ee's full of people celebratin, an' tis all because you picked Violet May t' come out t' us. I knaw th't I sh'll be always grateful to you fer that, and I knaw that mother and father will be too, and tis only left fer me to tell ee that you sh'll always be welcome at Stoney Downe. Well tha's all I c'n think of, except, thank you all very much, for bein yer with us today.'

Now that wasn't a bad effort on Joe's part, and he got a good bit of applause for it, but gradually the celebrations came to an end, and as is usual, the first to leave were the newlyweds.

But not before Violet May went to her father. 'What else could there be to make this day any more perfect?' she said to him. 'After all the worry of you being far away and in so much danger, now there will only be a short distance between us and I know you'll be safe here at Pottles Cross.'

Reg smiled at his daughter. 'I can see your mother in you today,' he said. 'You take care and don't worry about me. The only danger I'm in now is living next door to Mrs. Cherry. I think she's got some more ideas about me getting involved with the school, and getting paid for it too! I'm invited in for supper this evening to talk about it.' As he took his daughter's hand to say his farewell, she said, 'Don't worry about me either, Dad. This is just the way I want things to be. You have a nice evening and come out to the farm soon. And I love you too.'

She and Joe then had to go through the ritual of confetti throwing and cheering and shouting before jumping into the family's old Austin Six which, for once in its life, had been cleaned up for this special occasion, and with Joe at the wheel they sped quickly out of the village.

'Us ant 'eard nort bout where they'm gwain to for the 'unneymoon,' remarked one of the village ladies who was standing next to Bess as they watched the car disappear from view.

'Well, they bant gwain nowhere,' said Bess, 'Father an' me said they coulda gone up to a cousin of e's what farm's up t'other side o' Lanson, but no! All they wanted to do was get 'ome to Stoney Downe an' tha's where they'm gone to, an' I reck'n they'll 'ave done 'alf the milkin 'fore us get back.'

'Tis easy to see that Joe've found 'isself a good little partner there,' observed another of the ladies.

'Aw aise,' replied Bess, 'tiz a blessed day for all of us, sure 'nough. Now where's that George Mattford got to I wonder? He's gwain give me an' Tom a lift 'ome in 'e's van. I just hope e've 'membered to put somethin in the back fer us t'sit on, tha's all!'

The village hall was empty now, except for the Chapel Ladies who were clearing things away and tackling the mammoth job of washing up. Then George and Kathy Mattford appeared with their van and, without too much trouble, got Bess and Tom comfortably on board sitting on a wooden box upon which Kathy had thoughtfully placed a couple of cushions. She and Bess had most to say on the journey back, commenting mostly on how well things had gone.

When they arrived at the yard gate of Stoney Downe, Tom said 'You'm welcome to come in George,' as he and Bess climbed out of van, 'but I knaw you got things to do, same as us.'

'Aise, us won't stop now Tom,' replied George. 'Kathy an me'll be busy fer couple hours I reck'n, but us will come down in a day'r two, won't us, maid?' He turned to Kathy to verify his answer.

'Yes, 'course us will,' answered Kathy, 'but us'll give ee few days to recover from all the excitement!'

'Well, wish-ee-well, both of ee,' said Tom 'and thanks for comin. You knaw 'twould'n 'ave been the same without ee. Now us better way get in and see what they two be 'bout.'

And as George's old van chugged up the road and the evening shadows began to creep in, Violet May and Joe were seeing to the eighteen cows that had to be milked, the numerous calves and pigs that had to be fed, getting the horses stabled and settled down, all upon their Wedding Day.

But Tom would be there soon to help, whilst Bess busied herself in the kitchen preparing yet another meal. Violet May's happiness, however, knew no bounds, her life was complete. She was a Dryfield now, and no longer the farm's Land Army Girl. The whole world was hers, and it was all there at Stoney Downe Farm.

At last it was all done, and the family were sitting down in the farm kitchen enjoying their supper. Soon it would be time for the newly-weds to be leaving, and this presented a strange feeling for Joe, because for the first time in his life, he would not spend the night under the same roof as his parents. It didn't bother him unduly, but he felt slightly awkward about how to say 'Goodnight'. Bess could see it though, and put a motherly arm on his shoulder and said 'Goodnight, my 'andsome, see ee in the mornin.'

Violet May went to her then, and warmly embraced her new mother-in-law. 'Thanks, Mam,' she said. 'Thanks for everything, and especially for Joe.'

Joe turned to his father. 'G'night, Dad,' was all he said. But it was enough. Tom saw the gratitude in his son's face, and he needed no more.

'G'night, boy,' he replied.

And so the young couple departed. They made their way slowly across the yard and out through the gate towards Johnny Crickett's Cottage. It wasn't far to walk, and they didn't hurry. Bess and Violet May had worked hard in the past weeks, cleaning and sprucing the old place up ready for the big event, and now it was theirs. Her's and Joe's. Perhaps they would give it a new name, but for sure they would thank the Good Lord in heaven for their little bit of heaven on earth.

§

Back inside the farmhouse, Bess and Tom had retired for the night and were about to settle back on their pillows. Tom blew out the candle and wished his wife 'Goodnight.'

Bess, however, was still savouring the memories of the day and was not yet ready to go to sleep.

'Went off perty well, all of it. Don' ee think, Tom?' she asked.

'Aise,' answered Tom, stifling a yawn.

'The maid looked beautiful, didn' 'er. Abs'lutely

beautiful, don' ee think so?'

'Aise, 'er looked abs'lutely beautiful,' replied Tom. He lay there in the bed, full of food and drink, and would have quickly nodded off if she'd only be quiet.

'Course, Joe looked as smart's a pear, and stood up to it well I thought, and made a good speech, say what you like!' Bess still wasn't yet ready to go to sleep.

'Aise,' said Tom with another yawn, this time unstifled. 'Stood up to it well.'

There was silence for a good half minute, and Tom was very near to his first snore. Then....

'I wonder 'ow they'm gettin on in th' ol' cottage?'

Tom was forced to open his eyes again and frowned in the darkness. 'Now 'ow do I knaw that,' he said crossly. 'What do ee want t' knaw that fer? They'm as right as ninepence I 'spect. Now come on, tis time us went slape!'

But Bess still wasn't ready for sleep. 'I wuz only wonderin, tha's all,' she said.

Silence reigned for almost another half a minute. Then....

'Tom, be you still 'wake?'

'Mmmmm,' said Tom.

'I bin keep on thinkin about our first night when us wuz married. I'll bet a shillin you can't remember what wuz the first thing you done t' me that night.'

Tom's eyes opened wide, and his eyebrows moved up in the darkness as he tried with his fuddled brain to recall the happenings on a night some twenty five years ago. 'What-hevver be you on bout now?' he asked. 'Ow d'you 'spect me to 'member ort about that?'

'Well if you don't knaw, I'll tell ee,' she said. 'Fust thing you done t' me wuz, you bit my blimmin ear-awl!'

'Ahhhh,' said Tom, and followed it up with 'Awwww.' Then something approaching a smile tugged at his features, and the smile broadened as he slowly sat up in the bed, fumbled around for the matches and relit the candle.

'Tom,' she said, frowning, 'what be bout, my 'andsome, what be lightin the candle fer?'

There was a little bit of a pause, before he said,

'....I'm lookin' fer me teeth.'

It was quite some time then before she could say anything, and when at last she was able to speak, all she could think of saying was....

'Oh, my dear soul an' days.'

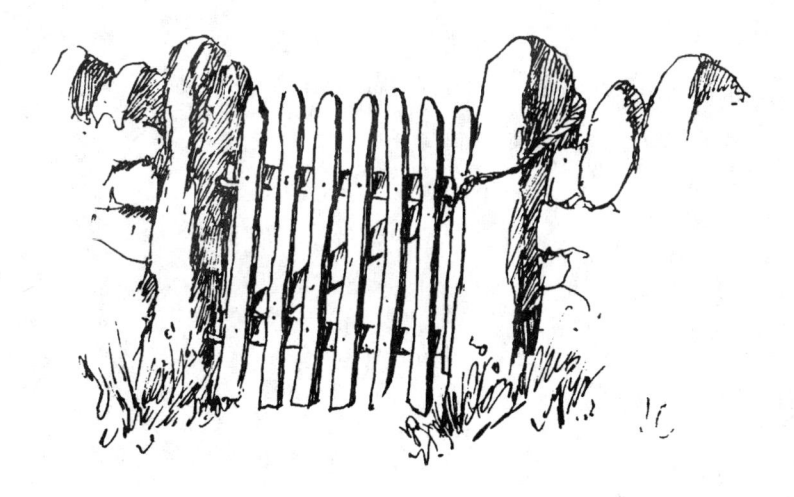

The End